4/95

NIGHTLINES

NIGHTLINES

John Lutz

St. Martin's Press
New York

Library of Congress Cataloging in Publication Data

Lutz, John, 1939–
    Nightlines.

    I. Title.
PS3562.U854N5   1985   813'.54   84–22871
ISBN 0–312–57324–3

First Edition

10 9 8 7 6 5 4 3 2 1

Dark the night
Yet is she bright
For in her dark she brings the mystic star
Trembling yet strong, as is the voice of love
From some unknown afar.

—George Eliot
Spanish Gypsy

NIGHTLINES

ONE

A wind-driven sheet of rain hit Nudger's office window, making a fierce rattling sound, like something with claws clambering to get in. Sometimes being a private investigator wasn't so bad. This was just like being in a movie. Or a dream. Or a dream of a movie. Real atmosphere.

He looked across his desk at the young blonde seated calmly before him. She had one of those passive, finely boned faces that lend an otherwise plain woman a serene kind of near-beauty. Even beneath the thick raincoat that she hadn't removed, only unbuttoned, there was disturbingly evident a petite, shapely figure, lovely swell of breast, sleek turn of ankle. Nice, nice, nice.

But it was the face that Nudger remembered, the slanted gray eyes and neatly arched eyebrows, the short, haughty nose that belonged on a department-store mannequin. Then, when she introduced herself, her name struck the same note in his memory as had her face.

"I saw your picture in the paper last week," he told her. "Under it they said you were dead."

"Obviously, that wasn't me," she answered in a cool, level voice that matched her calm demeanor. "I'm Jeanette Boyington, the murder victim is my twin sister, Jenine."

Nudger picked up a pencil from his desk and uneasily nibbled on some number 2 lead. Jenine Boyington had been found in her Beale Street apartment with her throat slashed. That sort of thing inspired abject fear in Nudger.

"I think I should tell you," he said, "that it isn't a good idea to hire a private investigator to work on the same case that the police are trying to puzzle out."

"I'm sure you're correct," Jeanette Boyington said, "but if you'll agree to take on this job, I can assure you that you'll be approaching it from an angle entirely different from that of the police department's. There'll be no duplication of effort. If that weren't true, there'd be no reason for me to be here."

Nudger's nervous stomach gave a couple of strong kicks, cautioning him to disassociate himself now from this cool prospective client. There was an indefinable something about her. He remembered the time he'd been driving along Cabanne Avenue, in a rough section of town, and almost run over a kitten. He'd thought he'd struck it, but when he got out of the car he found a small bundle of black fur cowering against the curb, uninjured but immobilized with terror. Not knowing what to do with the kitten, which was without collar and tag, he'd put it in the car and driven a few 'blocks, when he saw a knot of boys playing on some tenement steps. He gave them the kitten and smugly thought he'd done everyone a good turn, but as he drove away he glanced in the rear-view mirror and saw one of the boys place the kitten on the sidewalk with slow deliberation and then stamp on it.

Nudger had backed up the car in a rage. The boys magically disappeared in the way of preteen boys; the kitten remained sprawled dead on the pavement, its head grotesquely misshapen. Nudger didn't understand some people. The boy who had killed the kitten probably forgot the incident by the next evening. It had happened two years ago, and Nudger still remembered it. For some reason Jeanette Boyington had reminded him. He wasn't sure if that was because of the boy or the kitten.

"Do you know something the police don't, Miss Boyington?"

She aimed her perfect indomitable nose at Nudger and smiled without candle power. "Jeanette, please. And I should hope I know something the police don't. I know, for instance, that you're often underestimated, but very good at your job. A friend of my mother, Adelaide Lacy, recommended you. She said you helped her find out what happened to her sister."

"I wouldn't say I helped her," Nudger told Jeanette. "I merely confirmed her despair." He reflected that too many of his cases seemed to end that way.

The gray eyes that zeroed in on Nudger could have sunk the *Titanic*. And even as he sat there he knew he wouldn't change course.

There was, besides the obvious sexual attraction, something in Jeanette Boyington that tugged at Nudger even as it repelled. Her coldness suggested an isolation, a loneliness. A slow cancer of the psyche was loneliness. It was a disease that Nudger understood. He sympathized with Jeanette Boyington because of what he assumed must be her affliction. He felt that he should help her, almost as if he were duty-bound. Weren't they in the same leaky boat? He thought again of the *Titanic*.

"There are two reasons I'm telling this to you instead of to the police," Jeanette said. "One: I don't want anyone else to know what I'm going to share with you when I become your client. Two: The police would be skeptical of my theory."

"Theory?"

"That Jenine was the victim of a mass murderer operating in this city."

"Then where is the inevitable mass of victims?" Nudger asked flatly, determined not to be thrown.

"Lost," Jeanette said. "Lost in the overwhelming statistics; hundreds of people are murdered in this city each year. Lost because in each case it's obvious that the victim knew her killer, yet there is apparently no link between killer and victim for the law to latch on to."

"I couldn't help but notice you said apparently," Nudger told her. He began tapping the pencil point on the desk in time with the spastic twitching of his stomach, creating a new pattern of black dots on the old scarred wood. He studied the dots as if by chance they might impart some message. They might be as accurate as tea leaves.

"Jenine had a social life no one but she and I knew about," Jeanette said. She tilted back her head ever so slightly, seemed to feel cautiously around in her mind for words. "She was . . . into something unusual."

"Go on," Nudger said, an edge of curiosity in his voice.

Jeanette smiled with her lips closed, enigmatically, like a cold blond Mona Lisa. Then she said, "The rest will cost me. Are you hired, or do I look elsewhere for an investigator?"

Nudger could feel himself being reeled in, sensed the danger yet couldn't spit out the bait. He was intrigued. And he needed money badly, as usual. He watched Jeanette watch him. She appeared as sublimely amused as he was uneasy.

When he opened a desk drawer and got out a standard contract for her to sign, making her his client and saddling him with the power and obligation of confidentiality, she smiled again. This time he saw that her teeth were white and sharp.

As she glanced over the contract and dashed off her signature with a ballpoint pen, Nudger noticed her shoes, silver-blue high heels with black bows. His ex-wife, Eileen, often had worn a pair exactly like them. Another disquieting omen. He peeled the aluminum foil from the end of a fresh roll of antacid tablets and popped two of the chalky white disks into his mouth.

"Ulcer?" Jeanette asked, glancing at the roll of tablets as he chewed and countersigned.

"I don't know," Nudger said. "I'm afraid to see a doctor and find out."

"That's ridiculous."

"I'm interested in Jenine's social life," he said.

For all the expression they radiated, Jeanette's cool gray eyes might have been the glass orbs of a doll. "Of all Jenine's family and acquaintances, I'm the only one who knew that she liked men more than she should have. She confided in me because we were unusually close; we were twins. And because we were twins, she . . . well, she thought I might have the same inclinations." The slanted gray eyes shot icicles into Nudger. "I don't."

"Of course not." Message received. "Where did she meet these men?"

"On the lines."

Nudger rolled his cylinder of antacid tablets in a tight little circle on his desk. Rain slammed into the window again. He jumped. Jeanette didn't.

She explained: "During daylight hours there are several telephone numbers that phone company repairmen and installers use to test equipment. But in the late night and early morning hours, these lines are used by people who somehow get the numbers. They get to know each other without seeing the other party. Then maybe they make an appointment to meet somewhere, usually in a crowded public place, like a shopping mall. When they get there they look each other over as strangers, without being absolutely sure who they're looking at. If they like what they see, they make or accept overtures; if they don't see someone they want to get to know personally, they simply turn and walk away without making contact. It's nothing new; it's been going on in most big cities for years. There are people who've met through the lines and later married."

"Is using the lines legal?" Nudger asked.

"Technically, no. But the phone company puts up with what's going on. They don't use the lines during those hours anyway. And if they prosecuted these people, there would be nothing in it for them other than some bad publicity. People in trouble who need someone they can pour out their problems to, someone who can't even find out who they are, use the lines. Gays use them to meet partners. So do people like my sister."

For the first time Nudger glimpsed the agony within Jeanette, and it was a nailed-down and writhing thing that frightened him. How would a twin feel about the other twin's being murdered? Maybe a bit of Jeanette had died along with her sister. Maybe the half of the twins that survived became obsessed with retribution. Nudger decided that he was getting carried away and shook these metaphysical musings from his mind.

"There is in almost every large city a secret subculture of people who regularly talk on the lines," Jeanette told him, "people who usually are in no way connected in the daytime world. It's a desperate, troubled subculture, a lonely side of life that few people know exists. Jenine was part of it and it killed her."

"And you don't want the police to know Jenine used the lines."

"If the police were to know, then the family, and maybe everybody else, would find out. I don't want that to happen."

Nudger knew the police, knew the news media, here in St. Louis. He knew Jeanette was right. And she might be right about something else.

"What makes you think a mass killer of women is using the lines to meet his victims?" he asked.

"Another woman was murdered in her apartment last year, by someone the victim obviously knew and had entertained. Jenine was upset about it because she recognized the woman's name in the news-paper, and though they had never met, she knew her well through the lines. Using the lines, Jenine checked around and found out that there were at least three other female murder victims during the last three years who had regularly used the lines to meet partners. Two were slashed to death in bathtubs."

Nudger snapped an antacid tablet in half, then changed his mind and slipped both halves into his mouth and chewed. "For now," he said, "let's concentrate on Jenine. Which of the numbers did she use?"

"I don't know for sure. They all start with the prefix six-six-six, then the other four digits vary. And I don't know where Jenine got the number. I don't even know how many such lines are in service."

"She probably had the number written down," Nudger said. "People tend to write down important phone numbers, whether they can remember them or not."

"Even a number like that?" Jeanette asked. "One she wouldn't have wanted anyone to find?" She sounded dubious to the point of incredulity.

"Especially a number like that." Nudger scratched his chin, notic-ing absently that he hadn't shaved today. Poverty made a man lax. "Might Jenine have used more than one of these lines?"

"It's possible, but the numbers aren't easy to obtain. Usually a phone company employee, or a bartender, or maybe even someone on the line who uses more than one number, gives them out, but not to just anyone. I think the odds are good that Jenine only used one line, but of course we can't be sure. Some of the other victims used other lines as well as the one Jenine talked on."

"Do you have a key to your sister's apartment?" Nudger asked.

"Yes, and the police are finished there."

Nudger stood up, slipped his roll of antacid tablets into his shirt pocket, and shrugged into his sport jacket and light raincoat. Jeanette sat watching him in her eerily unruffled and efficient manner.

"We'll take my car," he said.

"The police have been all over Jenine's apartment," she told him. "They would have found the number if she'd written it somewhere there. I'm sure they would have."

"The six-six-six prefix is unforgettable," Nudger said, "and unwise to include in writing if secrecy enters into it. The police see phone numbers as seven digits; we're looking for four."

With another slow backward tilt of her head, Jeanette seemed to consider this and conclude that it made sense enough to act upon. She stood, glanced out the rain-distorted window, and buttoned her raincoat. "We can share my umbrella," she said, with a few degrees of warmth in her voice but not in her eyes.

Friends at last, Nudger told himself, and they left.

He was regretting his involvement with Jeanette Boyington, both consciously and on an instinctual level beyond consciousness. A subtle motion of events seemed to be stirring around him, like the hint of violent vortex movement a victim senses at the edges of a whirlpool in otherwise gentle water.

He swam on.

TWO

Jenine Boyington's apartment was still and drab, as if somberly reflecting its former occupant's death. The decor was neatly arranged hodgepodge. Over everything there was a thin film of dust that seemed to mute the light and give the furniture an odd waxy appearance. It reminded Nudger of the hue and texture of flesh after life had left it.

Jeanette shivered, then quickly tip-tapped across the room in her high heels and opened some drapes. The only effect was to admit more gloom from outside.

"Where do we start looking?" she asked, framed by gray sky beyond the window.

"Around the telephone," Nudger said, seeing a standard push-button phone on a small wooden table in the hall. There was a low stool near the phone, and on the table legs' cross braces rested a fat telephone directory.

Nudger's knees popped like Rice Krispies as he stooped and hoisted the thick directory. He checked the covers and front and back pages. A few phone numbers were penned or penciled inside the front cover, but they usually were accompanied by a name and all were prefixed by familiar three-digit exchanges. Nudger let his fingers do the walking through the interior pages but found no more handwritten numbers.

He scanned the wall near the phone, then examined the table's underside. No number. He helped Jeanette rummage through her dead twin's desk and dresser drawers, also without results.

Feeling more and more as if they were wasting time, he began to search in unlikely places. Maybe the damned number was written in code.

It was painstaking, discouraging work, and forty-five minutes had passed before Nudger said, "Gotcha!" and with a wide smile stood holding the telephone upside down and beckoning Jeanette.

"Jenine must have been given the number over the phone and didn't have a pen or pencil handy," he said. He held out the upside-down telephone for Jeanette to see, watched her lean close to it and squint somewhat myopically.

On the metal base of the phone was indented a long serial number. Four of the numerals—2,7,8,3—were traversed by deep scratches that might have been made by a pin or perhaps the tip of a key.

"The numbers aren't likely to be in the correct order," Jeanette said.

Nudger held the phone out in brighter light that slanted through the window. There seemed to be no distinction between the scratches; they were all approximately the same length, about two inches, and even slashed at the same angle.

"There are only four digits," he said. "We'll try them in various sequences with the six-six-six prefix."

Using a pen and paper from the desk to keep track of what sequences he'd tried, Nudger sat on the ridiculously small stool in the hall and began punching the phone's buttons.

What he got each time was a recording politely but acidly berating him for dialing incorrectly and suggesting that he please try again. He felt just like Beaver Cleaver being reprimanded by his TV series mother.

He kept trying, as the honey-voiced recording had urged.

On the fifth attempt he got a dial tone. He hung up the phone and jotted down the four numbers in the sequence that had accomplished this and slipped the paper into his pocket, immensely pleased with himself.

Jeanette was smiling down at him, apparently impressed at last. Nudger's ego inflated a couple of more pounds per square inch.

"Everything's elementary if approached in a simple-enough fashion," she said, shrinking him once more to doltish proportions.

"That's me," Nudger told her, "I'm simple and I work cheap."

"Don't be hard on yourself," Jeanette said. "Remember the model T Ford. Reliable if not swift. The favorite of millions."

They left Jenine's depressing apartment and Nudger drove Jeanette back to her car, parked outside his office.

His spirits perked up as he pulled to the curb in front of the building and switched off the engine; he was lucky enough to get the parking space with the broken meter. Fortune's wheel on the upswing?

"It smells terrific around here," Jeanette said, as he walked with her to her very practical blue sedan.

"That's the doughnut shop located directly below my office," Nudger told her. "Don't be fooled by the aroma."

"That's always been my philosophy," she said, unlocking and opening her car door. Before getting behind the steering wheel she asked, "What now?"

"As I am an investigator," Nudger said, "I will commence to investigate. I'm going to find out more about those numbers; I'm well connected at the phone company."

She lowered her neat frame and scooted onto the seat, fishing in her oversized white vinyl purse for her keys. "You'll call me?"

"When I have something worth saying."

Her face was as placid and unexpressive as ever as she drove away. She could have been one of the gang on Mount Rushmore.

Nudger realized suddenly that a cool drizzle was falling on him and that it was past lunchtime. Probably he should have invited the unresponsive Jeanette to dine with him. That would have been the gentlemanly and professional thing to do, even though he didn't want to take time for lunch.

Dodging traffic, he crossed the street, but before trudging up the narrow flight of stairs to his office, he ducked into Danny's Donuts. He would assuage hunger and at the same time do penance for his lack of manners by eating an iced Danny's Dunker Delite, and so kill two birds with one stone.

Chewing antacid tablets as if they were addictive, Nudger left his office and bounced across St. Louis in his dented vintage Volkswagen beetle to his appointment with Sam Fisher, a phone company programmer who made most of his income with his lucrative side business.

"So whose phone do you want bugged, Nudge?" Fisher asked, as Nudger settled into a chair in Fisher's semi-private, glassed-in office. The place was like an aquarium.

Nudger's stomach did a quick somersault and he glanced around nervously at the scores of employees milling about beyond the clear glass walls of the cubicle. He felt as if he and Fisher were on display. "Aren't you, er, afraid someone might overhear?"

Fisher smiled beneath his wide graying mustache. He had the eyes of an anarchist. "I do the overhearing around here." He waved an arm, gold wristwatch glinting. "Nobody'll hear us in here; I took precautions."

"Good," Nudger said, "because I came here for information."

Not telling Fisher why he wanted that information, Nudger explained what he needed to know. Fisher confirmed that there were such service numbers, and that it was common knowledge within the company that they were used for illegal late night conversations but that nothing was being done about it. The reasons he gave for the phone company's inaction were the same that Jeanette had stated.

"There are five such numbers, Nudge," Fisher said. "The caller dials, hears a tone, then waits until someone dials the corresponding number that makes the connection. The line will stay open until that happens."

"There's no ring?" Nudger asked.

"Not on these lines," Fisher said. "During the day they're kept open for installers and repairmen. At night the weirdos get on the lines and wait for a similar weirdo to make a connection. Weird talk ensues. Nobody knows exactly how these numbers become known to the public, but people have a way of finding out, especially the kinds of people who might use the lines at night."

"Can more than two people use one line at the same time?"

"No. They're not like party or conference lines. Anyone wanting to use a busy line has to wait until one of the callers has hung up."

"Would there be any permanent record of such calls from a particular number?"

Fisher shook his head. "None."

An impeccably groomed executive type in a three-piece pinstripe suit knocked on the glass cubicle and pointedly held up his wristwatch, apparently reminding Sam Fisher of an appointment, probably for lunch. Fisher waved and the man went away.

"What I need to know, Sam . . ." Nudger said.

But Fisher was already jotting down the five phone numbers on his memo pad. He was probably hungry. He ripped off the sheet of paper and handed it to Nudger.

Nudger thanked him.

"I'll send you a bill," Fisher said, "just like the telephone company."

After Nudger left phone company headquarters, he drove to a restaurant on Washington Avenue and ordered a bacon omelet and a glass of milk. His waitress was a coltish teenage girl with a hundred fiery pimples. She almost dropped or spilled everything and smiled a lot with self-conscious charm.

He sat picking at his food and staring out the grease-spotted window at the traffic on Washington, thinking about how things didn't feel right the way they were shaping up. Nudger didn't like danger, and in the manner of any sensible citizen did what he could to avoid it. Of course in his occupation that wasn't always possible, not unless one tried extra hard. He tried extra hard, always, and had developed a warning sense like that of a ten-point deer during hunting season. That warning tingle at the base of his spine was fairly screaming at him that this time he had stepped into something particularly nasty. He felt like Alice after falling down the rabbit hole, only everybody was trying to keep it from him that he was in Wonderland.

Leaving half the glass of milk and most of the undercooked omelet, he paid his check and left a reasonable tip for the acne-marred teenager. He hoped she realized that someday she would be a beauty. Just as he stepped from the restaurant door onto the sidewalk, it began to rain again. This city and its come-and-go weather.

Nudger returned to his office, locked the door, and got out the army surplus cot and his sleeping bag from the closet. After checking the answering machine for phone messages and hearing about past-due bills and a limited discount on lakeside resort property, he set his wristwatch's alarm for midnight. Then he stretched out on his back on the cot, not bothering to get into the sleeping bag.

He laced his hands behind his head and closed his eyes, listening to the oddly comforting faint rattle and pop of steam pipes, the inter-mittent soft swishing sound of traffic on the rain-swept street two stories below. At least for the time being things were under his con-trol and manageable.

He was forty-three years old. He was tired. The two facts were not unrelated. He had no trouble falling asleep.

The innocent sleep blissfully. So do the unsuspecting.

THREE

Each shrill, penetrating bleep of his wristwatch alarm was like the point of a needle probing the tissue of Nudger's brain. Something similarly sharp had been scraped across the base of Jenine Boy-ington's phone, he told himself foggily in his world of uneasy dreams.

As Nudger came awake, he groped for the ridiculously tiny watch stem and switched off the alarm, then pressed another stem and saw by the glow produced that it was two minutes past midnight. His office was dimly illuminated from the street lamp on the corner. Ev-erything was quiet; even the steam pipes were taking a rest from their cacophony of popping and hissing.

Nudger sat on the edge of the cot, his head resting in his hands. His throat was dry; his tongue was thick and seemed to be covered with that stuff used to fasten coats without buttons or zippers. It was the witching hour and cold and dark, so what was he doing still in his office? What was he doing struggling out of bed? What was he doing in this business? But he knew; he was eating regularly and sometimes paying the bills. The stuff of life.

He stood up, went into the small half-bath and splashed cold water onto his face and rinsed out his mouth. He glanced at his reflection in the mirror above the washbasin, winced, looked away, and went back into the office and sat behind his desk. His swivel chair squealed loud enough to wake the doughnuts downstairs.

After switching on his yellow-shaded desk lamp, Nudger reached for the phone and dragged it to him. He tried the number from the base of Jenine's phone and got a busy signal. Then he tried all the numbers Fisher had given him and was surprised to keep getting busy signals. He decided to try only the number from Jenine's apartment and sat punching it out every half minute until he got a dial tone.

Within seconds there was a loud click in the receiver. A male voice said, "Are you there, sweet thing?"

"I'm here," Nudger said. "How sweet I am is debatable."

"What's not debatable," the man said, "is that you're not my kind of sweet. That is, unless you've got an awfully deep voice to match perfect thirty-six C-cup lung power."

"I wear a forty-four-long suitcoat," Nudger said, "sometimes triple-knit, usually a bit frayed at the cuffs and elbows. Still interested?"

The man laughed. "Sure, but not in you, pal. I got a feeling we're looking for the same thing." He hung up.

Very possible, Nudger thought, staying on the line.

Another click.

"I'm a Nordic-type music lover in my early thirties, and I prefer the muscular Mediterranean macho type," a man said, sounding like one of those classified ads in the personal column of the *National Enquirer*. "I can be sheep or wolf, if anyone is listening. Also I'm into rubber. Hello, hello, are you there, lover? Are you assimilating my red-hot vibes?"

"I'm assimilating them," Nudger said, "but I'm not quite on the same wave length. I'm into chocolate frosting."

"Sounds divine."

"That's what Betty Crocker says."

"You jest?"

"I jest."

"*Ciao,* then." *Click*.

There was something more than a little sad in all of this, Nudger thought, as he shifted position in his chair. It reminded him of forced gaiety on New Year's Eve, when everybody realized that time was slipping away from them, but wore funny hats and tooted horns and then riotously sang "Auld Lang Syne," essentially a sad song.

As if from a great distance, a woman's gentle voice inquired, "Is anyone there? Anyone? Please?"

"I'm here," Nudger told her, pressing the receiver tighter to his ear.

"I'm lonely and I'm going to kill myself," the woman said. She said it as if she meant it.

Nudger sat up straight. What the French call a *frisson* raised the hair on the nape of his neck. "Don't do that, please."

"It's closing in on me," the woman said. "Everything's closing in on me. I don't think there's any other way to stop it."

"I understand how you feel," Nudger told her, "really I do."

"You don't. You can't. It's asinine of you to say you understand."

"Maybe I can't know for sure whether I understand," Nudger conceded, "but I've had the feeling you just described, where it seems that every available move will lose the game."

"What do you do?"

"I move, I lose, I start over."

She laughed. It was a sad laugh, a manifestation of hopelessness.

"I've had some experience with suicides," Nudger said. "None of the people you leave behind will feel sorry for you. Oh, maybe they will at first, but within a short time they'll be angry about what you did. They'll stay angry for a long while, maybe the rest of their lives."

"What possible difference will that make to me when I'm dead?"

There was sound logic in that, all right, Nudger admitted to himself.

"When life becomes unbearable," the woman said, "why should we continue to suffer?" More logic. Damn!

"Because we only *think* life is unbearable. If we hang on a while, the situation usually eases up, or maybe it gets worse in a way that might be a little more interesting."

The woman laughed again, not quite so hopelessly this time.

"Maybe you ought to try seeing a doctor," Nudger suggested, "a professional who can help you in some way you can't imagine."

"I've been to a psychiatrist. He listened to me, just like you, only he took notes. Are you taking notes?"

"No, but I would if I thought it would stop you from taking your life. Why don't you tell me what's bothering you. It might help you if you share your misery."

"Do you believe in hell?"

"No."

"I do. I'm in it."

"Don't be too sure," Nudger said. "You've got nothing to compare it with."

"Do you really think there is something to compare?"

"I think death is nothingness," Nudger told her. "It scares me."

"I take it back; you're not like the psychiatrist."

"Do you like gorilla jokes?" Nudger asked.

Again the laugh, briefer but brighter. "What a mundane thing to ask a potential suicide."

"Death is mundane. There is nothing more mundane. Talk to me tomorrow and I'll tell you some gorilla jokes."

She didn't say anything for a long time. Nudger thought she might not still be on the line. Then she said, "I don't want to hear the one about where they sleep."

"My gorilla jokes are much more sophisticated than that. Talk to me tomorrow night. Promise me." He sensed that he almost had her.

Another pause. "Are gorilla jokes worth staying alive for?"

"Mine are. Anything is worth staying alive for. Talk to me tomorrow on this line. You'll see. Everyone likes good gorilla jokes. They're a positive force in this world."

"All right," she said. "But I don't promise. I can't."

"Sure," Nudger told her. "Same time?"

"Same time," she said, and abruptly hung up.

Nudger replaced his own receiver. He realized that the woman had somehow become more than just a disembodied voice in the night, more than a stranger; their conversation had been piercingly intimate, and he felt as if he knew her, cared about her. Was that what Sam Fisher would describe as weird? Was it so bad? She had been reaching out for human contact, talking and not killing herself.

The office was quiet, the air motionless and thick, almost like liquid. Nudger's right hand still rested on the flesh-warm receiver. He was clenching his free fist hard enough for his fingernails to indent his palm, and he was perspiring heavily. There was more electricity on the nighttime service lines than was supplied by the phone company.

Nudger usually spared his intestines the rigors of coping with alcohol, but now he got up and walked to the file cabinet where he kept a bottle of Johnny Walker red label for special occasions and his very best clients. He poured himself a generous slug of the amber stuff in a rinsed-out coffee cup, drank it down and felt its warm bite. He went to the window and stood looking down at the street, at the faint greenish neon glow from the Danny's Donuts sign directly below. He wished the shop were open with doleful Danny down there behind the counter, grayish towel tucked in his belt, packing his greasy merchandise in fold-up cardboard boxes for carry-out orders for the workers in the surrounding shops and office buildings. It would be nice to talk with someone face-to-face. To read expressions.

Instead, Nudger set the empty cup on the windowsill and returned to his desk and the telephone.

He made several more contacts, had more lengthy conversations, before sitting back and considering it a night's work. He looked at his watch and was surprised to see that it was almost 5 A.M. Nudger had wanted to acquire a feel for what went over the lines and he'd gotten it. It had sobered him.

He stretched his arms and back, exhaling loudly. Then he made one more phone call, to the Third District, and left a message for Lieutenant Jack Hammersmith, who didn't come on duty until seven o'clock. When he had hung up, he reset his alarm and lay down again on the sagging cot, this time unable to sleep.

Around him the city gradually awakened, and the nighttime lines were claimed by the daylight hours and became once more the province of telephone company employees conducting routine business.

But a piece of the night had claimed Nudger, with its accompanying very real but indecipherable apprehensions. Like a child, he was afraid of the dark. And he was trapped in it.

FOUR

Hammersmith sat behind his desk in his Third District office and gazed at Nudger through a greenish haze of smoke emitted by one of his incredibly foul-smelling cigars. He was a corpulent Buddha of a man now, so unlike the sleekly handsome officer who had charmed and cajoled the ladies when he and Nudger were partners a decade ago in a two-man patrol car. Time did that sort of thing to people, Nudger mused, sitting down in the hard oak chair before Hammersmith's desk. He wondered fleetingly what time was doing to him, then promptly forced such depressing speculation from his consciousness. Why stick pins in oneself?

"What are you on to now, Nudge?" Hammersmith asked.

"I need to know about the Jenine Boyington murder," Nudger said, breathing shallowly to inhale as little secondhand smoke as possible. He understood why the Geneva Convention had outlawed chemical warfare.

Hammersmith seemed to read his mind, drew on the cigar and exhaled another green billow. "Medium-height-and-weight female Caucasian," he said, "found fully clothed in her bathtub with her throat slashed. There was alcohol in her blood—what was left of it when we met her. The killing was a nice neat job. No arrests, no suspects."

"All of that was in the newspapers," Nudger said.

Hammersmith narrowed sharp blue eyes within pads of flesh. "Are you on the case?"

Nudger nodded.

"We don't like that, Nudge. Anybody else I'd tell to butt out."

"I'll stay out of your way. Really."

"No need to promise," Hammersmith told him. "Who's your client?"

"Jeanette Boyington, the victim's twin sister."

"What do you know that we should?" Hammersmith asked.

Client confidentiality or not, Nudger knew that withholding evidence in a homicide case was illegal and would at the very least get his license suspended. That was one of the reasons he had come here, to protect himself. He could divulge such information to Hammersmith and keep it reasonably confidential unless it proved to be the crux of the investigation.

"My client and I wouldn't want this information spread around," Nudger said.

"It won't be. Do I need to promise?"

Nudger smiled. "No." He wondered sometimes at the bond formed between two men who spent countless hours in a cramped patrol car, depending upon each other day after day for their very lives. "Jenine Boyington had a habit of making late-night phone calls and meeting men," he said. And he explained to Hammersmith about the phone company service lines and their bizarre and desperate nighttime use.

"All of that might not be relevant," Hammersmith said, when Nudger had finished. But both men knew better. Hammersmith was playing the game and would explore the new avenue of investigation as quietly as possible. He had always been nifty at stealth.

"Time now for the other end of the trade," Nudger said. He was aware that often the police held back some pertinent piece of information from the news media. Aside from this helping them to screen the inevitable procession of cranks who confessed to every sensational homicide, it gave them a hole card to play against the murderer.

Hammersmith didn't try to be evasive. He took another pull on his cigar, exhaled a thundercloud, and said, "There were a few strands of blond hair under one of the victim's broken fingernails."

"The victim was a blonde," Nudger said.

Hammersmith shook his head, his heavy jowls undulating. "It

wasn't her hair. Jenine Boyington's hair was straight. These strands of hair were about six inches long and came from the head of somebody with very curly blond hair. They almost have to be the killer's." Another draw on the cigar. "And something else. We got a set of smudged prints, useless except that they indicate by the wide spread of the fingers that the perpetrator has abnormally large hands. Huge hands."

"Have any other women been murdered in their bathtubs during the last few years?" Nudger asked.

"Sure. But then bathtubs are a common enough place to find female murder victims. What could be more traditional?"

Nudger thanked Hammersmith and stood up from the hard oak chair. The chair was so uncomfortable that it was impossible to sit in for more than about ten minutes. Hammersmith knew it; he was a workaholic and didn't like to be disturbed for longer than that by visitors. Nudger wondered if he'd had the torturous chair custommade.

He was at the door when Hammersmith's voice stopped him.

"Your client, Nudge, is she an identical twin?"

"She looks exactly like her sister's newspaper photo," Nudger said.

"Sometimes," Hammersmith said, "one twin takes the death of the other unnaturally hard. It's like they think death ought to be shared between them like everything else."

"You worried about some compulsion for revenge?" Nudger asked.

"I'm telling you to worry about it. Keep an eye on your client. She might get cute."

"She already is cute, in a reptilian sort of way."

"And let me know if you find out anything else about those dead-of-night phone conversations."

"Some of the talk you hear on those lines can tear your heart," Nudger said. *Is anyone there? Anyone? Please?*

Hammersmith shrugged and picked up a pen from his desk. "My heart's been torn and torn. So has yours, but your problem is your heart grows no scar tissue. Get out."

Nudger got out.

*   *   *

When he returned to his office, Nudger found that Danny had let someone in to wait for him. That was the arrangement Nudger had with the doughnut-shop owner. Danny was less convenient but much cheaper than a secretary.

Even before she introduced herself, Nudger suspected the identity of the middle-aged, stiff-backed woman seated in the chair before his desk. She had to be well over fifty, but there was in her still composure, calm gray eyes, and petite curvaceousness a familiar chilly vitality.

"I'm Agnes Boyington," she said, half standing as Nudger entered. "Jeanette's mother." She offered a cool hand, which Nudger shook gently, then she sat back down and waited for him to circle his desk and settle into his swivel chair. She winced when the chair yowled.

"I assume Jeanette told you she hired me to investigate Jenine's murder," Nudger said.

"No, she didn't. But I came across your name and phone number when I was visiting Jeanette. Then I discovered that you were a private investigator."

Nudger smiled thinly. "It seems you've been doing some investigating yourself," he said, instinctively not liking this woman, not liking her at all.

"I bore Jeanette and Jenine late in life, Mr. Nudger," Agnes Boyington said, as if recalling with distaste the messy process of childbirth. "Perhaps for that reason I spoiled them, meddled too much in their affairs. Yes, I admit that. But I don't intend to confront Jeanette with what I've discovered and insist that she terminate her arrangement with you."

Nudger was ahead of Agnes Boyington. He knew she realized that dealing that way with her daughter would be futile. Jeanette would simply hire another investigator, taking pains to be more secretive. "Isn't my arrangement with her pretty much up to Jeanette, whether you confront her or not?" Nudger said. "She's how old . . . in her early twenties?"

"Twenty-eight," Agnes Boyington snapped, as if this were distinctly none of Nudger's business. He understood why and immediately raised his estimate of Jeanette's mother's age. "But she listens to her mother, usually."

"If you don't intend to interfere," Nudger said flatly, "why did you come here?"

Agnes Boyington leaned forward in her chair and fixed her unblinking eyes on Nudger, summoning her powers to persuade. "I'm here to try to convince you that the police should be left to handle alone the investigation of Jenine's murder. Jeanette was very close to her twin sister. Whatever she told you would be colored by her grief, and the emotional residue of her recent trouble. She would benefit from your benign neglect."

"Recent trouble?" Nudger said, grabbing at the brass ring that had been so obviously proffered.

"I regret the necessity to tell you this," Agnes Boyington lied, "and I am relying on your professional ethics to ensure your silence. Just a few months ago Jenine underwent an abortion."

"I thought you said the recent trouble was Jeanette's."

Agnes Boyington removed a long, slender brown cigarette from her purse and lit it with a silver lighter that worked on the first try. She had about her the air of a woman who was used to things working on the first attempt, a woman whose daughters, especially Jenine, had been an aggravation in an otherwise perfectly controlled existence. After making sure the cigarette was burning adequately, she condescended to speak to Nudger.

"Jeanette got into an argument with the man who impregnated Jenine," she said. "They fought over who was to pay for the abortion, and I'm sure they had other matters over which to fight. He beat her up badly, then left the city. The girls thought they were keeping it a secret from me, but of course they weren't." She sighed and gazed for a moment at the ceiling, as if seeking tolerance to cope with this world that didn't measure up to her standards. "It was I who eventually paid for Jenine's abortion, under the guise of a loan for a different purpose. I have paid for my daughters' mistakes all their lives. It's the cross God has given me to bear."

"What's the man's name?" Nudger asked.

"It doesn't matter. I want to maintain some discretion. I'm only here to try to impress upon you the fact that Jeanette isn't thinking clearly right now; she's suffered two traumatic experiences in the past eight weeks. Be advised, do not take what she says as gospel truth."

She stood up. She had the carriage and suppleness of a much younger woman. Age had somehow overlooked her. Or maybe she'd made a deal with the devil, something to ease the burden of that cross.

"So you want me to drop the case without telling Jeanette," Nudger said, still seated.

She smiled very faintly, pointing her smoldering long cigarette at him as if it were a magic wand that could in a wink make him disappear if she so chose. "Exactly, Mr. Nudger. Though I don't know you, since you move with at least some competence upon the less genteel and more demanding underside of life, I am assuming that you are a man of some practical wisdom and judgment. The police will find Jenine's murderer, *if* he can be found." She snuffed out the just-lighted cigarette in the ashtray on the corner of the desk, a gesture done entirely for effect, theatrical yet low-key. "Let me know what you decide, at your convenience. I'll send you a check of a more than generous amount."

Nudger was struck again by the woman's similarity to her daughter. Was there a mold somewhere turning out these shapely, cool, and distant women? He couldn't resist asking, "Are you a twin, Mrs. Boyington?"

"No. Twins run in families, Mr. Nudger, but usually they occur every other generation. My mother was a twin."

"Is Jeanette's father alive?"

"Herbert died twenty-five years ago. I never remarried. Why do you ask?"

"Curiosity, Mrs. Boyington." Nudger smiled and shrugged. "That's why I'm a detective." He didn't tell her it had crossed his mind that spiders sometimes devour their mates.

"You *will* consider my proposition?" she said. It was not really a question, rather a command.

"Oh, I try to consider everything. A closed mind is the devil's workshop."

"That's 'idle hands,' Mr. Nudger."

"I wasn't quoting."

She shot a withering glance at him, nodded, and stalked from the office, leaving in her wake a scent more like disinfectant than perfume.

Nudger listened to her measured steps on the narrow wooden stairs that led to the street door, heard it open and close and felt the subtle change of temperature in a draft across his ankles. It felt warmer, now that Agnes Boyington had gone.

Nudger drummed his fingers on the desk for a few minutes. Then he stood up and went downstairs, out the street door, and made a tight turn and entered the warm and cloying atmosphere of Danny's Donuts.

Danny was alone in the shop, as usual. Nudger often wondered how he stayed in business. But then he was sure Danny wondered the same thing about him. Neither of them was considering tax-free municipals.

Danny's basset-hound features brightened when he saw Nudger, and he poured a cup of his acidic coffee and placed it on the counter in front of Nudger's customary stool near the serving door.

Nudger sat and sipped. It was the polite thing to do. Danny plunked down a leadlike glazed doughnut next to the cup. Nudger knew that Danny's freebies were leftovers from yesterday's unsold pastry, and he was not so polite that he would eat *that* deadly morsel, despite Danny's extreme sensitivity about the quality of his product.

"I was upstairs thinking," Nudger said.

"That's your line of business, Nudge."

"Yeah. Didn't you once tell me you were a twin?"

"That's right. I had an identical twin brother. Sammy was his name. Samuel and Daniel."

"Where is Samuel now?" Nudger asked.

Danny smiled, but there was a gleam of old sadness in his brown eyes. "Sammy died when we were six," he said.

"Being twins," Nudger said, "do you think you were closer than other brothers?"

Danny began carefully wiping down the stainless-steel counter. It didn't need it. "I don't know, Nudge. How could I be sure; I never had another brother, and we were so young when he died."

"Have you ever worried about him dying young?" Nudger asked. "I mean, aren't identical twins genetically the same, so that their organs are subject to the same weaknesses, the same diseases?"

"It never worried me, Nudge," Danny said with that same sad

smile that Nudger had never seen before today. "Sammy was hit and killed by a car."

"I see." Nudger sipped his coffee, burned his tongue, decided he had it coming. "I'm sorry to pry, Danny."

Danny shrugged and tucked his gray dish towel into his belt. "Been a long time ago, Nudge."

But not so long that it didn't still bring pain, Nudger thought. And Jeanette Boyington had lost her twin sister only last week.

"You mixed up in a case with twins?" Danny asked.

"'Mixed up' describes what I am exactly."

"Well, I'll help you if I can. You know that, don't you?"

"I know," Nudger said. And he did know. Some things you don't doubt.

"That all you wanted, Nudge?" Danny asked.

"That and this," Nudger said, and girded himself and took a bite of the stale doughnut. He watched with satisfaction the slow formation of Danny's customary amiable smile.

Outside the doughnut-shop window, a hulking man in a tan windbreaker and a bright yellow, billed cap was squinting through the glass at Nudger. His coarse features—flattened nose, shelflike eyebrows, outthrust wide jaw—registered subtle satisfaction as he impressed Nudger's face upon his memory. He would know Nudger instantly if he saw him again, anywhere.

He turned from the doughnut-shop window and lumbered halfway down the street to where his car was parked. It was a brown ten-year-old Buick, faded and rusty and as hulking as its owner. As the man got behind the steering wheel and slammed the door, the rearview mirror wobbled and dropped to a crooked position from the impact. He started the car and pulled away from the curb, and was only a few blocks away when he automatically reached for a small red rubber ball on the seat beside him. He began to squeeze the ball rhythmically as he drove, exercising the already powerful forearm rippling beneath the windbreaker sleeve.

As he stopped for a traffic light, he glanced down at the ball expanding and contracting between his fingers and figured that it was probably just about the size of Nudger's Adam's apple. He smiled, not at all with his eyes, and with only one corner of his mouth.

Then the light changed and for the time being he completely forgot about Nudger. Squeezing the ball and driving occupied his entire capacity for concentration.

FIVE

"Mother has always been a snoop and an interloper," Jeanette said, later that day in Nudger's office.

Nudger made a tent with his fingers, just like Sidney Greenstreet used to do in Bogart movies, and stared candidly at Jeanette. "I'm playing this game honestly with you," he said. "Which is why I told you about your mother's visit. And I need complete honesty from you. What's the name of the man who got Jenine pregnant and beat up on you?"

"Wally. Wallace Everest. But he didn't."

"Didn't what?"

Jeanette uncrossed her shapely legs, planted her dainty silver high heels firmly on the floor, and aimed eyes like her mother's at Nudger. "You wanted honesty, and that's what you're going to get." She made it sound like a threat, and maybe it was. "Mother doesn't know everything. She doesn't know that I was the one seeing Wally, the one he made pregnant, the one who had the abortion."

"Prolong the honesty and explain," Nudger said.

"I'd been seeing Wally for several months. When he found out I was expecting his baby, he was angry instead of happy. He said he was leaving me and never wanted to see me again. Then he suggested the abortion. When I cried on Jenine's shoulder and told her what had happened, she came up with a plan."

There were curves that you could see and curves that you couldn't in the Boyington family, Nudger reflected. "Plan?" he said, and listened with some apprehension.

"Jenine confided in me that she'd already had three abortions," Jeanette said. "She suggested that rather than create a black mark against me and possibly incur the rage of Mother, she'd be the one to have the abortion instead of me. Abortion number four would mean little to her, or to Mother if she found out, considering Jenine's other activities and previous abortions, which Mother's spying might any day uncover. Mother is not a liberal or understanding person."

Some understatement, Nudger thought. "Didn't this plan pose somewhat of a medical problem?" he asked.

"Not one we couldn't solve. I simply went to an abortion clinic as Jenine, with all of her identification, including driver's license with photograph. So as far as anyone, even the doctor, knows, it was Jenine who had the abortion."

"I can guess the rest," Nudger said. "When you saw Wally Everest after the abortion, you tried to take up where you'd left off, but he still didn't want to see you and you fought." Nudger was only speculating, but he wanted to give Jeanette a version that might get her angry and crack her hard exterior so that he might gauge the truth inside. He waited for the fury of a woman presumed scorned, but it never made itself evident. Her serene yet oddly predatory features remained calm. It was as if she were a member of another species.

"I never wanted to lay eyes on Wally again and still don't," she said. "I went to him to get the money to pay for the abortion, the money he'd promised to give me so I'd terminate the pregnancy. But he backed down on the deal and refused to give me anything, got angry and called me names and then laughed at me. I lost my temper and struck him. It was all the excuse he needed. He beat me badly enough to put me in the hospital for two days. I never felt so much pain and fear."

"How do you feel about Wally now?"

"I hate him, of course."

"Have you seen him since the beating?"

"No. He left town while I was in the hospital. At least that's what I was told by his landlady and a few of his acquaintances. They said he moved to Cincinnati to start a new salesman's job. Wally sells religious textbooks; he's very good at it."

Nudger felt like reaching into his bottom desk drawer for the thermos of warm milk he kept there, but he decided that wouldn't seem very businesslike.

He waited until Jeanette had left, then he reached instead for the telephone and called Jack Hammersmith.

When he came to the phone Hammersmith asked, "Do you have something to tell me that will break the Jenine Boyington case wide open?"

"I never saw a case break wide open," Nudger said. "I don't know exactly what that expression means."

"But you do have some tidbit of information for me?"

"No. I don't know what a tidbit is, and I called to *ask* for information."

"You're like the rest of the world." Hammersmith sounded betrayed.

"Out here in the world away from Headquarters lives a guy named Wallace Everest. Know anything about him?"

"All I need to know, Nudge. He's the victim's ex-boyfriend. A bad sort. The mother told us about him. He's got an ironclad alibi in Cincinnati for the time of the murder. And he has dark hair."

"Thanks," Nudger told him. "You're on top of things."

"It's slippery up here, Nudge."

"I know. Everything that slides off falls on us folks down here."

He said good-bye to Hammersmith and quickly hung up before the lieutenant could reply. Hammersmith was accustomed to having the last word and would be irritated and chomp his poisonous cigar and literally fume about not having it this time. Good.

Nudger didn't dwell long on Hammersmith. He was thinking about how his options had narrowed, how the twists and turns of the Boyington women had brought him smack up against one obvious course of action. It was a plan he hadn't wanted to put into effect, because it was dangerous for him and dangerous for Jeanette Boyington.

But now it seemed to be that or nothing. In such situations, Nudger always chose that. It was the only way he could manage to stay in business.

"I want you to talk to men on the lines at night," Nudger told Jeanette that evening. "I want you to make appointments with them, if that's what they ask for. Tell them you'll meet them at some busy public place, preferably a large shopping mall."

Jeanette sat across from Nudger's desk and nodded somberly as he spoke, as if each of his words were physically penetrating her mind to be lodged solidly forever in the gray matter of her memory. He

could tell, watching her, that she'd meant it when she said she
wanted to help find her twin sister's killer, meant it perhaps more
strongly than she had revealed.

"Do you want me to meet these men?" she asked. He saw that she
was willing to undergo that danger. In fact, she was downright eager.

"No," Nudger told her, "I'll get their descriptions from you, then
go to the appointed place and look them over. If one of them happens
to have curly blond hair and oversized hands, I'll follow him when he
leaves disappointed and find out who he is."

"And then?"

"Then we'll watch him and decide whether the fish we've hooked
is legal and should be reeled in." Nudger studied her eyes as he
spoke. They were flat gray in his dimly lighted office and made him
wonder if her lifeless expression was the result of her sister's death;
Hammersmith had said some twins thought that way.

"Jenine told me she usually talked on the lines about three A.M.,"
Jeanette said, "when she couldn't sleep and was depressed. She said
three A.M. was the perilous hour, a time perfectly balanced between
darkness and light, joy and despair in the human soul."

"She had a poetic turn of mind."

"Had . . ." Jeanette repeated, twisting her lips as if she loathed the
taste of the word. "I'll make my phone calls between the hours of
two and four A.M. That should increase the chances of making connections with the man who killed Jenine."

"Remember that we're not sure someone she met through talking
on the lines is her killer," Nudger cautioned.

"I think we're sure," Jeanette said, decisive as always. "He killed
her and he killed those other women, and probably he killed more
women he met over the lines."

"All right," Nudger conceded, "we're sure. Sure enough, anyway.
What we're trying to do now is determine if we're right."

"Agreed," she said, obviously not meaning it. Nudger wondered if
she had doubted herself even once since she had popped from the
womb.

"Your phone conversations will require some convincing acting,"
he said.

"Don't worry, my heart will be in it." She seemed to turn her attention inward, as if seeking pain, like a method actor gearing up for a role, "Do you think this plan will produce results?"

"It might, if we have enough patience."

"Ever seen a cat poised patiently watching a mouse hole?" Jeanette asked.

"Only in a cartoon."

"Well, that's how patient I am. Like that cat." There was nothing cartoonlike about the intensity in her voice. Or in her eyes.

After she'd left with a list of phone company service-line numbers, Nudger sat for a long time at his desk, chewing antacid tablets and watching the office darken as the evening sun forsook the city.

He thought that if he were a mouse he wouldn't go outside his door.

SIX

Nudger's stomach lay weighty and solid as cement just beneath his rib cage. He was at his desk in his dim office, watching the big hand of the clock with the intentness of a school kid eager for the bell. The telephone receiver was jammed against his ear and he could hear his own pulse pounding on the line, merged with the faint hissings and distant clickings of the phone company's electronic monolith. It was as if the phone were draining him of something that it needed in order for its infinitely complex whole to exist and disseminate information and gossip and dispatch monthly bills.

He'd been on the line for almost an hour, discouraging hopeful romantics and listening to outpourings of desperation and sometimes madness. And waiting. It was thirty-five minutes past midnight.

At sixteen minutes to one, she was there. Nudger recognized her beaten, tenuous voice immediately as she asked if anyone was on the line.

"I'm here," he said. "I've been waiting for you."

"Were you worried about me again?"

"Yes."

"But you don't even know me."

"I was worried about you."

She let go of the subject. Nudger hoped she believed him. "It's odd," she told him, faintly amused through her despondency, "but I found myself actually looking forward to hearing your gorilla jokes."

"Not so odd," Nudger said. "Millions of people stay alive for nothing more intriguing than their golf games."

"How drab."

"Sub-par to you but important to them. It's a subjective thing."

"Okay, let's have it," she said wearily. "This gorilla walks into a bar and . . ."

"Exactly!" Nudger said with enthusiasm. "But stop me if you've—"

"Please!"

"Okay, this gorilla walks into this bar where there's nobody but the bartender, polishing glasses. So the guy looks up and is astounded to see a gorilla, more astounded when the gorilla saunters over and sits on a bar stool."

"I'm properly astounded. Get on with it."

"The bartender goes to the owner in the back room and says, 'A huge gorilla just walked in and sat at the bar. What do I do now?' 'So ask him what he's drinking,' the owner says."

"So the bartender goes back . . ."

"Right, the bartender goes back and says—"

" 'What'll you have?' "

"Very good. And the gorilla growls, 'Beer.' The bartender checks with the owner, who says, 'Well, give him a beer.' When the bartender sets the mug on the bar, the gorilla hands him a ten-dollar bill. So the bartender goes back to the owner and says in a shocked voice, 'That gorilla gave me a ten. What do I do?' 'Gorillas aren't very smart,' the owner says, 'so give him back a dollar for change.' The bartender does that and gets by with it, and starts polishing glasses again and is getting very nervous because the gorilla just sits there silently, sipping beer and staring straight ahead. Finally the bartender leans an elbow on the bar, to look casual, and says in a shaky voice just to make conversation and ease the tension, 'You know, we don't get many gorillas in here.' "

"And the gorilla says?"

"'I guess not, at nine dollars a beer.'"

Nudger waited. Static on the line, no laughter. But then he hadn't really expected any.

"Is that the end?" she asked finally.

"Uh, yeah. It's one of those 'all hell must have broken loose' jokes. You know the type. Based on the listener's imagination. Rooted in the future."

"Very apropos, not very funny."

"More interesting than a golf game."

"I'm not so sure."

"How do you feel tonight?" Nudger asked. "About the future?"

"Not much different."

"But different?"

"Jesus, I don't know. You didn't save my life with that gorilla joke."

"I know more of them."

"Don't threaten me." Her voice became calmer, more serious. "I did want to talk with you again. I don't know why, except that for some reason you seemed . . ."

"To understand?"

"No, not that. You seemed to care, even though we're strangers."

Nudger looked at the blackness outside his window. "Sometimes two strangers can talk for a few minutes and then not be strangers. A rapport is there that springs from something deeper than they know, like the confluence of rivers underground."

"Very eloquent. Probably nonsense."

"If you took your life, I'd care a great deal. Do you believe that?"

"I'm not sure. I seem to believe it, despite myself."

"What's your name?" Nudger asked. "What's your conventional phone number?"

"No!" she blurted, almost shouted the word.

Too fast, Nudger warned himself, *too fast*. "Take it easy," he said gently. "I'll give you my name. It's Nudger, Alo Nudger. Short for Aloysius. Everyone just calls me Nudger."

"I never met anyone actually named Aloysius. I'm sorry for you."

"Will you tell me your first name?" He felt like a teenager coaxing a reluctant sophomore virgin.

"It's Claudia," she said. She spoke the name as if she disliked it.

"Would you like to have my phone number, Claudia? In case you want to get in touch with me during the day."

"No."

"Can we talk again this way, then? I'll tell you more gorilla jokes."

"We can talk again only if you do *not* tell me more gorilla jokes."

"That seems unreasonable."

"Most of the good things in life are unreasonable."

Nudger had never really thought about that. It might be true. "Will you tell me more about yourself, Claudia?"

"No."

"That leaves me as the subject of conversation. I'm quite handsome, with a large disposable income, and enough suffering in my past to be graced with wisdom and nobility."

"Bullshit."

"That, too."

"Your suffering is going on right now, only you seem to have learned to live with it, almost to regard it as an unwelcome old acquaintance that's moved in with you and won't go away. You've come to an accommodation. Maybe that's what there is about you that is more interesting than your gorilla jokes, so-called."

Nudger smiled slightly and licked his lips, tasting the salt of his perspiration. This wasn't suicide talk at all. "You're a damned good psychoanalyst," he said.

"I've learned from experts."

"Why don't you tell me—"

"Tomorrow, Nudger."

"—at least some trivial thing about yourself?"

But she had hung up. The vacated line sighed in Nudger's ear like the plaintive echoes of a vast lifeless ocean heard in a seashell. It was a lonely sound, a residue of pain.

He replaced the receiver in its cradle and leaned back in his swivel chair. He was pleased. Claudia was her name and for the moment she was no longer bent on suicide. That was progress. Gorilla jokes seldom failed altogether.

Nudger rested his elbows on the desk, stared at the telephone and wondered. Why *did* he care about her to such a large degree? Claudia was, after all, a stranger to him. Even she had referred to herself as such.

But he knew better. She actually was more than a stranger. Rapport, subterranean rivers flowing to a dark confluence, mystical oneness. He did feel that way. And so must she. Maybe that was all that was keeping her alive. Maybe. What was he to her? Who was she, really? What was she to him? Could the rights to this be sold to one of the networks for a new soap opera?

No, Nudger didn't feel as if he were embroiled in a soap opera. This was more of a Greek tragedy, with its bizarre upstage chorus and an innate engine of fate propelling its characters to destinies they didn't understand and couldn't escape. Sophocles by phone.

He stood up and stretched, then exhaled with a great rush of breath. It was frustrating to sit at his desk and think about Claudia. He didn't want to think about anything at all. He wanted to sleep.

After turning out the lights and locking the door carefully behind him, Nudger descended the dimly lit narrow stairway to the street, drove to his apartment and went immediately to bed.

The telephone shrilled beside him like a nagging wife. "Eileen . . ." he muttered. But it had been years since she'd shared his bed. Nudger came awake enough to realize that the phone was ringing and lifted the receiver to quiet the damned thing.

Morning light was angling in where the drapes didn't quite meet, lancing across the bedroom to lie in a streak of brilliance across the foot of the bed. Nudger looked at his watch. Ten forty-five. He put ear to receiver and said a sleep-thickened hello.

"Mr. Nudger, this is Jeanette. I've got two."

"You've got to what?"

"No, no. *T-w-o.* Two men made dates with me over the lines last night. I'm supposed to meet them this afternoon by the fountain in the Twin Oaks Mall."

"Good," Nudger told her. "I'm assuming you made these dates for different times."

"Of course." Jeanette's voice was icy enough to wither the last vestiges of sleep in Nudger's mind. "I'm to meet the first one at two o'clock, the second at two-thirty. Frank and Sandy, but that's not their real names."

"Did you learn anything else from your conversations with them?"

"Only what they like."

"Do they like the same things?"

"No."

"Do either of them like what Jenine liked?"

"I don't know," Jeanette said. "Jenine and I never talked about things like that. Frank seems pretty conventional. Sandy suggested—"

"Never mind," Nudger interrupted, "I don't want to know. Who's the two o'clock?"

"Frank. He'll be wearing brown slacks and a yellow sweater. At two-thirty Sandy should show up wearing vinyl boots and a black vinyl cowboy hat."

"Did you say vinyl?"

"That's right. Maybe he's too poor to be into leather."

Nudger realized with incredulity that she seemed serious.

"I'll be at the mall to look these two hopefuls over," he told her.

"If one of them fits the description," Jeanette said, "phone me as soon as you learn anything about him."

"That's what you're paying me for."

"That's right, Mr. Nudger. Good-bye."

Nudger hung up the phone, rolled onto his side in the fetal position and tried to go back to sleep. He seemed to get wider awake by the minute. Finally he got out of bed and showered and dressed.

The shopping mall was only half an hour from his apartment, so there was no rush. He went through the routine with Mr. Coffee, poured himself a cup of the strong brew, disdaining cream and sugar, then sat in the living room, sipping while he watched the news on cable TV. Big trouble. There was big trouble everywhere.

After a while Nudger used the remote control to switch off the TV and then simply sat in the increasing warmth of the living room. The apartment was small and cluttered, comfortable by chance. The furniture was a potpourri of styles and periods, running to overstuffed and old. Nudger figured that in a few years he and the furniture would be perfectly compatible. There was nothing in the apartment left over from his days with Eileen. He had gotten rid of all that in the first year after the divorce.

When his cup was empty, Nudger got up and went into the kitchen to prepare brunch. He poured another cup of coffee and a tall glass of chilled orange juice, then broke four eggs and got out some cheese and cooked up an omelet.

He had never acquired the knack in the kitchen. He cooked the omelet too long and it took on the thickness and texture of leather, but it tasted like vinyl.

SEVEN

Nudger decided to drop by his office on the way to Twin Oaks Mall and look over his mail. He was expecting a check from a Mrs. Mallowan, a West Side woman whose stolen Pekingese he'd traced and recovered. She'd said that Ringo was a pedigreed show dog, leading Nudger to believe that the animal was worth hundreds of dollars per pound and that Mrs. Mallowan could well afford his fee.

As he cornered the Volkswagen, he noticed that the bite marks on the back of his hand had almost faded away. Ringo hadn't the amiable disposition of a show dog and had bitten Nudger. The dog's owner had also put the bite on Nudger, and had owed him over nine hundred dollars for the past three months.

"No more animal cases," he vowed again aloud, as he parked the Volkswagen in a remarkably small space that he would have trouble getting it out of unless one of the cars inches from each bumper was moved. How he had maneuvered into the space with such ease was a mystery. This was pretty much the way his life went.

He jogged across the street, deftly dodging traffic like a scared broken-field runner without blockers, and headed for his office.

There was only one item in the mail, a Grand Prize notification that he'd won either a trip to Spain, a color TV, a three-thousand-dollar stereo system, or a pen that wrote in three colors. All he had to do to collect was drive a hundred miles, match his computerized number with a prize number, and tour something called Rocky Glen Estates, about which scant information was furnished. Nudger had plenty of pens. He tossed his Grand Prize notification into the waste-basket, where it landed on edge and made a hollow thunking sound.

He went back out onto the landing and locked the office door behind him, then took the steep wooden stairs down, pushed open the street door, and stepped outside.

The sun had had enough of clouds and was exercising its clout. The afternoon was brilliant with promise. On a ledge of the building across the street, pigeons were lined up like smug sentinels, feathers puffed out and colorful in the direct sunlight. Half a dozen women from the offices in the building, probably on their lunch hour, were walking along the sidewalk, also luxuriating in the fine weather, heads and shoulders thrown back, long legs kicking out in spirited strides. Nudger felt like whistling at them. Several of them glanced across the street at him and then looked away. He was glad he hadn't whistled. He veered to enter Danny's Donuts.

There were no customers inside, only Danny. The doughnuts sold here were too concretelike for lunch fare, and palpably dripping with grease and calories. Danny made his pittance in the mornings. Still, the place smelled good as usual, if a bit nauseatingly sweet.

Nudger smiled and nodded at Danny. "Anybody been around?"

Danny wiped his hands on his ragged gray towel. "Not in a business sense."

"Some other sense?"

"An animal of a guy's been watching your office from across the street." Danny glanced out through the grease-marked window as if checking to make sure he wasn't being overheard through the glass. "He stood over there most of the morning, but I ain't seen him now for about an hour."

"What do you mean by 'animal'?" Nudger asked, settling onto a red vinyl stool at the counter. "Did he have fur, horns, hooves? An old cow hand?"

"Big," Danny said simply.

Danny sometimes communicated like he manufactured doughnuts. Heavily, full of holes. "What's 'big'?"

"Big is tall," Danny said. "Big is wide. Big is ugly. I think the guy is maybe an ex-fighter, Nudge. Even from here I could tell he had that look about him. You know, outa-plumb nose, and lumps of scar tissue over the eyes."

An ex-fighter. Nudger rummaged through his memory but came up with no former pugilist who might be looking for him. "Did you notice what he was wearing?"

"Yeah. A light tan jacket, it looked like, and a bright yellow cap, like a baseball cap, with lettering across the front."

"Could you make out what the lettering said?"

"Nope, he was too far away. My eyes ain't what they used to be, Nudge."

"How long by the clock would you say he was out there?"

"About two hours, acting like he was waiting for you. Every now and then he'd glance up at your office window, like he wasn't sure whether you were in or out."

Nudger doubted that the man was an emissary of Ringo's owner, here to pay him his nine hundred dollars. Tall, wide, ugly, and waiting for him. He didn't need this. Neither did his stomach. It kicked and growled mightily, as if urging extreme caution.

"You say something, Nudge?"

Nudger shook his head and popped an antacid tablet.

"Stomach acting up again?"

"Never really quits." Nudger swiveled and climbed down from the stool. "If Eileen calls or comes by here, trying to find me to talk about back alimony, tell her I've gone to meet Frank and Sandy."

"Sure. She know who they are?"

"No. Tell her they're bankers."

Danny nodded. He held up a large foam cup. "You want a coffee to go?"

"No, thanks," Nudger said, "I'm regular enough without it."

Danny's sad eyes lowered in rejection. Was he becoming as sensitive about his coffee as about his doughnuts? Damned wimp.

"On second thought," Nudger said, "maybe about half full, with cream and sugar."

Carrying his coffee, he pushed out the door and stepped onto the sidewalk. There was no point in not leaving before tall, wide, and ugly reappeared. Waiting around for trouble was a lot like looking for it.

Of course, there were times when someone plying Nudger's uncertain trade earned his fee by waiting for trouble. Which was what

Nudger was doing as he took up position near the fountain in Twin Oaks Mall.

He was sitting on a bench outside Woolworth's in the vast indoor mall, with seeming casualness observing the shoppers milling around the large, gently splashing fountain that was illuminated by recessed colored spotlights. There was a circular raised concrete ledge around the fountain, serving as a bench, and several bullet-shaped trash receptacles and some plastic potted plants were scattered about. Nudger, who appeared to be simply another patient husband waiting for his wife to finish browsing, sat and watched two old women with sore feet and huge shopping bags lounge on the bench and discuss a purchase. The women finally left and several preteen boys ambled up, leaned precariously over the ledge and spat toward the fountain. An exhausted obese woman lugging an irritated infant sighed and plopped down on the bench near them. An elderly man wearing a hearing aid sat not far from her and placidly smoked a pipe. The usual shopping-mall gang.

Nudger checked his wristwatch, as if wondering how much longer he'd have to wait for his errant spouse who'd lost track of time among miles of Sears goodies. A stereotypic but effective ruse. It was five minutes past two. Where was Frank? Was this lack of punctuality a wise way to begin a romance? Or a murder?

Then Nudger saw a short, slender man wearing brown slacks and a yellow sweater tentatively approach the fountain. The sweater either was stained or had one of the currently popular tiny animals embossed on the left breast. The man stood for a minute near the circular concrete bench as if debating whether to sit, decided to stand, and moved off about fifty feet to the side to slouch self-consciously before a window display of jogging shoes. He was in his late fifties or early sixties, and what hair he had left was in a wispy white fringe above his ears.

The man stood in 'he same position for about ten minutes, frequently glancing at his wristwatch. He lit a cigarette, took a few puffs, then crossed to a pedestal ashtray and ground it out as if it had all been a big mistake. Returning to his original position, he craned his neck to gaze about the sparsely occupied mall, then settled again into his slouched position, spine arched out like a cat's and hands crammed in pockets. Frank, all right.

Frank was game. He waited until almost two-thirty, then the look of perplexity on his flushed face changed to anger, and he lit another cigarette. This one he didn't put out immediately. Puffing furiously and trailing smoke like a locomotive, he strode with a dejected yet springy stride down the mall, keeping well to one side near the display windows as if afraid something might fall on him if he ventured too far from a wall. There was a kind of wary resilience in his bearing that Nudger found admirable.

Almost as soon as Frank had gone, Sandy showed up.

"Ah'll b'damned," Nudger muttered, as he saw that Sandy actually was wearing glistening black vinyl boots and a wide-brimmed cowboy hat with a chrome-studded band. He also had on black vinyl wristbands, remarkably tight-fitting jeans, and a bright plaid western-cut shirt with pearl snaps instead of buttons. His shirt sleeves were rolled up above his elbows, as if he'd just been out mending fence, and instead of a pistol on his hip a massive ring of keys dangled from his belt and faintly jingle-jangle-jingled when he walked. From beneath his hat, which was shoved back on his head, protruded long blond hair. Sandy brushed back a strand of it to reveal briefly a gold stud in his left ear. Some buckaroo.

Nudger's momentary hope died as he surreptitiously studied Sandy more carefully. Though the wrangler's hair was blond, it was fine and perfectly straight. And the hand Sandy was using to rotate a tattered toothpick between his front teeth was so dainty he probably needed help turning doorknobs. Nudger sighed and stood up from the hard bench. Sandy was no more a murderer than he was a cowboy.

As Nudger walked past him, their eyes met and Nudger nodded pleasantly. He had nothing against Sandy; life was tough on and off the prairie. He hoped Sandy could someday work his way up to real leather. This was the land of sexual opportunity for almost everyone other than cattle. He wondered what all the urban cowboys or preppies would studiously dress up as next. Maybe giant chickens. Whatever they could be sold. It was all okay with Nudger, who wore white J. C. Penney underwear.

Nudger left the mall and stood for a few seconds staring at the vast sloping parking lot and the rows of brightly colored car roofs glinting in the sun like newly dyed Easter eggs. It always took him a while in places like this to remember where he'd parked his car. At one time he'd had one of those plastic bananas on top of the Volkswagen's antenna so he could spot the car easier in crowded lots. But the banana caused the antenna to whip around in the wind when he drove fast, and it was not unobtrusive enough during stakeouts, so he had abandoned it. Maybe he'd get one of those plastic daisies for the antenna; you used to see as many of them as you did the bananas, but not anymore.

He remembered then: halfway up the aisle straight down from the "G" in DRUGSTORE. He found the Volkswagen hiding behind a fancy travel van, got in and rolled down the windows to allow some of the superheated air to escape, and then drove from the lot.

On Manchester Road, halfway back to the office, he became increasingly interested in the old Buick that had been lumbering along behind him for the past two miles. He made a few turns, a slight detour that brought him back to Manchester Road, traveling in the same direction.

The Buick remained behind him, its weary chrome face smiling a sad and implacable gape-grilled grin.

Nudger reached for his antacid tablets and thumbed back the aluminum foil. He made it a double, chewing the two tablets in time with the clattering tempo of the engine as he drove toward the Third District Police Station.

Periodic checks in the rearview mirror indicated that the Buick was steady on the pace, perhaps even closer, still grinning knowingly at him like a wily, patient predator. This must be what Satchel Paige had warned about. Nudger's stomach turned in on itself like one of the legendary black pitcher's hard curveballs.

He speeded up. The Buick gained speed as if attached by a string to the Volkswagen's rear bumper. The old car's windshield was tinted and Nudger couldn't get so much as a glimpse of the driver, but he had a firm idea of who might be behind the wheel.

Nudger took the sweeping cloverleaf onto the highway to downtown, gripping the steering wheel with both hands and holding his speed at a steady, legal fifty-five. The Buick stayed with him, hovering near like the angel of death. Those old cars sure had personalities.

The people in the cars passing Nudger didn't glance at him; they were totally unaware of their near-proximity to such acute fear. It gave Nudger a helpless, lonely feeling. The worst thing about any kind of real suffering was that it was a solitary exercise.

He didn't feel the grip of that fear begin to loosen until he exited on Twelfth Street, drove several blocks, and turned into the blacktop parking lot behind the Third District Station. He pulled the Volkswagen into a slot near the brick building, turned off the engine, and leaned back in his sticky vinyl seat in relief.

Then he glanced into the side mirror and fear lanced through his bowels like a shaft of ice, stunning him.

Incredible! Nudger had been followed before and successfully used this ploy to find sanctuary. But not this time. The hulking Buick had followed him right into the police department's parking lot.

It lurched to a stop close behind him and sat blocking the Volkswagen in its parking slot, its prehistoric giant engine rumbling with throaty, ominous power.

The rusty door on the driver's side swung open. A man got out and stood up straight. He was wearing a bright yellow, billed cap with CATERPILLAR lettered in black across the front. "Caterpillar" was a brand of bulldozers and other earth-moving and heavy equipment. The man looked like heavy equipment, himself. He was tall, wide, and ugly.

EIGHT

Nudger reluctantly got out of his car and stood waiting for the big man who had emerged like Prometheus from the Buick. There was no doubt that this was the man Danny had described, the man who had waited for Nudger across the street from the doughnut shop. He was several inches over six feet tall, with a bull neck that strained his shirt collar and merged with wide sloping shoulders. He had an often-broken nose, and a brow built up by scar tissue from inept cornermen who didn't know how to treat cuts. His lantern jaw suggested he'd been a boxer who could take a punch and absorb much punishment, and who had paid in blood for his dubious ability to continue standing. He bunched his shoulders and slowly advanced on Nudger with ponderous and obvious malevolence.

When he was about ten feet away, he smiled with bad teeth. Even with good teeth, it wouldn't have been a smile to thaw cold hearts.

"Nudger," he said, "you an' me are gonna have an unfriendly little chat."

Nudger glanced around desperately at the dozens of empty cars baking in the sun. This was the lot where most of the on-duty cops left their private cars. Near the far exit were a couple of parked cruisers, representing the only city vehicles. There wasn't a uniform in sight. Nudger's stomach felt as if it were searching for a way out as frantically as he was. It emitted a growl that sounded something like "Please!" He gulped back the bitter bile of fear as he saw the huge man's powerful gnarled fingers flexing and unflexing around a defenseless red rubber ball.

"They say that's great for strengthening the forearms," Nudger said, pointing to the tortured, misshapen ball. He thought that if a ball could scream, this one would be howling.

"What they say is true," the man said. His stained, crooked smile turned absolutely nasty.

Nudger's gaze fixed for a hopeful few seconds on the double doors of the building's rear exit. He prayed that a dozen blue uniforms would pour out on their way to lunch or anywhere else. Wasn't this about the time for a shift change? Maybe the entire day shift would suddenly emerge, streaming toward their cars. Maybe the cavalry would charge right onto the parking lot. Custer, Lieutenant Reno, the Johns Payne and Wayne. All of them, riding hell-for-leather, maybe singing.

It hadn't happened yet, except on screen. And Nudger knew he hadn't paid admission or tuned in the television Late Show. He was on his own.

"This is an odd place for our conversation," he croaked, stringing out time. "Right here in the police department parking lot."

The big man's wide jaw dropped a few notches. Doubt changed to slow comprehension in his eyes as he glanced around seeking repudiation of what Nudger had said.

Nudger managed to draw a breath. Was this possible? It had never occurred to him that the man might have followed him automatically, might not know where they were standing.

The shelflike brow knotted in a frown. Nudger saw the man's lips move as he read the black-and-white sign near the corner of the building, dread words mouthed silently: THIRD DISTRICT, SAINT LOUIS METROPOLITAN POLICE DEPARTMENT.

Just then a uniformed cop appeared on the sidewalk bordering the lot, munching an apple as he walked toward one of the parked cruisers.

The big man saw him and reeled backward, stunned by total realization, and the rubber ball dropped from his uncurled fingers, bounced against the side of Nudger's car, and then rolled back toward the man's size "huge" wingtip shoes. Then under one of the shoes, as the man began hurrying back toward the Buick. He slipped, grunted in surprise as he flailed backward, and hit the blacktop as if a crane had dropped him from twenty feet up. Nudger winced at the melon-hollow sound of the massive head bouncing off the hard surface.

He started to yell to attract the cop's attention, then realized that the fallen giant was blocked from view by the parked cars and decided it would be wiser to remain silent. Besides, it seemed sinful to disturb a man enjoying an apple in the Eden of the inner city.

Nudger knelt and worked the prone man's wallet out from his hip pocket, flipped it open and found identification. The man groaned and started to sit up.

Nudger dropped the wallet, stood tall and shouted, "Hey!"

The uniform had been about to climb into the nearest parked cruiser. He stared at Nudger, then slammed the car door behind him as he started to walk across the lot. When he caught sight of the large wingtip shoes protruding from behind the Volkswagen, he tossed his apple core aside and his stride became more purposeful.

"What's happening here?" he asked, when he'd seen what was attached to the shoes. He was a middle-aged cop with narrow wise eyes and an expanded waistline. There was a tiny piece of apple stuck to his clean-shaven chin, and when he noticed Nudger staring at it he wiped it away.

"I slipped an' fell," the big man said, lowering the Volkswagen several inches as he rested a giant hand on it to lever himself to his feet. "Hit my head." He was holding his yellow cap that had fallen off. He replaced it on his head at a cockeyed angle.

Nudger realized that the man hadn't actually done anything to him. Hadn't actually said anything that constituted a physical threat. Then he remembered the wallet at his feet. He stooped and retrieved it. "You dropped this." He held out the wallet for the big man to take.

The cop looked at the wallet, then looked hard at Nudger, reappraising the situation.

The big man finally grasped the meaning and treated them with his nasty smile. But the smile disappeared as slowly as it had formed, when he realized that if he accused Nudger of trying to steal the wallet, he would have to go into the station and answer some potentially revealing questions.

"Musta slipped outa my pocket when I fell," he said. He took the wallet and counted the folding money laboriously. "All there." He closed the wallet so that the two halves snapped together loudly, like voracious jaws, then jammed it back into his hip pocket so hard he almost ripped his pants seams.

"Which one of you yelled for me to come over here?" the cop asked. He was a thinker, even though unsuspecting of the truth. Probably he'd make detective.

"I called you," Nudger said.

The man who had accosted him sullenly nodded. "That's right," he confirmed. "He seen me fall, I guess, and wanted to help."

"Do you need medical attention?" the cop asked.

The big man removed his cap and probed a lump that was forming on the back of his head, as if he'd just remembered he'd been hurt. "Nope, I'm okay." He smoothed back his thinning oily black hair, straightened his clothes and brushed them off. Then he replaced his cap, nodded to Nudger and the cop, and climbed back into the old Buick. The ancient behemoth left a low cloud of dark exhaust smoke as it rumbled from the parking lot. A peeling sticker on the rust-pocked rear bumper read: GOD SAID IT, I BELIEVE IT, THAT SETTLES IT.

"He really ought to get a ticket for polluting," Nudger said.

"I'm not in Traffic," the cop explained.

He was still standing motionless with his fists on his hips, staring suspiciously as Nudger went inside.

Nudger inquired at the desk. Crime was slow. Hammersmith was in.

After the duty sergeant had alerted him by phone of Nudger's presence, Hammersmith appeared in the hall outside his office door and waved for Nudger to enter.

Nudger perched on the uncomfortable oak chair and waited to speak until Hammersmith had situated his bulk in his deep leather executive chair. Hammersmith's smooth, fleshy pink hand moved toward the box of cigars on his desk, hesitated, then withdrew. Only a threat.

"I was accosted in the parking lot," Nudger told him.

"Accosted. That's an old-fashioned word."

"I almost went into an old-fashioned swoon. The gunsel who accosted me was almost big enough to be snow-peaked."

"Gunsel? Really, Nudge." Hammersmith's blue eyes were as merry as Santa's in his flesh-padded cheeks. "Was the subject armed? Were threats made?"

"Implied."

Hammersmith did remove a cigar from the box now, and methodically peeled the cellophane wrapper from it. He gazed at it as if it were a woman he'd just undressed but made no move to light it. "Explain how all this came to pass," he suggested.

Nudger explained.

"Did you get the Buick's license number?" Hammersmith asked.

"I did, but we don't need it. I got the man's name."

Hammersmith did light the cigar now. He exhaled a green death cloud and raised his eyebrows incredulously, crinkling his smooth forehead. "He followed you right into the station-house parking lot without knowing it, then was dumb enough to give you his name?"

"I forgot to mention," Nudger said, "that before dropping the wallet when he started to come around, I looked inside and checked his identification. He's a Hugo Rumbo."

"Hm, sounds like a dance craze."

"His address is over on Russell, that stretch of run-down apartment buildings."

"He obviously isn't a pro bone crusher," Hammersmith said, "because he didn't know the location of the station house. And because of the way he handled the situation when he did find out where he was."

"I'd like you to goose the machinery," Nudger said. "Find out who and what Hugo Rumbo is, and why he might be interested in me."

"That might not be so easy," Hammersmith said, "with just his description, license plate number, name and address." He leaned back and exhaled another cumulonimbus. "Though in this, the age of the microchip, computers do work magic."

"You're taking this kind of light and loose," Nudger said. "This Rumbo was about to commence pounding on me right in the police station parking lot. How would that have looked in tomorrow's newspapers? Or on the evening local TV news? Remember, I used to be Coppy the Clown. I can ham it up for the minicameras even from a hospital bed."

Hammersmith extended his lower lip and somberly nodded. "You make a salient point." He placed the greenish cigar back in his mouth, clamped down on it but didn't inhale. "Don't you have any idea as to why this Rumbo thing was following you?"

"None."

"Do you owe anyone money?"

"Almost everyone, but no one who'd . . ." Nudger sat up straighter. "Eileen, maybe."

Hammersmith appeared disgusted. "Stay serious, Nudge." He had always liked Eileen.

"I owe her almost a thousand dollars in back alimony."

"Eileen wouldn't hire an enforcer and you know it."

Nudger nodded resignedly. Hammersmith was right. Not as right as he assumed, but right. It would be silly of Eileen to risk messing herself up in court and killing the goose that laid the brass eggs.

"Are you still working on that twins case?" Hammersmith asked.

"Sure, but I doubt if there's a connection with Rumbo."

"Oh? What else are you working on?"

Nudger saw what Hammersmith meant. But he couldn't imagine Agnes Boyington hiring a professional leg breaker any more than he could really picture Eileen arranging a serious beating for him. And it didn't seem possible that Jenine's killer could know at this point that Nudger was on his trail.

Unless the murderer knew Jeanette, or Agnes Boyington, or anyone else who had found out what Nudger was working on. Those people included Danny, Fisher at the phone company, Hammersmith, and those on the case's periphery whom he'd questioned indirectly about the Boyington murder. It might be absurd to suspect any of them, yet people talked. And people listened. Word spread like the proverbial ripples in a pond, signaling both prey and predator.

"I'll run a check on Rumbo," Hammersmith said. He said it reassuringly, reading Nudger's mind with his cop's honed insight. "We'll get some answers."

"And probably raise some questions."

"It usually works that way. But it's better than walking around in complete ignorance."

"I'm not so sure," Nudger said, "and I've walked around in both conditions. My problem is, I need to learn enough answers to be able to collect my fee. Sometimes that turns out to be a few answers too many."

Not joking in the slightest, Hammersmith said, "I have a feeling you're going to more than earn your fee this time, Nudge."

Nudger offered no contradiction. He shared Hammersmith's ominous premonition, and he had a personal stake in its accuracy.

He said good-bye and walked from Hammersmith's smoke-fouled office, down the hall, past the booking desk and outside, pausing halfway out the door to stand on the top concrete step. The early evening sky was mottled by gray, illuminated clouds, blasted with light by the lowering sun to make it look like a scene from one of those dime-store religious prints that depressed rather than inspired. A southwest breeze whispered confidentially that there would surely be rain by nightfall. In the booking area, the droning metallic voice of a dispatcher directed a patrol car to a trouble spot somewhere in the darkening city. Telephones rang in remote offices, were answered with reasonable promptness. The place was humming with efficient, well-practiced activity, comforting sounds of Law and Order.

Nudger started toward his car.

When the station house's heavy doors clicked shut behind him, he felt naked.

NINE

"Do you wonder what I look like?"

"I'm glad you're curious about whether I do," Nudger told Claudia. He was seated again at midnight in the dimness of his office, wrapped in the soft yellow illumination from his desk lamp, the telephone receiver gripped like a handle affixed to the side of his face. "It suggests that you might be interested."

"In you?"

"No," he told her, "in you."

"Maybe it amounts to the same thing."

"Oh, it does. And I do wonder, Claudia. Why don't you describe yourself?"

She didn't speak for a while. There was a sound in the phone that Nudger couldn't identify, a rising and falling, a distant, rushing roar. Not interference on the line; he was sure of that.

"I'm . . . average," she said at last.

Nudger harrumphed into the phone. "Average, huh? Tall? Short? Blue eyes, or brown? Young, old, fat, lean, brunette, blonde, straight, or stooped? Nobody's average. Only people who sell things believe that."

He thought she might be annoyed by his persistence, but she wasn't. "All right," she said, with subsurface laughter in her voice, "I'm thirty-six-years old, medium height, brunette with brown eyes, not too fat or thin, with reasonably good posture."

"Sounds average," Nudger said.

"I warned you. I never claimed I was a finalist in a beauty contest."

"Who would want you to be? Anyway, a thing so slight as a twitch in the flank can knock you out of the finals in those contests. And maybe I'm enamored of average. Maybe I like ranch houses, four-door sedans, two-fifty hitters, and plain vanilla ice cream—two scoops."

"No," she said, "you're not average."

"I strive not to be," Nudger admitted. "For instance, I often wear

my brown shoes with my gray suit, just to shake things up. I try to
vary my schedule in all things. Maybe it would be a good idea for us
to get out of this rut and talk when the sun is out."

"I work during the day," she said simply.

"Every day?"

"Almost. But not tomorrow." Again Nudger heard that soft, peculiar rushing sound on the other end of the connection, a murmur at
first, building to a crescendo and then tapering to silence. He considered asking Claudia what the sound was, then decided not to tip
her to the one clue he had as to her whereabouts. "Maybe we can talk
again tomorrow," she said, almost grudgingly. "Will you be at your
number in the afternoon?"

"I can't promise," Nudger told her. "Why don't you give me a
definite time?"

"No," she said. "If you don't answer the phone, I'll try to get
through to you again."

"Do *you* promise?"

"Of course not."

"It would be easier if we simply met somewhere," Nudger suggested. "Are you afraid you'll be disappointed?"

"No. And I'm not afraid you will. Isn't that really what you were
implying?"

"Don't get all defensive on me, please," Nudger said.

He heard her breathe out into the receiver. "All right, I'm sorry.
It's just that if we talk in person, there'll be no way to cut short a
gorilla joke."

Actually, her defensiveness was exactly the sort of response
Nudger wanted from her. She seemed to have acquired a degree of
resilience. She seemed to have moved much farther away from the
gun, rope, pills, or whatever means she had been considering to fur-
nish her transportation beyond this vale of tears. But Nudger knew
the unpredictability of people actually contemplating suicide, the dark
cloud on the mind, unexplainable, that came and went as if by whims
of capricious breezes. A distorted face flashed vividly in Nudger's
mind. It belonged to a man he and Hammersmith had found over ten
years ago hanging in a garage. He was dressed in women's clothing

and had killed that side of himself he loathed. Nudger had been told it wasn't uncommon.

"I don't mean to push," he told Claudia, still haunted by the macabre memory.

She must have picked up the concern in his voice. "You don't push," she said. "I say ouch too quickly; I admit that." Again the rushing roar, then silence.

"Don't say ouch, Claudia, just push back. I won't mind. I have a thick skin."

She laughed loudly, a little too shrilly. "No, you don't. That's one reason you were able to . . . draw me back from where I was going. When we talked that first night, I somehow knew right away that you were as vulnerable as I."

Nudger felt the heat of an almost adolescent blush. This was absurd, to form a close electronic relationship with a woman he'd never met. A relationship so intimate that she could make him react this way. This was self-deception raised to an art. This was the masochism of truth.

"If I've touched a sensitive nerve, embarrassed you . . ." Her voice was apologetic.

"No," Nudger lied, "you haven't embarrassed me. Or if you have, I deserve it." The hell with this pain of revelation. "I still think we should get together, lie to each other like other people. It might be refreshing not to suffer."

"Maybe someday," she said. "I'm going to hang up now, Nudger. I've got to get some sleep so I'll be able to get out of bed to go to work tomorrow."

"You told me you were off tomorrow."

"I'm only working in the morning. You probably have to go to work, too."

"Not me. I've got nothing to do but amble to my safety deposit box and clip coupons, then phone my broker. I usually start around noon. It's a good life even if somewhat monotonous."

When she didn't speak, Nudger thought she might have taken him seriously.

"Actually," he said, "I was lying. The only coupons I clip are the kind that save a dime at the supermarket, and my broker doesn't return my calls."

"You weren't lying, Nudger. You were just telling the truth in your own way. A kind of reverse English."

"Freud is dead," he snapped at her, but she had hung up.

He fitted the receiver in its cradle and, with his fingertips still resting on it, sat in the warm dimness trying to figure out the source of the sound he'd heard in Claudia's phone.

Not intermittent rushes of nearby traffic, not distant trains or planes or . . . ships.

The sea! That was what the sound reminded him of more than anything else. The occasional rush of a wave onto the beach, a loud sigh of surf that reached a higher decibel range when the infrequent huge breaker roared in from the sea.

He rubbed his hand over his face, as if to erase worry lines, and shook his head. The trouble with the surf theory was that the nightlines were strictly local, and the nearest ocean to St. Louis was almost a thousand miles away.

Nudger decided not to think about Claudia or the eerie sound on the phone or anything else for a while. He was tired enough to have slumped in his chair without realizing it, and gravity was getting the better of his eyelids. Forcing himself to sit up straight, he considered drinking a cup of coffee.

Then he decided that staying awake would be pointless. Whatever he might accomplish tonight—this morning—would be easier done after he'd slept. He was at the point where whatever drowsiness he endured now would simply add to his sluggishness after sunup. Rather than fight his weariness, he leaned over the desk, cradled his head in his arms, and dozed with the scent of old varnished wood inches below his nose. There was a memory jogger. Nap time in elementary school. "Heads on those desks, children." Catching a stolen wink or two in high school or college. "Are we disturbing your slumber, young Mr. Nudger?"

He ignored the teacher. He was on the beach, his cheek pressed into a rough, warm towel that gave with the soft sand beneath it. A hot sun made his bare back tingle pleasantly. He heard the ocean nearby, sighing deeply and evenly like something gigantic in hibernation in a dark cave of the mind. A gull screamed. A gull rang. A spindly-legged sandpiper hopped delicately across the hot beach to Nudger, extended a fingertipped wing, and, raising his sunglasses so it could see his eyes, said, "It's for you. Rates are cheaper after nine. Reach out and—"

Nudger was awake in the morning-bright office and the receiver was in his hand. He must have reached for it in his sleep. He brought it to his ear. Danny's voice said, "Short notice, Nudge, but I thought you'd wanna know trouble's coming your way."

Nudger was aware of footsteps, someone climbing the narrow stairs from the street door. He thanked Danny for the warning and hung up the phone, picturing the substantial Hugo Rumbo while trying to recall if he'd locked the office door. He had, he hadn't, he had, he hadn't. He hadn't!

A board on the landing creaked. A familiar sound. Whoever was out there was at the top of the stairs. Nudger would have opened a desk drawer and reached for his gun, if he'd owned a gun. His stomach and heart seemed to be fighting for the same cramped space in his throat as he stood up and leaned steeply forward, supporting himself shakily with his arms locked at the elbows and his hands palms-down on the desk. He found himself unable to look away from the prismatic glass doorknob on his office door.

The knob rotated. The door opened.

Eileen stepped in.

"Startle you?" she asked.

Nudger sat down, leaned back, and breathed out hard. "You startled me," he confirmed.

"I meant to. It seems to be the only way I can capture your attention."

Nudger smoothed back his hair with his fingers, straightened his collar, and gave her his attention. She was still an attractive woman, trim and neatly groomed, with a kind of wholesomeness about her that would have carried her far as an actress playing typical homemakers in television commercials. Though a delicate woman with a certain frilliness about her, she had a robust complexion, large and perfectly aligned very white teeth, and shapely, strong-looking hands. It all suggested that good health meant good sex, and wasn't far off the mark.

Why had they lost both love and lust for each other? Nudger

thought sometimes that it was the ungodly and unpredictable hours he worked. Or was it the sterility of the suburban plat they had called home? Whatever had caused the widening gap between them was still a mystery, as it probably remained in most divorces. Nudger only knew that when she suggested the divorce he had felt not only shock but also undeniable relief. A lightning comprehension—or admission. He, too, wanted to live a life different from the one they shared. Eileen had seen that in him as soon as she'd brought up the subject of a divorce as a possible alternative, and that was that. In that instant it had been transformed from an alternative to an inevitability.

Such were the complexities of the human heart. Or maybe it was simpler and less poetic than that. Maybe he'd decided subconsciously to leave her when he heard her use the word "cute" three times in one sentence, there on the phone in that suburban frame house that was like the neighboring houses on either side. But he was being unfair. He knew that his reaction to that triple-cute was probably only symptomatic of their real problem.

"You still have it," he told her.

She smiled. "Thank you."

"I mean, you still have my attention." He hadn't meant to hurt her.

Smile gone. "And you still have a way with words, and I still don't have my money. Almost a thousand dollars now in back alimony."

"Eight hundred fifty-three dollars and some odd cents," Nudger corrected.

"Nine hundred."

He shrugged. "Whatever." Or did he enjoy taunting her? "I have the exact amount written down."

"But not written where it counts—on a check made out to me." He had made her angry. She began to stalk about the office, rotating her high heels slightly with each slow step as if grinding despicable small objects into the floor. She had on those silver shoes with the tiny black bows, like the pair Jeanette Boyington wore. Nudger felt that he might be developing a dislike for those shoes.

"You'll get the money," he said. "You know that."

She stopped pacing and wheeled to glare at him. "But I want *you* to know that. If I don't have a check in my mail by the end of next week, I'm taking you back to court."

"Eileen, you know what they say about not being able to squeeze blood from a turnip."

He could almost feel the heat from her eyes as she said, "I'll settle for whatever oozes out."

Nudger's nervous stomach growled. It seemed to develop a language all its own when Eileen was around. It was a good thing she didn't know what she had just been called.

"I'm giving you more than a week," she reminded him. "That should leave you plenty of time to raise the money."

"What I don't have is plenty of collateral."

She lifted her shoulders eloquently, flicked lint from her sleeve onto his floor. "That's a problem you let develop. You should have gone back on the police force. You should have been paying me all along."

He smiled and shook his head sadly. "I couldn't go back, Eileen. And I can't get a loan."

She advanced a step and cocked her head sharply sideways. "Are you saying you're not going to pay me?" A long-nailed forefinger was aimed like a gun at him, loaded with ammunition provided by a divorce court judge. They were bullets that stayed in the wounds and festered.

Nudger stared at that steady finger and remembered the divorce proceedings. Eileen's lawyer was about the slickest courtroom manipulator he had ever seen. So convincing was the man that even Nudger thought the exorbitant alimony Eileen had been granted was justifiable, until several hours had passed in the real world outside the illusionary but credible world the lawyer had created for just long enough inside the courtroom. By then it was too late. His own lawyer had phoned to apologize, cutting the conversation short so he wouldn't be late for his remedial law classes.

"Of course I plan to pay you," Nudger said to Eileen, wondering how the two of them had come to this. And if they would have if the divorce had been over something simple, or at least definable, like an extramarital affair. They were both basically decent people.

"When and how much?" she asked.

"Soon, and all—well, half."

She smiled as if she'd caught him breaking his diet at midnight. He remembered that beautiful, impenetrable skepticism. "I thought you had no collateral, no resources."

"Someone owes me money from a job," he said.

"And when will you be paid so I can be?"

"That depends. Should be any day. The Ringo case has been wrapped up for weeks."

"Ringo? Sounds like a bookie or police character. What makes you think this Ringo pays his bills?"

"He'll pay. He's from a good family. Breeding tells."

She sighed and scowled at him. Such a naughty boy he was. "All right," she said. "I expect five hundred dollars by the end of next week, or it's back to court. No more deals."

"That's reasonable enough," Nudger said, reinforcing her spirit of compromise.

"And if this Ringo tells you he can't pay, I want to know about it."

"He's not the type to tell anyone that," Nudger assured her.

As Eileen started toward the door, she paused and looked around the office as if finally noticing her surroundings. Her upper lip curled as if she'd just discovered a hair in her salad. Nudger knew that she was making plenty of money selling one of those all-purpose home product lines while recruiting more salespeople. It was like a pyramid. She was a distributor now, with her own network of salespeople and a disproportionate cut of everyone's take. To her, way up near the peak of the pyramid, this was poverty.

"How can you stand it here?" she asked.

Nudger felt anger dig its claws into his guts. But he knew the folly of stumbling into an argument with Eileen at this point. She was inviting him to thrash around in quicksand.

"The roof doesn't leak," he said, "and the rent is cheap, so I can save up and make alimony payments."

She was smiling as she left. He didn't get up to show her out.

To think that theirs had begun as an amicable divorce.

She certainly wasn't the woman he'd married. But didn't every divorced man think that about his ex? And since she'd gotten into sales, Eileen had become particularly bitchy and aggressive. Perhaps

that rapacious aspect of her personality had been there all along beneath the surface, held submerged by her socially imposed self-image
and the demanding but stifling roles of helpmate and homemaker, and
the divorce had freed that part of her. Whatever the reason, the beast
was on the loose. Nudger had married a female Dr. Jekyll; now he
was contending with Ms. Hyde. These things happened in the chem-
istry of human relationships. Maybe people should never marry;
maybe it was tinkering with the laws of nature and that's why staying
married was so tough. It was something for the marriage counselors
and psychologists to consider.

Nudger returned his head to the cradle of his arms, and dreamed
again of the sea.

TEN

Nudger was told at the Third District that Hammersmith had just
gone out to eat lunch. He'd left a message for Nudger, inviting him
to join him at Ricardo's in the adjoining Fourth District.

Nudger was familiar with Ricardo's, though he hadn't been there
in the past several years. The restaurant had been in existence at the
same location on Ninth and Locust for more than a decade. Nudger
remembered eating there when he was a police rookie attending the
Academy, and he and Hammersmith had stopped in there a few times
when they were assigned to the same two-man patrol car. It had become one of Hammersmith's favorite restaurants.

As Nudger tugged open a heavy wood door with a stained-glass
insert and stepped into Ricardo's, he was struck by the size of the
place. The owner, Gino Ricardo, must have leased the space next
door and eliminated a wall. The long mahogany bar was where
Nudger recalled, along the north wall, to the left of the door, and the
general decor seemed much the same. There were the heavy dark
drapes, plush carpet, and red tablecloths. Thick oak partitions af-
forded privacy and provided only occasional glimpses of the tops of

heads of tall diners. Ricardo's was a restaurant where, even when it was crowded, a conversation could be carried on with reasonable assurance that it wouldn't be overheard. Though within walking distance of Police Headquarters at Tucker and Clark, it was the scene of countless tense and confidential exchanges between the police and their informants.

Ricardo's was crowded now. The long bar was two-deep with customers drinking or waiting for drinks, some of them marking time until a table became available. Waitresses and busboys scurried around among the oak partitions like industrious mice in a maze they had mastered. A maître d' in a serious blue suit was approaching to ask Nudger if he had a reservation, when Nudger caught familiar movement from the corner of his vision. Hammersmith had sat where he could see the entrance and was standing now and motioning Nudger over to his table.

Nudger sat down across from Hammersmith, who had before him an awesomely large pizza whose embellishments ran the gamut of the garden, and a tall frosted stein of draft beer. Nudger ordered a chicken salad sandwich and a glass of milk from a waitress who looked like a young, skinny Gina Lollobrigida.

"Don't be crazy," Hammersmith said. "This is a great Italian restaurant. They've got lasagna and cannelloni and fettuccine. They've got pizza any size and way, spaghetti and ravioli and other olis and onis and inis. And you ask for—"

"My stomach's been bothering me," Nudger interrupted. He could understand how Hammersmith had reached his corpulent state. There was real passion in his voice when he spoke of food. "Besides, if I order light, you might offer to pick up the check."

"You look glum," Hammersmith said, changing the subject. "Something the matter?"

"I had a visit from Eileen."

Hammersmith took a wolfish bite of pizza, used a plump finger to tuck in a string of cheese that was dangling from the corner of his mouth, and nodded in understanding. When he'd chewed and swallowed, he said, "Nice woman, Eileen."

"For somebody else, not for me."

"The divorce was your fault. You bring out the worst in women, Nudge."

Nudger said nothing as the waitress brought his sandwich and milk. He took a cautious bite of the sandwich. It was delicious, despite its lack of ethnicity. Hammersmith could be wrong.

Neither man said anything until Nudger had finished eating. Then Hammersmith offered him one of the three remaining oversized slices of pizza and Nudger declined. Around them were the muted sounds of flatware and china in subdued cacophony. Buzz of conversation, occasional laughter, clink of ice cubes against glass. Nudger rested the back of his head against the oak partition behind his chair and waited.

Hammersmith enjoyed a long swig of beer and set the stein down on the red tablecloth. "Hugo Rumbo is his real name," he said, "and he hasn't got much of an arrest record. Stole a car when he was a teenager, and an assault charge four years ago. He's forty years old, had some amateur fights and a few matches as a pro boxer. Nobody ever compared him to Marciano. The way I heard it, his feet and hands were always fighting in two different rounds, and he got hurt bad and had to quit the fight game. Now he picks up money as a sparring partner over at the South Broadway Gym, and besides his old Buick he has a pickup truck and does yardwork and hauling. Other than the usual shady characters who hang around boxing, he has no disreputable friends and no mob connections. He's ornery and clumsy and washed up, not a pro either in or out of the ring."

"Did somebody talk with him?"

"No, he has no idea we checked into his background. If he means you bodily harm, we wouldn't want to frighten him away."

The waitress came over and cleared away some of the dishes, placed the point of a pencil to the dimple on her chin, and asked if there would be anything else. Hammersmith said no, he'd already eaten two Gourmet Deluxe pizzas and drunk two steins of beer. Nudger asked for another small glass of milk. The waitress scrawled the order on a pad and hurried away with the impatient, fluid gait of the very young.

"The thing you should know," Hammersmith said, "is that one of the people Rumbo frequently does work for is Agnes Boyington."

Nudger wasn't surprised, now that he knew Rumbo wasn't a professional enforcer. "She tried to buy me off the case," he said.

"Why? Her daughter was murdered and you're trying to find the perp. You should be chief among the good guys."

"She doesn't want her other daughter suffering mental strain, but above all she doesn't want the family name besmirched by what might be revealed in the press about the dead twin. The Puritans have nothing on Agnes Boyington. She runs a tight little matriarchy."

"I gathered she was one of those." Hammersmith tilted back his head to drain the last of his beer, then pushed the empty mug away to the center of the table. "Could be coincidence," he said. "Maybe you cut Rumbo off when you made a left turn, and he sulked and followed you so he could set you straight about rules of the road. Maybe what happened has nothing to do with Agnes Boyington. Actually, she doesn't seem like the sort to hire a thug."

"She's the sort that will do what's necessary to get what she wants. You're fooling yourself with that coincidence talk."

"I'm not fooling myself," Hammersmith said. "I just wanted to see what you thought of the idea."

"What I think is that I need to have a talk with Agnes Boyington."

The waitress appeared again, and placed Nudger's glass of milk on the table along with the check. She smiled and commanded them to have a nice day and discreetly withdrew.

Hammersmith transferred his wadded red napkin from his lap to the table and stood up, brushing crumbs from his paunch. "I've got to get back to the station house," he said. "Crime doesn't stop for lunch, you know." He scrutinized the check and placed some folding money on the table. "This'll take care of half," he said.

"Sometimes crime goes to lunch at Ricardo's," Nudger told him.

Hammersmith smiled, said good-bye, and walked away. Nudger saw him nod to the maître d' and light up a cigar as he pushed through the door to the street.

Nudger took his time finishing his second glass of milk, enjoying the restaurant's warm and garlicky ambience. Then he summoned the waitress and paid the check, leaving most of Hammersmith's "half" for the tip.

He drove from Ricardo's back to his office. When he checked his telephone recorder he found that Claudia hadn't called but Jeanette Boyington had.

When Nudger returned Jeanette's call she told him angrily that she'd phoned him four times and had gotten only the recorder. She'd made another appointment, for two o'clock, at the fountain again in the Twin Oaks Mall. She was to meet a lonely man named Rudy.

"This one has blond hair," she said. "I got him to tell me that on the phone. It's easy to get them to trade general descriptions, and if they have dark hair I don't make an appointment with them." She told Nudger what Rudy would be wearing. He was the white-belt, polyester type. A step up from Sandy.

"You sound as if you're enjoying yourself," Nudger said, catching a smug sense of power in her tone that gave him a chill.

"I am. I feel that we're doing something that will result in the apprehension of my sister's murderer, without him even suspecting. That's the only part of this I'm enjoying, but I'm enjoying it immensely, to the very depths of my soul." Her voice crackled with cold fury.

Some family, Nudger thought, hanging up the phone. There were flaws, aberrations, genetic and otherwise, that were passed down from generation to generation in certain families, affecting differently each person contracting them. He reflected that it would be an exercise of morbid fascination to trace the Boyington family tree back to its diseased and twisted roots.

Rudy must have had second thoughts. Or maybe since 3 A.M. he'd met someone more his type. For whatever reason, he didn't show up for his appointment with Jeanette at the fountain in Twin Oaks Mall. Nudger watched for him until half past two before giving up and going back to the office.

The morning mail had arrived during the afternoon. Hidden among the advertisements and incredible offers was a note from Mrs. Natalie Mallowan, Ringo's owner, explaining that she would be somewhat later than she'd anticipated with the nine hundred dollars she owed Nudger. She assured him that Ringo was well and seemed to be suffering no ill effects from his time away from her.

Nudger was glad about Ringo, but he hoped Natalie Mallowan could come up with his fee before the end of next week.

If only he could introduce Eileen to Natalie and explain that there was no need to transfer the money twice and they might as well leave him out of it. Natalie could owe Eileen, okay?

But that sort of thing hadn't worked since his schoolyard days. It was a character-builder to make paying one's debts as difficult as possible. Even banks wouldn't let you assume loans anymore.

The desk phone rang. Hammersmith calling. Nudger recognized the special edge in his voice; it went back years.

"I'm at an apartment over on Spring," Hammersmith said. "It's leased to a woman named Grace Valpone. I think you should come right over here, Nudge."

Nudger felt the old hollow coldness in the pit of his stomach, the heady shortness of breath. "Who's Grace Valpone?" he asked.

"We don't know. She can't tell us. She's in her bathtub, not taking a bath. She's dead."

ELEVEN

Grace Valpone's apartment was in an old U-shaped brick building with ornate gray stone cornices. There was a circular area that had once been a garden in the center of the network of walkways to the entrances. Now it was bare earth with a few withered azaleas in the middle and a futile sprinkling of grass seed, bisected by what looked like tricycle tracks. A few dozen neighbors were milling around the many police cars blocking the quiet residential street and parked at crazy angles to the curb. Uniformed cops kept the gawkers out of harm's way. Some of the patrol cars' roof lights were still on and rotating, casting pale hues against the slanted late afternoon sunlight. One of the cars' radios, tuned to top volume, sputtered and crackled occasionally with code numbers, car designations, and addresses. Official stuff. The neighbors were impressed. They shifted about uneasily, exchanging comments and I-told-you-so's, excited and a little scared.

A calm, striped cat disdainfully observed Nudger from a perch on a windowsill as he gave the hard-faced cop at the building's west entrance his ID and explained that Hammersmith was expecting him. The cop nodded, stepping aside to give him room to pass.

Nudger's stomach was becoming light and queasy. "Is it a messy one?" he asked.

"She's been dead a couple of days," the cop said.

Nudger swallowed the acidic, coppery taste along the edges of his tongue. The cop smiled. The cat didn't blink.

"First floor, at the end of the hall," the cop said, as Nudger pushed open the door and entered a vestibule profaned with graffiti.

There had been no need for directions. From halfway up the stairs Nudger could see plenty of activity in the hall, and, through the wide-open door, in the apartment's living room.

As he entered, a familiar, faintly medicinal scent wafted to him, then was gone. He tried to identify it but couldn't.

The apartment was surprisingly large, sparsely and cheaply furnished, with threadbare oriental rugs over hardwood floors, mismatched furniture, and a very old console TV with a round bulging screen like an insect's eye. Large prints of show-business personalities or reproductions of thirties movie posters decorated the rough plaster walls. There was Bela Lugosi hovering over a coffin, disturbingly apropos. There was Bogie, blowing a whiff of smoke from the barrel of a blue steel automatic while a young Lauren Bacall watched with disinterest. There was King Kong taking a poke at a biplane.

There was Hammersmith, in the ample flesh, motioning for Nudger to join him. Nudger nodded to an assistant ME he knew slightly and circled a knot of plainclothes detectives to get to Hammersmith.

"C'mon," Hammersmith said. "She's still in the bathroom."

Nudger braced himself and followed Hammersmith down a short hall.

The bathroom was also a very large room, lined with green tile from floor to ceiling. Grace Valpone didn't look as bad as Nudger had anticipated. She was so pale she was almost the grayish white of the claw-footed porcelain tub wherein she reclined. One slender white leg was draped over the side of the tub. Her head was resting on the porcelain slope of the tub's back. No one had closed her eyes.

She was a beautiful woman, probably more so in death than she'd been in life. Her expression was one of dignified, laconic annoyance, as if she resented the intimacy of her bath being invaded by the clods from Homicide, the fingerprint crew just now closing up shop, the police photographer still snapping shots from various angles with his instant-print Japanese camera. Horror without gore. Hitchcock couldn't have staged it better.

Nudger stepped closer and his stomach lurched. Different movie. The bottom of the tub was caked reddish brown, and the lower portion of Grace Valpone's body was slashed and mutilated. Her nipples were gone; there were several deep defense wounds on the palms of her hands.

Nudger stepped back. "Good Christ," he said softly.

Hammersmith clapped him on the shoulder. "You never could take it, could you, Nudge?"

No need for a reply. Both men knew how it was. Nudger had never become accustomed to the sight of violent death. It was one of the reasons his police career had been cut short.

They left the pale lady and went into the living room. Some of the bustle was dying down as various technicians who'd finished their tasks were leaving the crime scene, casually chatting, occasionally grinning, as if drifting away from a cocktail party. All very convivial. Soon the hostess would be removed in a rubber body bag.

Nudger and Hammersmith sat on the sofa. Hammersmith stared at Nudger for a moment and suddenly seemed uneasy and solicitous, as if any second he might try to smooth things over by offering Nudger tea.

"I didn't figure it would be such a shock to your system, Nudge. Honest."

"The hell with that," Nudger said. "Do you think this was done by Jenine Boyington's killer?"

Hammersmith drew a cigar from his shirt pocket, glanced guiltily at Nudger and then returned it. "There are obvious similarities, and dissimilarities. The picture isn't clear yet. This one's been dead since night before last; a friend found her a few hours ago. We'll know more when we get a lab report, and after we question her family and friends."

"The two crimes might tie in," Nudger said. "Fingerprints, hair, the Valpone woman's love life . . . any of them could make the link." Nudger imagined the killer sitting where he now sat, in the corner of the sofa, watching Grace Valpone and building to the moment. "It almost has to be."

"Fingerprints we know about," Hammersmith said. "The apartment's full of them, of course, but none of them are the killer's. The fingerprint boys said right away that whoever murdered Grace Valpone wore gloves. So there's one dissimilarity in the two crimes. And there were no correlative prints to determine the size of this killer's hands."

"What about similarities? Other than the fact that Grace Valpone and Jenine Boyington were stabbed to death in bathtubs."

"There was no sign of forced entry in either case. And the crimes were tidy. Notice there's no blood anywhere but in the tub. It was the same way with Jenine Boyington. The two women were placed in their bathtubs alive and then killed. Jenine's throat was opened up, this woman's wasn't. But who knows, maybe the lab can tie it to the same knife. There was no semen in Jenine. We'll have to wait for the report on Grace Valpone."

"Dissimilarities?" Nudger asked.

"Grace Valpone was nude; Jenine Boyington was fully clothed. They were ten years apart in age; the Valpone woman was thirty-eight, in a stage of life different from Jenine's. Jenine did temporary office work; Grace Valpone was a beautician. They lived and died in different sections of town. Boyington had never married; Valpone was divorced and had a ten-year-old son living with his father. Boyington's apartment wasn't bothered; this place was rummaged through. Boyington liked to party; neighbors say Valpone might as well have been a nun." Hammersmith languidly waved a ruddy, manicured hand. "'It goes on and on,' as the widow said to the bishop."

"What we need to find out," Nudger said, "is whether Grace Valpone used the nightlines."

"Correct," Hammersmith said. "We're going to turn this place all ways but loose looking for one of those six-six-six phone numbers, hoping we don't find it."

Nudger understood. "You don't like the idea of a mass murderer," he said. "You want her boyfriend or a neighbor to have done it and confess and hand over the weapon."

"Exactly. The last thing anybody in this city needs, except for the news media, is a knife-happy series killer roaming around keeping in practice. I don't *want* there to be any connection between this and the Boyington murder, Nudge."

Nudger looked closely at Hammersmith. The sleek and handsome fat man had crescents of loose flesh beneath his eyes, and vertical frown lines above the bridge of his nose. He was deeply concerned, as well he should be. Blood was being spilled in copious amounts right here in his bailiwick. Still, Nudger could offer him no comfort.

"I think there is a connection," he said. "So do you."

"Of course I do," Hammersmith said. "Or at least I think there might be. But as long as the two crimes aren't officially related, I can move more freely in trying to solve them. The media, the Chief of Police, the mayor, the chronic confessors, all those people who make a cop's life complicated, won't be involved. It's pointless to operate in a pressure cooker if you can stay out on the range."

Nudger watched two white-uniformed morgue attendants saunter through the apartment and go down the hall toward the bathroom. Conversation and laughter drifted out, then the harsh ripping sound of the rubber body bag being zipped. A few minutes later they carried out the wrapped thing that had been Grace Valpone. Residual rigor mortis kept the limbs bent in the slumped position the body had assumed in the bathtub, giving the grotesque impression that the corpse was attempting to push its way out of the black bag. *She'll suffocate in there*! Nudger thought inanely.

"Always a cheering sight," Hammersmith said. "I'll let you know if we come up with anything that connects Grace Valpone with Jenine Boyington, Nudge. In the meantime, is there anything you've found out that we should know?"

"I haven't learned anything that would be of much help," Nudger said. He told Hammersmith about Wallace Everest's being Jeanette's lover, and about the abortion under a false identity.

"That totally evaporates Wally Everest's motive to kill Jenine,"

Hammersmith observed, "and still leaves him in Cincinnati at the time of the murder."

"I told you it wouldn't help."

Hammersmith stood up. He did fire up a cigar now, concentrating entirely on that task for a few minutes while greenish billows fouled the room. For once Nudger didn't mind the cigar; its pungent odor overpowered the faint but unmistakable scent of death.

"I wanted to talk to you about this Valpone murder, Nudge," Hammersmith said, "but there's another reason I asked you to come down here. You haven't been a cop for a long time, and I know the kinds of cases you've worked as a private investigator. Divorces, dips into the till, missing library books. Weren't you even working on a dog-napping?"

"I cracked that one," Nudger said.

Hammersmith regarded him with calm appraisal through a greenish haze. "The police are taking the possibility of a series killer quite seriously now, Nudge. We're very, very interested. And I wanted you to see Grace Valpone so you'd realized what you might be up against, so you'd be careful and remember not to exclude us entirely from your plans. Your police department cares."

A pale vision of Grace Valpone in her claw-footed bathtub flashed like a Kodak slide on Nudger's mind. "Your psychology is sound."

"I hope it's effective." Hammersmith crossed his arms over his protruding stomach. Ashes from his cigar dropped onto the floor. "We won't start to toss this place for another hour, Nudge. Want to go out for some supper? I'll buy."

Nudger's stomach was doing gymnastics. Not perfect ten scores, too herky-jerky. "I think I'll diet until tomorrow," he said.

Hammersmith smiled. That was the answer he'd been seeking.

As he left the apartment building, Nudger passed the same dreary graffiti, the same hard-faced cop, the same striped cat staring at him smugly, as if it knew that the way out was *always* the same as the way in and was enjoying the joke.

When Nudger got back to his office, he checked the answering machine and heard Claudia's voice tell him she was tired of trying to reach him and they could talk tonight in the usual way at the usual time. She sounded somewhat bemused that she would want to talk with him, maybe even slightly irritated. It was as if the recorder's tone had sounded before she could hang up, signaling go, and she'd had little choice but to be polite and postpone the conversation rather than cancel it. One of life's little electronic traps.

Quite an invention, the telephone. Nudger wondered if Alexander Graham Bell had ever suspected that someday the thing would speak back of its own accord, that it would bring so much heartache as well as convenience. He might have. Maybe he'd mentioned it. Nudger tried to remember the Don Ameche film but couldn't.

He got the phone directory from the desk's bottom left drawer and leafed through its dog-eared thin pages, squinting at its headache-inducing fine print until he found a listing for A. Boyington. There was no Agnes Boyington listed. A. Boyington's address was in the city's fashionable central west end.

Nudger slid the phone over to him and began to punch out the number, then he hesitated and replaced the receiver. He decided not to use the phone.

The A. Boyington in the directory might not be Agnes, but the chance that it was made it worth Nudger's time to drive to the address to try to take her by surprise, so she'd be unprepared for their conversation.

Nudger thought it might be fun to catch her in her old clothes painting the porch glider. Or cleaning up after the dog or masturbating or watching "Family Feud" on TV.

If Agnes Boyington did such things.

TWELVE

The A. Boyington address belonged to a large, squarish two-story house on Lindell Boulevard, a wide four-lane street bordering Forest Park. Though Lindell was heavily traveled, especially during morning and evening rush hours, the houses were divorced from the traffic, set well back on meticulously tended artificial-looking green lawns, and were expensive and luxurious. This house was of white brick, with a red tile roof, black shutters, and a colonial porch that boasted tall fluted white columns supporting a peaked roof with its own tiny cupola.

Nudger looked the place over with some envy and an inevitable subtle feeling of inferiority, as if he had no business being here in his down-at-the-heels shoes and clattering little car. His very presence was an affront. Agnes Boyington was a woman of at least moderate wealth; Nudger was no stranger to the cluttered aisles of K-mart.

He drove up the hedge-bordered, smooth blacktop driveway and parked by the porch. As he climbed from the car he noticed that shade trees—oaks and fast-growing maples—had been strategically planted so that the street was barely visible despite its relative nearness. The occasional swishing of passing cars was a mere suggestion of Lindell Boulevard's presence. From the rise on which the house sat, he could see the park across the street, a leafy expanse of green.

On the porch was a push button for a doorbell, as well as a fancy brass knocker at eye level on the door. Nudger ignored the button. He'd rattled the round brass knocker only once before Agnes Boyington opened the door.

Cool air from the house drifted out. Or was Agnes Boyington emitting that coolness?

"So, Mr. Nudger," she said, as if not at all surprised to find him standing on her porch. She was dressed up, wearing a dark blue dress, navy-blue high heels, an expensive-looking double-looped pearl necklace. She was also wearing white gloves that extended most of the way up her forearms. Nudger didn't think anyone wore white gloves anymore except to keep their hands warm. Yet here it was a hot summer evening and Agnes Boyington had on spotless soft white gloves. Nudger supposed that was class. He could think of no other explanation.

"We have matters to discuss," Nudger said.

"I have an appointment in half an hour," she told him, "but I suppose I have time to write your check." She turned and went back inside, leaving the tall door open as an invitation to Nudger. Or maybe he was expected to wait on the porch. He walked inside.

He was standing in a hall with white walls and a terrazzo floor of many subdued colors. There were no wall hangings and only a few pieces of furniture: a complexly constructed brass coatrack that looked like a metallic tree without leaves, an oval mahogany table on which sat a fancy fat lamp with a Tiffany glass shade. Agnes Boyington was leaning over the table, opening her purse to get out her checkbook.

"I didn't come for a check," Nudger told her.

She turned to face him, cocking her head back and to the side in the distinctive Boyington manner. "Oh? Then just why are you here?"

"To ask about Hugo Rumbo."

She gazed with icy appraisal at Nudger, as if trying to see right through the front of his skull into the machinations of his mind. She was an accomplished player on the board of life. She knew how to compete in whatever game he might intitiate. "I know Mr. Rumbo," she said. "Why are you inquiring about him? Do you need the services of a handyman?"

"I sift my own swimming pool," Nudger told her. "I'm inquiring to see if it was you who arranged an unpleasant encounter between Hugo Rumbo and me."

"Encounter?" She was amused.

"Yes, yesterday. It seemed to me that Rumbo was in a destructive frame of mind."

"He threatened you?" Nicely feigned disbelief.

"I think he intended to go beyond threats." Nudger mentally gagged himself. Why should he carry on this conversation on Agnes Boyington's genteel terms, using innuendos and euphemisms? He said, "He was determined to beat the shit out of me."

She raised her eyebrows, not from a shocked sense of propriety, but in mock concern. "Then he implied violence."

"He implied it strongly. There's no room for doubt; he was going to work me over."

"He struck you?"

"He would have hit me several times, I'm sure, only he was interrupted."

Agnes Boyington smiled and shook her head. "You're mistaken,

I'm certain. Oh, I can understand how it might happen. Mr. Rumbo has an assertive nature."

"So does an MX missile."

She zipped her purse closed. No check for Nudger now, even if he changed his mind. That was what happened to bad boys who balked, who had nasty tongues. "Mr. Rumbo also has a loyal and helpful nature. He's eager to please. It could be that he knew of my dealings with you and decided on his own to talk with you in a firm manner that might persuade you to see reason."

"You hired him to rough me up," Nudger told her, "so I'd accept your check and drop the case without telling Jeanette."

"I hire Mr. Rumbo for odd jobs," Agnes Boyington said, "not to commit mayhem. What he does on his own time, away from my property, is his business." Again the cold, sweet Boyington smile. "Of course I pay him very well."

Nudger saw that it was pointless to argue with Agnes Boyington. He'd learned what he came to find out. She'd had Hugo Rumbo follow him for the purpose of intimidation, as insurance that Nudger would accept her offer and, in effect, work for her instead of for Jeanette. He'd learned also the extent to which Agnes Boyington could deceive herself. It was probable that she habitually thought in the self-serving, convoluted fashion in which she'd just described her employment of Rumbo. Some people could rationalize anything. Nudger wouldn't be surprised if she and Rumbo really believed Rumbo had acted entirely on his own; they were both the type that drove polygraph operators to distraction.

"I do have to leave now, Mr. Nudger," Agnes said. She tugged at her white gloves to tighten them around her fingers. "I have an appointment that must be kept." Stepping adroitly around him, so as not to soil herself with physical contact, she reached, stretching, and opened the door for him.

Nudger didn't move. "I'm afraid of Hugo Rumbo," he said. "He might trip over his ankle and fall on me. I've been to the police about this, and if Rumbo slips his collar again and tries to attack me, they'll know you had something to do with it."

"But I thought I made it clear that I'm not responsible for Mr. Rumbo. And there's certainly no law against me talking to him as a friend and not an employer. If he finds out you've decided to reject my suggestion that you cease working for my daughter, it wouldn't surprise me if he decided to visit you on his own. He's a simple and dedicated man."

"He's a stupid and dangerous one," Nudger corrected. "Dangerous to me and to you."

She impatiently peeled back the top of one of her white gloves and glanced at a tiny square gold watch. "Mr. Nudger, I'm ready to leave."

Nudger nodded and walked past her out the door. As he stepped onto the porch, he heard a series of crisp snicking sounds coming from the side of the house. Almost like disapproving clucks of the tongue.

Agnes Boyington pointedly locked her door, then walked past him and through another door, leading into the attached garage. Nudger got into his Volkswagen and sat there until the garage's overhead door automatically opened. An old but mint-condition long gray Cadillac nosed out. As it emerged all the way, Nudger saw that it was even older than he'd thought, one of the models with fins. It looked like a long gray shark; it suited its owner.

The overhead door glided closed behind the car. Agnes Boyington let the Caddy coast down the driveway and made a left turn onto Lindell. She'd known that Nudger was still there but hadn't deigned to look at him.

Rumbo had filled her in on the day's activities, so Nudger's appearance at her door hadn't been unexpected. She'd known he'd talked to the police and she'd known he wasn't going to accept her check, but she'd acted out her scene with him without missing a beat or a cue, reciting her lines even when Nudger departed from the script. She was one of life's great troopers in her own long-running production, creating her own reality with the convincing force of her delusions.

Nudger found himself envying her. There had to be a warm security in being so unalterably correct in all matters. Possibly she was on her way to church, to interpret the sermon her way and sanctify her actions. There seemed to be an ugly outbreak of that kind of thing lately.

Snick! *Snick*! With the Volkswagen's windows rolled down, Nudger could hear the sound again clearly. Metal on metal. He got out of the car and walked across the spongy carpet of grass toward the corner of the garage.

Peering around a forsythia bush, he saw Hugo Rumbo in the side yard. He was shirtless and wearing blue bib overalls, standing about a hundred feet away and diligently trimming a squared-off privet hedge with a pair of long-bladed shears. As if sensing that a ring opponent was about to throw a sneak left hook at him, he raised a shoulder slightly, ducked his head and turned. He saw Nudger immediately and smiled his lopsided, unsettling little smile. Shifting the shears to his right hand, he took a step toward Nudger.

Nudger did what a hedge couldn't do. He backpedaled to the Volkswagen, clambered in, and had the engine started in a jiffy. As he backed the car all the way down the driveway to the street, he saw the overalled Hugo Rumbo round the corner of the garage, holding the long shears upright at his side, and stand staring at him in a kind of macho American-Gothic posture.

The little car's engine seemed to be clattering with fear as Nudger drove fast down Lindell Boulevard, as if agreeing with him that now wasn't a good time to talk with Hugo Rumbo.

Probably there was no good time.

In the glut of traffic on Kingshighway near the expressway, Nudger saw Agnes Boyington's gray Cadillac a block away, stopped for a red light. Maybe she wasn't going to church. Instead of turning west onto the expressway, he switched lanes and stayed on Kingshighway.

It might be worthwhile to follow Agnes Boyington. She could be on her way to meet someone else who wore white gloves.

THIRTEEN

Agnes Boyington drove south on Kingshighway, then took Highway 44 downtown to 55 and exited on Memorial Drive. Gothic church towers glided past Nudger, piercing the sky in contrast to the soft stroke of the Arch's caressing curve. Agnes stayed on Memorial, passing Busch Stadium and the Arch, then cut over to Market and headed west. She made a right on Seventh Street, and found a place to park near Seventh on Chestnut. It was the only empty parking space on the block, maybe a slot reserved for the genteel, and she effortlessly maneuvered the haughty gray lady of a Cadillac into it.

Nudger drove half a block past Agnes, hoping she wouldn't see him, and pulled to the curb near a fire hydrant.

He watched her in his rearview mirror as she crossed Chestnut and entered one of the office buildings that lined the block. The Hammond Building. This was the area of downtown where many of the city's high-priced lawyers kept their offices. That made Nudger wonder. He got out of the Volkswagen, hoping it wouldn't be ticketed or towed away, and jogged across the street and into the Hammond Building.

The lobby, adorned with gray marble and cigarette butts, was almost deserted. Most of the offices were closed at this hour, and only one elevator was in service. Nudger watched the brass indicator arrow on the veined marble above the elevator doors. It slowed, wobbled, then rested on the six.

He crossed the lobby and checked the building directory. There were enough law firms in the place to stall a thousand cases a thousand years. On the sixth floor there were three law offices, an architectural firm, and several businesses of nondescript corporate name. Nudger considered taking the elevator up and finding a spot in the hall from which he could see Agnes Boyington emerge from whatever office she'd entered. However, not knowing which office she was in made that too risky an idea to carry out. Besides, it was altogether possible that whatever business she had here didn't concern him.

He left the lobby, trudged back across hot concrete to the Volkswagen, and sat waiting. From his car window he could see the silver, soaring curve of the Arch, towering above even the newer downtown buildings. The Gateway to the West and to McDonald's floating restaurant. The Arch was Nudger's favorite memorial. It was so nonfunctional. Its stainless steel, inspirational arc was the sole reason for its existence. If it wasn't a joy forever, a lot of time and money had been wasted. What was it doing here in this conservative midwestern city where commerce was king? Or maybe its creation was inevitable. Perhaps out of all this flat, staid sanity it had to spring like joyful madness, a glittering dream-reflecting ribbon unfurling skyward to an exquisitely graceful apogee and then rushing earthward, like life itself.

Nudger was still contemplating the Arch fifteen minutes later when Agnes Boyington left the Hammond Building and got back into her car. The Cadillac glided past him. He was sure that Agnes hadn't seen him, with the Volkswagen tucked as it was between a larger car and a van. He started the engine, waited until she'd reached the corner, then followed.

She didn't drive far, only to Tucker and Clark, where she parked in a visitors' slot in the lot of Police Headquarters. After locking the Caddy, she strode with vigor and purpose around to the front of the imposing gray building and up the wide steps. She still looked cool as frozen custard in her blue dress and white gloves, and she certainly moved like a much younger woman. Nudger watched the metronome sway of her flared hips until she disappeared through the main entrance. She wasn't quite as impressive a piece of architecture as the Arch, but then she was older.

Nudger didn't follow Agnes Boyington into Police Headquarters. And when she left half an hour later, he didn't follow her disdainful finned Cadillac.

Instead he got out of the Volkswagen and went inside the building.

The Headquarters building was also the Fourth District station. Nudger recognized the desk sergeant, a thirtyish, dark-haired man named Mazzoli who was on desk duty because of a hip injury he'd suffered during a high-speed chase a few years ago. Mazzoli had been assigned to the Third, Hammersmith's district, at the time of the accident.

Nudger figured they were acquaintances if not friends. Mazzoli gazed flatly across the wide booking desk at him and seemed not to recognize him.

"Hey, Mo Mazzoli," Nudger said, smiling. "I knew you when you were in the Third. Remember me?"

"No," Mazzoli said. His cop's eyes stayed flat.

Well, he met a lot of people in his job. "I'm Nudger," Nudger said. "A friend of Lieutenant Hammersmith."

Ah, rank. The mention of lieutenanthood brought some amiability to Mazzoli's stern features. "Lieutenant Hammersmith's okay," he said.

"At select times," Nudger told him. "The woman who came in here a while ago, older, nice-looking . . ."

"Wearing gloves?"

"That's the one. What did she want?"

"I dunno. She wouldn't talk to me. She wanted to see someone with authority, she kept saying, so I sent her in to Lieutenant Springer."

"That's right," a sharp, clipped voice said behind Nudger, "he sent her in to me."

Nudger turned to see Lieutenant Leo Springer standing just outside his open office door. He was a tall, lean man with vivid dark features built around an oversized pockmarked nose. He looked as if someone with incredible strength had placed a hand on each side of his face and squeezed. Intensity gleamed in his close-set black eyes, and there was a permanent tenseness to his forward-tilted posture that gave the impression he'd be tireless at tennis. He wasn't one of Nudger's favorite people in the department. Or on planet earth.

"And I suppose what she wanted to see you about is a private matter," Nudger said.

Springer shot his underslung, shark's smile. He'd have looked great in Agnes Boyington's finned Cadillac. "Not at all," he said. "She wanted to see me about you. She'd just come from her lawyer. I was her second call."

"I know."

"Mrs. Boyington said you'd been following her," Springer said with an edge of triumph, like a real-life Columbo. "You just confirmed it."

Nudger's stomach fluttered. He felt himself getting angry. Springer could do that to him. "I haven't broken the law."

"That's always debatable," Springer said smoothly, verbally gliding around his prey like the ocean carnivore he resembled. "Mrs. Boyington said you're working for her daughter, and that the girl isn't thinking straight because of grief and shouldn't have hired you. You shouldn't have taken her on as a client. In effect, you're stealing her money. And it's a case you've got no business on anyway, a pending homicide. You've also been trying to convince Mrs. Boyington to pay you to drop the case on the sly while humoring the daughter and still collecting your fee. You tried to intimidate Mrs. Boyington; you implied threats. She has a handyman as a witness. Bunko, extortion, all sorts of laws apply here, Nudger."

"Then apply them!" Nudger snapped.

Springer stared at him with a contempt usually reserved for murderers set free on technicalities. "Unfortunately, I can't. Mrs. Boyington doesn't want to bring charges against you. She's too much of a lady. She only wants us to talk to you, so you'll leave her alone and she can have some peace of mind. You're here, being talked to. Leave this case alone. Leave her alone. If you bother Mrs. Boyington again, your investigator's license will be up for review, and before you can say 'Sam Spade,' you'll be toting a lunch bucket back and forth to work. If you can find work."

"Nice of you to listen to my side," Nudger said.

"You don't have a side, Nudger. You're just a guy in the way. Private investigators stir up the muck, is all. They create obstacles. Not that it isn't personal too, Nudger. I don't like you. You're a smart-ass. You've got smart ways and a smart mouth."

"You forgot smart dresser."

"No, I didn't. That jacket you're wearing's got so much synthetic fiber in it, the sun might melt it."

"How do you afford such high wool content on a lieutenant's salary, Springer?"

Springer's face revealed nothing, but his lean dark fingers flexed around a wood pencil he probably didn't even know he was holding, threatening to snap it. "I can possibly talk Mrs. Boyington into pressing charges," he said. "She's a woman who obviously has a deep respect for the law. She might go for the 'your responsibility as a citizen' approach." His strained voice hissed like the sibilant opening note of a teakettle. He was coming to a boil.

"You could talk her into nothing," Nudger told him, turning up the burner. "She only feeds when she's hungry."

Springer's eyes were like black laser beams. Nudger was winning this joust. "Get out, Nudger! You and your class of cop oughta live under rocks!"

"Class isn't sewn into your designer suits, Springer. I'm surprised someone wearing white gloves would even talk to you."

Nudger knew an exit line when he'd uttered one. So much in life was timing. He neatly about-faced and made for the door, paying no attention to the wooden pencil that bounced off the wall in front of him. Mazzoli, who had been listening to the confrontation, turned away from Springer and winked at Nudger without moving any other part of his face.

Nudger's stomach felt as if it were rolling in on itself, again and again, winching his body taut. He breathed deeply as he walked to his car, trying to exhale the tension he'd built up. He hated to get angry. And he knew that Agnes Boyington and not Springer was his real problem and the deep source of his rage. He would talk to Hammersmith about Springer, who was in Vice and had no business interfering with a homicide case.

By the time he drove from the parking lot, Nudger was calmer, but his metabolism still hadn't returned to normal. He went to Swensen's at Laclede's Landing and treated himself to a thick vanilla malted milk, sitting in a booth where he could see out the window and watch the tourists wandering about, the ritual of teenagers cruising in their highly glossed cars, the pretty girls gingerly probing and picking their way across the rough cobblestone street in their slender high heels. It was relaxing to watch the rest of humanity through a sheet of glass, separated from it, ignoring the sounds of the ice cream parlor and its other customers. It lent a sense of perspective.

Nudger sat sipping the criminally rich malted milk for almost an hour before paying and walking back to his car. The clawed creature in his stomach had retreated to wait for another day.

He'd finally cooled down, and so had the evening. The breeze swirling in through the car's open windows soothed him as he drove. He'd managed to put his conversation with Leo Springer in a time vault in his mind. He wouldn't think about it again until tomorrow morning.

As he was driving west on Walnut he heard a loud roar. He was near Busch Stadium, where the Cardinals must be playing a home ball game. And playing it right, judging by crowd reaction. Nudger wondered if someone had hit a home run. He wished he could hit some kind of home run in this life, just once. He'd even settle for a long triple.

Not until he was home in bed, about to drift into one of his frequent dreams of the sea, did he realize the roar of the stadium crowd had a surflike roll and rush to it that he'd heard recently somewhere else.

He was sure it was the mysterious sound in Claudia's phone.

FOURTEEN

Nudger hadn't slept well. He'd awakened twice during the night from dreams of walking on an empty beach, leaving a line of footprints just beyond the reach of crashing, hungry waves that were angrily devouring the wide slope of sand. There was no one in sight, not for miles up and down the coastline. A half-moon was so bright that it etched his black shadow in front of him, almost as if it were day rather than night. He was alone, never more alone, and gusting in from an indiscernible horizon were roiling dark clouds, dropping lower and lower, threatening to engulf and smother him when they reached the shore.

He tried not to think about last night's dreams as he sat eating an omelet and dry toast, grateful for the morning light cascading through the kitchen window, even though its glare worsened his dull headache. He seemed to be haunted by the same sorts of dreams, if not the same dreams. He was either by the sea, which might be in any of its varying moods, or he dreamed of falling from great heights. Sometimes the sea dreams were pleasant and reassuring. The dreams of falling always left him sweating and scared.

While he ate, he listened to an old Billie Holiday record from what was left of his jazz collection after last year's poverty-induced sale. That made him feel better. If he was down, Billie was lower; but something in her dulcet voice affirmed that it was possible to get up.

He left his dirty dishes in the sink, telling himself he'd wash them that evening. Sure. After switching off the stereo and replacing the record in its jacket, he draped his sport coat over his arm and left the apartment.

As he got out of his car and crossed the street to his office he was almost struck by a van with a thousand windows. Traffic was heavy on Manchester for this time of day. He reached the haven of the opposite sidewalk and squinted to see up the street. Cars were backed up beyond the traffic light, waiting to turn into the K-mart underground parking lot. There must have been coupons in the paper.

He trudged upstairs to his office, unlocked the door, and went inside. The place was hot, but he wasn't planning on being there long. There was no point in switching on the air conditioner. Listening to the traffic sounds from beyond the dirt-spotted window, he sat down behind his desk and punched buttons on the answering machine.

"This is Eileen," said the machine. "Just a reminder—" Nudger pressed Fast Forward.

"Jeanette here, Mr. Nudger. Only one appointment today. At noon by the Twin Oaks Mall fountain. His name's Jock. He'll be wearing dark slacks and a beige sport jacket, no tie. Personnel Pool sent me out on a temporary secretarial job today, so phone me late this evening and report." *Click.*

"Jack Hammersmith, Nudge. Call me at the Third when you get a chance. Some of us are pitching in for a birthday gift for Leo Springer. . . ." Hammersmith's cigar-distorted chortle came through before Nudger could punch the red Off button.

He'd heard enough for now. In a way it was nice to know that the temporary office help firm that sent Jeanette out on jobs had tucked her safely away where she couldn't bother him for a while.

Nudger stood up and walked over to where a *Globe-Democrat* lay folded on the cold radiator. When he examined the paper he was surprised to find that it was four days old and wouldn't tell him what he needed to know. Dropping the paper into the wastebasket, he sat down again at the desk and dialed Hammersmith's number at the Third District. Hammersmith knew about Agnes Boyington and should have no trouble getting Springer to back off.

"I'm busy, Nudge," Hammersmith said into the phone. "Not much time for you. Ever seen a man actually foam at the mouth?"

"Only in bad movies. I think they do it with some kind of chemical."

"Springer did it with only the forces of nature. He told me about his conversation with you. I set him straight. At least as straight as possible. He'll leave you alone, but not for long. I would describe him as incensed."

"What did you tell him?"

"Practically nothing. He doesn't deserve to know anything at all." Hammersmith was definitely annoyed. "There's plenty to do in Vice. The bastard had no business meddling in Homicide. Unless of course he wants to become a victim."

"I talked to Agnes Boyington at her house last night," Nudger said. "She as much as told me she hired Hugo Rumbo to help persuade me to accept her offer of a payoff to bow out of the case without telling her daughter. I think she was expecting me. Rumbo was there in the background, to protect her and intimidate me."

"I suppose when Hugo told her about yesterday's fun in the Third District parking lot, she decided her best defense would be immediate offense. Gutsy lady."

"She wears white gloves, even in this weather."

"Springer told me. He was genuinely impressed. I know a massage parlor where all the girls wear white gloves."

"Do you have anything yet that might tie in the Valpone murder with Jenine Boyington?"

"I was wondering when you'd ask," Hammersmith said. "The search of the Valpone apartment didn't turn up a six-six-six phone number, or anything else that proved useful. The autopsy report lists death by asphyxiation, from when her throat was slashed, but she was tortured before that. As badly as she was mutilated, she would have survived her injuries for at least an hour, though she wouldn't have been able to climb out of the bathtub. Maybe she tried; maybe that's why she had a leg draped over the side of the tub. Also, the lab report says there was no semen in her vagina, throat, or rectal tract, and no evidence of violent entry. So she wasn't raped or sodomized. But, like Jenine Boyington's murder, this is the worst kind of sex killing."

Nudger knew what Hammersmith meant. This sort of murder was

the giant, grisly step beyond rape. And it was a step that seldom allowed any backtracking. It was a step that led on, to more violent death. "But there's no strong link between the two crimes," Nudger said, disappointed.

"Nothing to rule it in, nothing to rule it out. But there is one other thing, Nudge. Turns out that Grace Valpone was engaged to be married. The date was set for next month."

"Have you questioned the intended?"

"Sure. Name's Vincent Javers. President of his own small company out in Westport. Guess what? He was in Hawaii at the time of the murder, at a tire wholesalers' convention."

"Hawaii, huh. Wally Everest was in Cincinnati when Jenine Boyington was killed. They're getting farther away."

"The Valpone murder has a lot of the earmarks of the Boyington job, Nudge, but there are things about it that bother me. It doesn't quite fit."

"Doesn't fit why?"

"Tell me, how likely is it that a woman engaged to be married would be setting up blind dates with who-knows-what over the nightlines a month before her wedding?"

"Not as likely as death or taxes," Nudger admitted.

"Maybe it was only a coincidence that Jenine Boyington talked on the nightlines and also got herself murdered. She and Grace Valpone could have been killed by the same perp, but the nightlines might have had nothing to do with it."

"Which would leave me way out at sea in my investigation," Nudger said.

"It's a good thing you swim well. And it looks as if you'd better start stroking." The tone of Hammersmith's voice suddenly changed. "Duty calling, Nudge. It sounds remarkably like the Chief of Police."

Nudger thanked Hammersmith and hung up.

He listened to the rest of his calls on the answering machine, hoping to hear Claudia's voice. But she hadn't phoned him. He got up from the desk and adjusted the Venetian blinds to a sharp downward angle to block the warming morning sunlight. His headache was gone. His stomach murmured something about being hungry. The omelet and dry toast hadn't been enough to eat. Nudger figured he'd been burning up a lot of calories lately just by worrying.

He closed the office, then went downstairs for a doughnut and a bracing cup of vile black coffee at Danny's.

Danny was alone except for an old woman hunched over a cup of coffee at the far end of the counter. She wore a faded dress with crescent stains of perspiration beneath the arms, and she was talking softly and earnestly to herself.

Nudger felt a current of pity for her as he sat as far away from her as possible, so as not to eavesdrop, and asked Danny for a small coffee and a Dunker Delite. Danny smiled and nervously wiped his hands on his gray towel as he headed for the coffee urn. He was glad not to be alone with the woman, who seemed harmless enough and more interested in staring at her coffee than in drinking it. Maybe it was the coffee that had caused her condition.

Nudger sipped his own coffee, then took a bite of a particularly large Dunker Delite. He used a paper napkin to wipe the grease from his fingers, then, like the woman down the counter, stared into his cup and thought about his world.

It occurred to him that the crowd roar he'd heard on Claudia's phone might have come from somewhere other than Busch Stadium. A television set or radio? Not likely. Nudger was sure he would have recognized a broadcast sound. Maybe Claudia lived near a Little League field or a park where high school or legion baseball was played.

No, Nudger decided. Not much baseball was played at one in the morning, not even major league ball. It could be that he was wrong about the source of the sound. Then he heard again the crowd's roar last night as he was driving near the stadium.

"Did the Cards play in town night before last?" he asked Danny.

Danny nodded, a gleam of interest in his dark, basset eyes. He was a baseball fan and an ardent Cardinals rooter. "They won thirteen to ten in extra innings," he said.

Nudger paused as he raised his foam coffee cup. "How many extra innings?"

"They played seventeen innings, their longest game of the season.

They won the game with two singles and a home run when they had two outs. If they get good pitching in September—"

"Never mind that. What time was the game over?"

Danny shrugged and leaned on the glass doughnut case. "Oh, I dunno, but it had to be awful late. You could find out what time, I guess." He stood up straight. "In fact, I know where you could find out. I still got that day's sports page in a stack of newspapers in the back room."

Nudger was about to ask Danny to get the sports page, but the doughnut shop entrepeneur was already shoving open the swinging door by the display case. From the back room came sounds of rummaging.

"Ain't fair," the old woman at the end of the counter was absently muttering again and again. "Ain't fair, ain't fair, ain't fair . . ."

Age had granted her wisdom. Nudger sat feeling sorry for her, then wondered if she might actually be better off than he was. Disoriented though she might be, she didn't have to cope with Hugo Rumbo and the Boyington women, not to mention a mass murderer.

Danny emerged within a few minutes clutching a grease-spotted sheet of newspaper. It featured a photo of a leaping ballplayer and the headline CARDS SMITE CUBS IN SEVENTEEN. He turned the paper so Nudger could read it, spreading it out on the stainless steel counter and smoothing it flat with a swipe of his hand.

The information Nudger sought was in the second paragraph. Forty thousand people had seen the Cardinals triumph when a ten-ten tie was broken in the bottom of the seventeenth inning by a pinch-hit home run with two men on base. Forty thousand people. How far from the stadium might the exuberant roar of that many fans carry, and still be loud enough to be picked up in a phone conversation? Three blocks? Ten?

Then Nudger remembered that the area around the stadium was almost exclusively commercial; there weren't that many apartment buildings. That would make his task possible, though not easy.

Leaving his coffee and doughnut, but no money, on the counter, he said a hasty good-bye to Danny and hurried from the doughnut shop to drive downtown.

"Hey, Nudge!" Danny called.

"Put it on my tab!"

"Ain't fair, ain't fair, ain't fair," the old woman repeated sagely, as the door swung closed behind Nudger.

Traffic was heavy downtown, the usual business crowd as well as a surprising number of summer tourists, come to see Missouri's Big City. Nudger drove around for a while, studying the buildings in the vicinity of Busch Stadium. There were only a few apartment buildings, but there were some business structures that might contain upstairs apartments.

He divided the area around the stadium into quadrants, parked the car, and began his search on foot. He felt like the love-crossed prince searching for Cinderella. All he needed was a glass slipper.

The first building was a gloomy old converted hotel. Nudger stood in the faded vestibule and studied the bank of brass mailboxes. Some of them had only last names printed on the cards showing above the slots. Nudger cursed and wiped his forehead with his forearm. Maybe he wasn't as close to Claudia as he thought. Or maybe closer. She might live right upstairs from where he stood, but he had no way to know from the mailboxes.

He began punching buttons above the boxes, asking if Claudia was home when he got an answer on the intercom. No Claudia lived here, he was told. No one in the building had even heard of a Claudia. At least no one who was home. Feeling better, but not completely satisfied that he could discount the building, Nudger moved on to the next challenge.

The day was getting hotter. He removed his sport jacket, slung it over his shoulder, and went through the mailbox procedure in a similar though smaller building two blocks away. No Claudia there. An apartment whose mailbox was simply labeled "Elwood" didn't answer his ring. He made a note of it as a possible and walked back to the Volkswagen, eager to get rid of his coat and tie in the heat.

He paid the two dollars he was charged to park, then drove to another pay parking lot in the second quadrant.

More hot, tedious work, without result. He was getting dehydrated. He entered a bar beneath a sign lettered ZIGZAG's and ordered a draft beer. It was a tiny, dim place with an overactive air condi-

tioner that made the ice-flecked mug of beer taste even colder than it
was. The bartender was a young, prematurely bald guy in a white
apron. Or maybe he shaved his head; Nudger couldn't keep up with
style. There were only two other customers, a harried businessman
type slouched at the bar, and a bearded man in a sleeveless shirt, cut-
off jeans, and sandals. On a hunch, Nudger carried his beer to where
the bartender was wrestling with some paperwork at the end of the
bar.

"Help you?" the bartender asked, lifting his pencil and looking up
at Nudger. His brown eyes were much too young for his bald pate.

"Does a girl named Claudia come in here?"

The bartender laughed. "The place is like a mortuary now, but
girls by the hundreds flock in here before and after ball games and on
Saturday nights. We got live music after eight," he added, as if that
explained such fervent female clientele.

"I mean a regular customer, a girl who lives in the area."

The bartender shook his gleaming head. "Sorry. But she oughta be
easy to find if she lives around here. The neighborhood's nearly all
commercial." He licked the point of his pencil and went reluctantly
back to his paperwork, copying numbers from a tiny calculator.

Nudger finished his beer and started to leave.

"You might try here after eight tonight," the bartender suggested
behind him. "Live music," he reminded.

Nudger thanked him and pushed out the door into heat that struck
like a hammer. It was still too early to drink alcohol. His head began
to throb in reproach for his dissolute ways.

In the only likely building in the third quadrant, on Spruce Street,
Nudger felt a cautious elation as he studied the mailboxes. There was
a "C. Davis." Also a "C. Bettencourt." Single women often listed
their names with only first initials in phone directories and on their
mailboxes, to give potential interlopers the impression that the occupant might be a 250-pound armed male with an extra Y chromosome
and a taste for combat.

This was a run-down, rent-subsidized building without intercoms.
It was the only apartment building in an area of closed office buildings converted to warehouses. The vestibule reeked of cooking odors
and bums' urine. Most of the apartments had only round blank holes

above their mailboxes, where push buttons for doorbells had been punched into oblivion and not replaced.

C. Davis was in apartment 2C. Nudger climbed the stairs, found the door halfway down a dim, littered hall. It was a heavy wood door whose dark enamel had shrunk and cracked like eroded soil, leaving a sharply angled network of shallow crevices. The "2C" was painted on the door with what looked like pink fingernail polish.

Nudger knocked, then stood patiently. A car horn honked outside. A distant siren gave its singsong frantic wail like a faraway creature in pain.

There was a change of light in the tiny glass peephole mounted in the door. Nudger smiled, trying not to look like an overheated insurance salesman or rent collector.

"Who is it?" a female voice called.

"My name's Nudger."

"So who's Nudger?" It was a black woman's voice, lilting and rich with accent.

"I'm looking for Claudia," he said. He waited.

A chain lock rattled and the door opened. A large ebony woman with wild straightened hair peered suspiciously out at him. "What Claudia?"

"I don't know her last name. I saw the C on your mailbox."

"The C happens to be my husband," the woman said. She had large, intelligent eyes, gentle and proud eyes that were measuring Nudger dubiously. Poverty, meet poverty. "You a friend of Claudia?"

Nudger tried not to show his excitement. "Very much a friend."

"She want to see you?"

"She should see me." He met the woman's soft, skeptical stare directly, not blinking. Neither of them blinked for a long time. Then Nudger blinked.

"Claudia's a good woman," C. Davis's wife said. "She don't need no bullshit."

"I know. That's why I came."

"You look like you been wandering around out in the desert, Nudger."

"I have been, like a prophet of old whose camel has died."

"Hm, yeah. Well, Claudia lives up in 4D, top of them stairs."

"Thank you. Is she home?"

"How do I know if she's home? I ain't no spy satellite. Could be she's working today. Go knock on her door, you want to find out."

"If she's not home and you see her later, do you intend to tell her I was around asking for her?"

"You better believe it, Nudger."

Nudger smiled at her. "Good. Nice meeting you, wife of C. Davis."

He knew she was watching him as he walked toward the stairs. Without looking back, he raised a hand in a listless wave and started up toward the fourth floor.

Someone else was already knocking on Claudia's door.

He was a slim, sharp-featured man wearing a dark suit and tie and carrying one of those slender leather briefcases that look like purses because they don't have handles.

Nudger didn't know quite what to do. He could hardly knock on the door to 4C and pretend that had been his destination. It could prove embarrassing, even dangerous in this neighborhood, if the door were opened. And there could be little doubt that he was heading toward 4D's door.

The man turned and gave him a long look. He had bushy dark eyebrows and high cheekbones. He would have been craggily handsome if it weren't for a skinny kind of meanness in his features.

"She's not home," he said, jerking his head toward Claudia's door. "I've been knocking for five minutes."

"I see," Nudger said, not knowing what else to say.

The man noticed Nudger's discomfort and stared at him with new interest. "You her boyfriend?"

Nudger followed his detective's instincts. "Yes, I am."

"I'm her husband," the man said.

Ho, boy! Nudger's stomach went into a spasm and made a sound like a cat meowing.

The man narrowed one eye and took a step toward Nudger, his suit coat open and flapping as if there were a breeze in the stifling hall. Or as if he were prepared for quick-draw gunplay, his holster in easy reach.

"You tell her when she gets home that I was here," he said. "And that I'm leaving town with the kids and she can't see them this weekend." He pointed a slender forefinger as if he could shoot lightning from it. "You got that?"

"Got it," Nudger said, trying to keep calm and size up what was happening, not having much success doing either.

The man clenched overdeveloped, bunchy jaw muscles, then strode past him and down the stairs. Nudger stood listening to his echoing, receding footfalls on the wooden steps, then heard the vacuumy clatter of the vestibule door opening and closing.

Nudger looked at 4D's closed door, its layered enamel cracked like the door to C. Davis's apartment, then rapped his knuckles on it three times, hard.

He stood stiffly, waiting.

No answer. No sound from the other side of the door. No hint of movement behind the peephole. No one home.

Maybe it was just as well, he thought, looking at his watch. He was sure now that this was Claudia's apartment. Claudia Bettencourt's. He repeated her full name to himself. Say it often enough and it became musical. Like Greta Boechner's, the girl he had loved in high school.

He knocked again on the door, in case she was home and for some reason hadn't heard his first knock.

Still no reply. He backed away from the door and started walking down the narrow hall. He would return this afternoon and try again to see Claudia Bettencourt.

On the way down the stairs, he waved again to the wife of C. Davis, who was standing staunchly outside her door staring. But he didn't take time to stop and chat. He was in a hurry. It was almost eleven-thirty, and he had a noon appointment with a nightline Romeo named Jock at Twin Oaks Mall.

FIFTEEN

Nudger took up his position near the Twin Oaks Mall fountain and waited. Between twelve and twelve-thirty, he saw four blond men wearing dark slacks and beige sport jackets. All of them could be ruled out for one reason or another as Jenine's murderer, and none of them appeared to be waiting for someone.

It occurred to him that the description Jeanette had given him was exceptionally vague for the basis of a rendezvous of strangers. For the first time, he wondered if Jeanette was playing their game totally within the rules he'd laid down. She was a manipulator, like her mother, and might act out of some devious scheme of her own, or only for the satisfaction of control over other people. Nudger had met other compulsive manipulators. High-level corporate executives, politicians, and tournament chess players usually had that kind of streak in them.

And it ran like a broad, deep current in the Boyington women.

Nudger craned his neck and glanced up and down the mall. Other than a young salesclerk lethargically applying a squeegee to the display window of a shoe store, there wasn't a blond man in sight. Nudger let himself relax.

He found it restful sitting in the cool indoor mall, listening to the gentle splashing of the fountain and watching the shoppers walk past. There was a controlled, protective atmosphere in a large shopping mall. It was a practical place of constant temperature, where rain never fell but where flowers and ornamental trees flourished. Inside every store's wide entrance were people paid to be polite, and almost every facet of suburban life was catered to here. There were several restaurants, a bank branch, drugstores, dime stores, department stores, and specialty stores. Bookstores, hardware stores, and software stores. Card shops, food shops, and antique shoppes. Merchandise for everyone from birth through all the stages of life. Everything but a funeral parlor. Shopping malls wanted no truck with death.

Nudger's pelvis felt as if it were grafted onto the hard concrete bench he was sitting on. It was twelve-forty, and still no blond Jock. Jeanette had been stood up again; Nudger had waited long enough.

He got to his feet and dodged a pert young woman pushing a baby stroller, then joined the stream of shoppers walking toward the escalators. From a shop that seemed to sell only electric organs, an elaborate but repetitive beat was drifting into the vast mall. It sounded like someone playing drums that wheezed, but it was kind of catchy and Nudger noticed that most of the shoppers were unconsciously walking to its relentless jaunty rhythm.

Nudger stopped suddenly. A man walking behind him bumped him, mumbled a "'Scuse me" and walked on, giving a little skip to recapture the beat.

Moving over against a display window, so he would no longer be an impediment in the flow of shoppers, Nudger stared across the mall.

There was Hugo Rumbo, standing next to a bullet-shaped trash receptacle, looking at Nudger with his dreamy half-smile and squeezing his rubber ball in perfect rhythm with the wheezing organ music. As Nudger watched, Rumbo slid the ball into his jacket pocket and drew out an orange. He held the orange over the trash container and smiled more broadly at Nudger as he slowly squeezed it, compressing it to juice and pulp that oozed from between his fingers to drop into the container. Then he wiped his fingers with a handkerchief very deliberatively, never looking away from Nudger. Here was an unmistakable message not of good cheer.

Nudger's stomach was tight, but he felt safe in the mall, surrounded by hundreds of people, standing right in front of B. Dalton. He walked across the red synthetic stone floor to where Hugo Rumbo towered motionless.

Rumbo hadn't expected that. His novocaine smile disappeared and he tried to look mean. He only managed ugly, but he managed that very well.

"I could show you how to peel one of those," Nudger offered.

Rumbo's little eyes darted around like blips on a video game, taking in the throng of shoppers. "You better watch out I don't peel you," he grunted.

"Did Agnes Boyington send you to follow me?" Nudger asked. He tried but couldn't imagine being peeled.

"Nobody sent me anyplace. This is a free society. I can go anywhere I want, and if it happens to be where you are, that's just too bad."

Nudger crossed his arms and looked up at Rumbo. "How long did it take you to memorize that?"

Rumbo crossed his own leg-sized arms and sneered. "You're pretty brave here, Nudger, with all these people around us."

"I'm not pretty brave anywhere," Nudger said. This conversation was stirring playground memories. "Tell Agnes she shouldn't have gone to the police and lied about me. And that you following me around isn't going to make me change my mind about her proposition."

Rumbo flexed his bulging biceps by way of a shrug. "I don't know nothin' about any of that stuff. You tell her whatever you want her to know."

"I already have. She doesn't seem willing to accept it. She's a headstrong woman, your employer. Or is she more than just your employer?"

Rumbo didn't respond to Nudger's probe. He got his rubber ball out of his pocket, looked for a moment as if he might ask Nudger to play catch, then hunched his powerful shoulders and began his rhythmic squeezing, working the red ball as if it were a tiny detached heart that he had to keep pumping.

"The kind of people who wear white gloves usually have flip sides," Nudger said. Silence. In, out, in, out went the ball. Talking to Rumbo was some chore. Nudger decided to be direct. "Do you sleep with Agnes Boyington?"

Rumbo stopped working the agonized ball. His glittering little eyes widened in shock as color rose on his bull neck. "That ain't a very nice thing to say, Nudger."

"I didn't say it, I asked it."

Now Rumbo was shuffling his huge feet in embarrassment. Like Agnes Boyington's, his was a puritanical heart, capable of limitless cruelty for a cause thought just. That really was the thing about the massive and ineffectual Rumbo that frightened Nudger.

"Same thing," Rumbo mumbled accusingly.

"Maybe so," Nudger conceded, still wondering if what he'd suggested happened to be true. The prospect was enough to make the

imagination run riot. But Rumbo probably would have responded to
the question the same way whatever his relationship with Agnes Boyington.

"I like you less every time I see you," Rumbo said, using bluff to
regain his composure. "But that's okay."

"Why is it okay?"

"'Cause eventually the time'll come when I'm gonna enjoy your
company, Nudger, but you ain't gonna enjoy mine." Rumbo flipped
the ball into the air, caught it one-handed, and walked ponderously
away in the direction of Sears.

Nudger thought that, considering Hugo Rumbo's obviously limited
mental capacity, his message had been succinctly put. No doubt he
and Nudger shared a piece of the troubled future.

Trying not to think about that future in graphic detail, Nudger
turned and resumed walking toward the parking lot.

Halfway there, he noticed that he was walking too fast and made
himself slow down. He had places to go, but since Jock hadn't shown
up and occupied his time, there was no need to hurry.

Fools didn't always rush in.

SIXTEEN

Nudger drove out to Westport, a modern business community five
miles beyond the western city limits. Most of the buildings had been
constructed ten or fifteen years ago—brick, squarish single-and mul-
tiple-story office buildings and warehouses, many of them still sitting
vacant with FOR LEASE signs in front of them. There were also a
high-priced pseudo-English Tudor-style shopping mall and apartments, on the western edge of Westport next to the interstate highway. The developers had wanted to attract all manner of businesses,
and had. Westport was a profitable venture, with a number of thriving companies located here, not a few of which would thrive only
briefly before being forced into liquidation or relocation by the fast-
rising rents. Law of the three-piece-suit jungle.

Several of the streets in Westport were named after astronauts. Javers' Tire-O-Rama was on Grissom Drive, in a low tan building that was shared with an electronics distributor. Nudger parked in the freshly blacktopped parking lot and listened to the soft tar suck at the soles of his shoes as he walked to the east entrance.

He found that he'd opened the wrong door and was in the warehouse. A sign proclaimed that Javers' Tire-O-Rama made direct retail sales here at discount prices. An equally large sign read MOUNT YOUR OWN AND SAVE! Tires were piled high and leaning crookedly in hundreds of stacks, fitted into and on top of metal tier racks. Against one wall rose a mountain of used tires. The acrid, oily smell of all that rubber was overpowering.

A hefty little man with a clipboard and an air of authority came over and directed Nudger to the door of the office.

Nudger thanked him and shoved open a green swinging door. He found himself in a large room containing an even dozen desks in two rows of six. Behind each desk sat someone working diligently, either poring over papers or talking on the phone. The oily rubber smell was as strong here as in the warehouse. It had probably permeated the entire building.

At the far end of the room, near the entrance Nudger should have come in, sat a receptionist at a curved counter. Nudger walked over and smiled down at her. She was a startlingly pretty dark-haired girl with rimless glasses and a turned-up nose. There was a decal of a tire with arms and legs and a happy hubcap face on her IBM Selectric.

"How long does it take to get used to the smell?" Nudger asked.

"What smell?"

"Never mind. Is Mr. Javers in?"

"Do you have an appointment?"

"No. My name is Nudger."

She rang her boss's office with apparent trepidation.

"Tell him it concerns Grace Valpone," Nudger added.

The receptionist did, then hung up the phone.

"Mr. Javers says to come right in," she told him. She seemed relieved that Javers had agreed to see Nudger. "Through that door on the left."

As Nudger crossed the room he overheard some of the phone conversations. Most of the people behind the desks were salespeople, using WATS lines to coax orders from out-of-town retail tire outlets.

Javers stood up from behind his desk when Nudger entered. He wasn't a very tall man, though well proportioned inside an expensive gray suit. He was about fifty, balding, with jet-black wings of hair that were meant to disguise protruding ears. Though his complexion was swarthy, there was an underlying pastiness to it. A small, neatly trimmed mustache writhed in an attempted smile that evolved into more of a grimace. Grief had made inroads on his face, lending it a wise but helpless expression that might soon become permanent.

Nudger introduced himself and shook Javers' hand.

"I thought you were from the police," Javers said, sitting back down behind his desk.

"I used to be," Nudger said. "Right now I'm working for a woman whose twin sister was murdered in much the same way as your fiancée. I'm sorry to intrude on such short notice, but I thought it would be a good idea if I asked you a few questions."

The mention of Grace Valpone's murder brought a momentary look of deep anguish to Javers' face. Nudger wouldn't have blamed the man for asking him to leave. Misery didn't really love company.

But Javers had as much control over his grief as he had over his employees conducting business as usual in the next room. He leaned forward over his wide desk. There was nothing on the gleaming surface of the desk except a pen set, a small Lucite clock, and an ashtray; Javers hadn't been hard at work. "Do you think the same man committed both murders?" he asked.

"It's an odds-on possibility," Nudger told him. "There are parallels. There are also inconsistencies."

"If you think one case might have a bearing on the other," Javers said, "I'll be glad to tell you anything you want to know. I want more than anything to see Grace's killer . . ." He let the words fade away, then swallowed hard and bowed his head. Light glanced off his taut, bald crown between the black wings of hair.

"I understand," Nudger said. He felt like walking over and patting Javers on the shoulder. But he didn't. Sympathy from a stranger was sometimes more confusing than comforting. He wondered how he'd be able to ask Javers what he needed to know.

"I want the man caught and punished," Javers said in a level voice, sitting up straighter. He had himself back in check.

"Had Ms. Valpone recently mentioned anything that struck you as unusual?" Nudger asked. He knew the police had already asked Javers the same question, but sometimes people overlooked things. Sometimes people answered the same question differently.

"No, she said nothing at all unusual."

"Was her behavior in any way out of the ordinary?"

"Grace's behavior right up until . . . she was found, seemed perfectly normal. Of course, I hadn't seen her for almost a week. I was in Honolulu, at a convention."

"What did she think of you going off to Hawaii alone for two weeks?"

Javers smiled sadly. "She didn't mind. I asked her to go with me, but she refused. She wanted to wait until after the marriage for that sort of thing. Grace didn't mind being thought of as old-fashioned, Mr. Nudger. In fact, she didn't mind at all what other people thought about her, as long as she felt she was doing the right thing. It was one of the reasons I loved her."

"Then things were going well between the two of you."

"Very well. We were both in love for the second time in our lives, enjoying it more than the first time." The acute anguish gouged its way across Javers' face again. "Romance tempered by maturity has a sweeter, more lasting quality than youthful love."

"I guess it would." Nudger paced nearer to the desk and wiped his perspiring hands on his pants legs. "Did Ms. Valpone ever mention any late-night phone conversations?"

Javers appeared puzzled. "Conversations with whom?"

"Anyone." Nudger tried a smile, couldn't tell from his side of it how well it worked. "It's probably nothing, Mr. Javers, but it might tie in with something else."

Javers accepted that weak explanation for Nudger's question. "No," he said, "she wasn't one of those women who enjoy talking for long hours on the phone, either day or night."

Nudger asked a few more questions, none of them really pertinent, all of them polite. It wouldn't hurt to sow a little goodwill, in case the police objected to his talking to Javers. If the police ever learned of it. Besides, Nudger liked Javers, and talking about Grace Valpone seemed to provide some sort of relief for the man. People didn't lose fiancées the way they did socks in dryers.

When Javers had wound down somewhat, Nudger thanked him and shook hands again, offering his condolences and meaning it. Javers got up from behind the desk and saw him out, assuring Nudger he'd do anything possible to cooperate in the investigation, so please to call on him. Nudger thanked him again and left Javers' Tire-O-Rama, using the right door this time, nodding somberly to the pretty receptionist with the insensitive nose.

What Nudger had learned here was that Grace Valpone by all outward appearances simply wasn't a candidate for the nighttime lines. Her future had been in order, her nights of loneliness numbered.

Or maybe there was a side to her that Javers didn't know about. That no one knew about. A hidden, agonized side. Wasn't that true of most of the nightline people?

He hurried across the blacktop parking lot to his car, breathing deeply of air that didn't smell like new rubber. The humid summer day seemed to have gotten ten degrees hotter during the short time he'd been inside the building. A bead of perspiration zigzagged crazily, like a disoriented insect, down his rib cage.

As he drove from the lot, a size 13 wingtip shoe made a sharp smacking sound as it was lifted heavily from the heat-softened tar. Half a minute later, another car left the lot and turned onto Grissom Drive in the direction Nudger had taken.

SEVENTEEN

The Volkswagen was an oven. Nudger sat inside it, across the street from Claudia's apartment building, and felt as if maybe he should be wrapped in aluminum foil so he'd bake evenly. The evening sun glinting off the dented hood hurt his eyes. He reached above the visor and slid his sunglasses out of their vinyl clip-on case, adjusting them with a deft tap of his forefinger to the bridge of his nose. The plastic frames were hot and sticky.

He wanted to approach Claudia before she had a chance to talk with the wife of C. Davis. She should be arriving home from work soon, and Nudger planned to get out of the car, cross the street, and confront her near the building entrance. For the past hour he'd been sweltering in the car, trying to think of an opening line. Finally he decided to let his and Claudia's impending conversation take care of itself, let it flow naturally and hope it wasn't a swirl down the drain.

A bedraggled brown stray dog trotted along the sidewalk and glared at Nudger. For a moment Nudger thought the dog might urinate on the car. It was that kind of look. But the dog paused, sniffed, then trotted on with sudden purpose as if it had business downtown.

Nudger watched it in the rearview mirror, feeling a kind of kinship with the stray dog, as if they shared the same futile destiny. He wondered what he'd do if Claudia had lied to him. What did she look like? What if she turned out to be hideous? Would they still be souls rushing toward confluence? Would he still approach her? He thought he would, but he didn't want to be put to the test.

No one had entered the building other than an elderly, stooped woman carrying a small shopping bag and advancing tediously with the aid of an aluminum walker. It was too hot today for anyone but fools and stray dogs to be meddling around outside unless it was absolutely necessary. Too hot for an aged semi-invalid even if it *was* necessary.

Nudger felt the vague beginnings of heartburn. He thumbed back the wrapping on a roll of antacid tablets and tried to head off discomfort before it got a firm bite on him. He was aging alone in a hard world.

He had just popped a tablet into his mouth when she arrived. At least he assumed that the woman was Claudia.

Seen from across the street, she was indeed an average sort, medium height, dark-haired, wearing a plain but attractive blue or black dress that showed off a shapely figure somewhat on the thin side. She moved well, with a dancer's unconscious grace; Nudger noticed that about her immediately because her smooth, elegant walk was in contrast to her angled, gritty surroundings. She was clutching a straw purse beneath her arm, walking fast toward the apartment building from the direction of the bus stop.

Nudger had to move fast himself if he was going to intercept her. Chewing and swallowing the antacid tablet so hurriedly that it made him cough, he opened the car door, tugged the sweat-plastered back of his shirt away from the upholstery, and climbed stiffly out.

Claudia—if she was Claudia—noticed him approaching and broke stride ever so slightly. Fear registered in the sudden mechanical deliberation of her walk, the squared set of her shoulders.

She got prettier as Nudger got closer. Dark eyes, lean face, nose straight but too large, the perfectly turned calves and ankles of a shoe model. His eyes took it all in. He decided the nose gave her a look of nobility. Nudger hoped this was Claudia.

Time to find out. When he was a few yards from her, standing between her and the building entrance, he said, "Claudia?"

She seemed ill at ease, yet somehow relieved that he knew her name. He wasn't a complete stranger, out to snatch purse or virtue, an urban predator. On the other hand, he wasn't a handsome priest.

"You're Nudger," she said, in a voice he recognized from the nightlines.

He moved closer, trying not to loom. "Are you angry because I found you?"

"No. I'm angry because you searched for me. Now that you're here, it doesn't seem to matter much."

Nudger was trying to figure out just how to interpret that remark when she stepped around him and continued walking toward the doorway. What the hell? He followed her into the vestibule. She seemed to expect it. Or did she?

"We should talk," he said, trying to get their meeting on less confusing ground. On any kind of ground at all.

"I guess so." She started up the stairs and he trudged behind her, unable to stop watching the rhythmic sway of the dark dress about her legs. He could hear the soft rustle of its material against nylon. "I'm inviting you up so I can get in out of the heat," she said, turning her head slightly so she could lob the words back over her shoulder.

Nudger said nothing as they scaled the four flights of stairs to her apartment. He decided that the dress might be a cocktail-waitress uniform. She was wearing brown sandals that didn't go with the dress but were easy on the feet, and he had a hunch she was carrying high-heeled shoes in her purse.

Without looking at him, she unlocked the door, pushed it open, and with a kind of shrug motioned for him to enter.

It was a small apartment, clean but in hectic disorder. Nudger could see into the kitchen. There were dishes, apparently washed and dried, stacked haphazardly on the sink counter. The living room, where he stood, was cluttered with paperback books, magazines, and newspapers. There was a threadbare green recliner in a corner, a sagging sofa, a coffee table marked with interlocking pale rings from damp glasses. On one end of the table sat an old Sylvania black-and-white portable TV, angled so it could be watched from the sofa. A print of water lilies, a Monet, hung on one of the pale-gray walls, and that was the only wall decoration. There were patches of gouged plaster and even a few nails protruding here and there, probably left by previous tenants. At the far end of the room was a closed door, no doubt leading to the bedroom. The telephone must be in the bedroom.

Claudia crossed the bare wood floor and switched on the window air conditioner. It rattled fiercely in protest, then settled into a steady hum and seemed resigned to doing the job.

"The place cools off fast," she said.

"Good," Nudger replied. He was still hot. His face felt greasy with perspiration. He wished he knew what to say to Claudia.

"Sit down, please," she invited.

He did, on the sofa. Its springs gave a metallic gurgle and it threatened to collapse. He watched Claudia. She watched him.

Crossing her arms tightly so that she was clutching her elbows, she said, "Now what? Gorilla jokes?"

"If you want to hear some."

"I don't."

"Downstairs on the sidewalk," Nudger said, "how did you know who I was?"

"Coreen phoned me at work and told me you'd been here."

"C. Davis's wife?"

"There is no C. Davis living downstairs other than Coreen. Single woman's subterfuge. It's necessary in this neighborhood."

Nudger stood up, paced to the window with his fingertips inserted in his back pockets, then turned to face Claudia. "I'm sorry. I shouldn't have tracked you down against your wishes, but I couldn't resist. It's part of my line of work. I'm a private detective."

"Christ, is there still such a thing?"

"Only the best of us survive at the trade. We're primitives. Like iguanas and cockroaches, only not so ugly."

"As which?"

"Ah, I detect a healthy nastiness here."

She smiled. "Good old Nudger talk. It comforts."

"I'm glad it does. Genuinely glad."

"I suspect that genuineness is your talent and weakness. How did you locate me?"

Nudger explained it to her. She seemed not at all impressed by his cleverness.

"Can I get you something to drink?" she asked, as if suddenly not wanting to be remiss as a hostess. But she didn't apologize for the apartment's messiness. "I think there's beer."

"Water will do fine," Nudger said. He didn't like it that she'd immediately thought of him as the beer type. Which he was.

While she walked into the kitchen and he heard tap water running, Nudger glanced at the titles of the reading material scattered around the room. There was fiction, nonfiction, mystery, mainstream, everything.

"You read a lot," Nudger told her, when she returned and handed him a drinking glass full of water. There were three square ice cubes suspended in it, very clear ones, imprisoning muted reflected images.

"It's escape," she said. "I escape as often as I can."

"From what?"

Instead of answering, she turned, went back into the kitchen, and ran a glass of water for herself. When she returned she said, "Now what again?"

"When I was here earlier today there was a man knocking on your door. A skinny, annoyed little guy with dark hair. Looked like an ugly young Frank Sinatra. He wanted me to deliver a message to you. He and the kids will be out of town this weekend, so you can't see the kids. Who is he? Who are the kids?" That should give her plenty to chew on, Nudger thought.

Claudia raised her ice water to her lips and sipped, gazing calmly over the glass rim at Nudger, not answering.

"Another painful subject?"

She seemed to deliberate for a moment, then she said, "The man is Ralph Ferris, my former husband. The kids are Nora and Joan, our daughters."

And that gave Nudger plenty to chew on. "How old are Nora and Joan?"

"Twelve and ten."

Nudger glanced around the apartment; no sign of children. "Do the girls live with Ralph?"

Something seemed to draw Claudia into herself and cause discomfort. "Yes."

"I instinctively disliked Ralph," Nudger said. "Was I right?"

"Ralph's okay. The marriage would have worked out, only . . ."

Obviously she didn't want to finish such a revealing sentence. Not yet, anyway.

"Bettencourt's my maiden name," she said, changing the subject just enough. All of a sudden she seemed embarrassed. She placed her glass on the coffee table. "Nudger, I never met anone else after talking to them on the lines. I mean, I don't use the lines for what you might be thinking."

"I know why you use them. I'm glad we talked to each other. It's okay." He was trying to soothe her; she seemed seconds away from an emotional explosion. Nudger glimpsed something dark in her that had a hold on her, a voracious thing that fed on her insides and waited for opportune moments to inflict pain.

She picked up her glass and sipped more cold water. That seemed to calm the thing.

"Have you had dinner?" Nudger asked.

She shook her head no. There was a beaten quality about her that saddened him and evoked pity.

"I know a little bar near here called Zigzag's," he told her. "They serve great hamburgers. They have live music after eight o'clock. I hear it's really something."

She pursed her lips and he thought she was going to refuse him. But she said, "Let me change out of this dress, okay?"

"Okay," he said, smiling.

She smiled back, a bit whimsically, and followed her noble nose into the bedroom.

When she returned a few minutes later she was wearing very practical Levi's, the same brown sandals, and a white cotton blouse. The Levi's weren't form-fitting, but she had enough form to look good in them nonetheless.

"You're much prettier than just average," Nudger told her, as they walked from the apartment. He meant it. She seemed pleased, maybe amused, by the directness of the compliment.

As they descended the stairs, Nudger was becoming more at ease, more confident. Claudia in the flesh was becoming real to him in a way that Claudia on the phone could never be, exerting a pull on him that was sensuous and easy to understand. This was far from the darkness of their phone conversations. This might turn out to be a monumental rendezvous, yet at the same time an ordinary date, something he could comprehend, cope with, and enjoy. Normality.

On the second landing, she turned to him and held up her wrists to the light streaming through the cracked window.

"See the scars?" she said. "They're from when I tried to kill myself."

Zigzag's actually did serve hamburgers, Nudger was relieved to discover. He and Claudia sat in a dim booth near the back of the place, beyond the bar. When a barmaid came over, Claudia asked for a whiskey sour and excused herself to go to the restroom. Nudger ordered a beer for himself and a hamburger and french fries for each of them, slyly instructing the barmaid to have the kitchen hold the onions. "The future's not ours to see," according to Plato. Or was it Doris Day?

The drinks were on the table when Claudia returned. Nudger watched her walk across the room, claiming the attention of a few of the male clientele. Hers was a subtle magnetism. She was the sort of woman that wasn't striking, yet seemed more pleasing to the eye with each glance. Her features were unremarkable, but in harmony.

As she sat down, Nudger said, "I ordered burgers and fries. Now you owe me. Want to tell me about Ralph?"

Claudia didn't go deaf this time. She sampled her whiskey sour and seemed to find it to her liking, then said, "He's my former loving husband, is all."

Nudger knew that wasn't all, but that it had better be all for now. "Where do you work?" he asked. A mundane enough question. He downed half of his icy beer and waited for a mundane answer.

"I'm a waitress at Kimball's Restaurant."

"A four-star eatery. Gourmet food."

"Are you a gourmet?" she asked.

"No, I'm more of a great white shark. I like most any kind of food. Only my stomach is more particular. Tell me about waitressing. Do you enjoy it?"

"It makes your feet sore and you have to take a lot of abuse from some of the customers. On weekends, when I serve more liquor, the tips are good, but the abuse quotient rises too. There are worse jobs." She raised her glass again. She didn't seem to be a practiced drinker, and there were no physical signs of the lush about her. "Tell me about detectiving, Nudger."

"Oh, it's pretty much what I'm doing now, asking questions. We detectives are a curious lot."

"'Curious' can be an adjective used to describe an unusual object," she said.

"I know, teacher. It's been applied that way to me."

She looked at him with a faintly startled expression.

"Which daughter is how old?" he asked.

"Nora's the twelve-year-old; Joan's ten."

"Are they beautiful in the manner of their mother?"

"More beautiful. In their own manner."

The hamburgers arrived, beautiful in their own beef-and-bun way. They were as tasty as they looked, and the fries were greasy and salty, the way Nudger unfortunately liked them. He ordered another beer. Claudia asked the barmaid if she could have some onions for her hamburger.

Nudger said nothing more probing than "Please pass the catsup" until they'd finished eating. He asked Claudia if she wanted another whiskey sour, and she said she'd prefer coffee. That was easy enough to get at Zigzag's, even though the barmaid was taking a break. The same young, bald-headed bartender who had been on duty earlier today brought over two steaming white mugs on a tray.

"I see you found her," he said to Nudger, placing the mugs before them and clearing the table of dishes and glasses.

"What did he mean?" Claudia asked, watching the bald-headed man walk away.

Nudger shrugged. "I don't know. Bartender talk, I guess."

They sat saying little over their coffee, oddly at ease in each other's company, until the live music began at eight o'clock. A slightly raised stage that Nudger hadn't noticed was abruptly bathed in red and green light, and two middle-aged men with punk haircuts and steel guitars began to twang and sing insolently of petty injustices. Nudger winced and looked across the table at Claudia. She grinned. They agreed that the hard rock at Zigzag's wasn't in the same class as the hamburgers.

The barmaid had disappeared for good, apparently, so Nudger walked over to the bald-headed barkeep and paid the check. Zigzag's was becoming crowded despite the Hard Timers, as the two middle-aged punk rockers called themselves, so Nudger moved in front of Claudia, clearing a way to the door.

"I mean t'git down an' be mean!" screamed the Hard Timers in perfect discord. One of them did a screeching slide on the guitar.

Nudger and Claudia emerged from the din, tobacco smoke, and dimness into an evening that had cooled off and conjured up stars. The door swung shut and muted the music to loud.

Claudia politely thanked Nudger for dinner. First-date patter.

"Walk a while?" he asked.

She hesitated, then nodded.

He took the curbside like a gentleman and set off in a direction away from her apartment building. He didn't want the evening to end prematurely, still heavy with unanswered questions.

For a long time they were quiet as they walked, listening to the counterpoint rhythm of their footfalls. Nudger liked it that way but couldn't figure out why. There was much he wanted to know about Claudia. On the other hand, maybe he was finding out something very important this way. It seemed that there could never be an awkward silence between them. Could love be mute as well as blind?

It was Claudia who finally spoke. "You said you were a private investigator. Am I part of a case you're working on?"

"Only indirectly. The nightlines are part of the case. That's why I was talking on the lines the night we made contact; I was trying to get a feel for what was going over the wires."

"Then you don't talk regularly on the lines." She seemed pleased.

"No. Do you?"

"More often than I'd like. I can't sleep. The early morning hours are a lonely time. Occasionally I just have to talk to someone. Regardless of their reason for listening, they provide human contact."

Nudger smiled at her as they stepped down from a high curb. "You're clean and attractive. Aren't there more conventional ways to find human contact?"

"I don't want any of the conventional ways, any of their complications." She shifted the focus of the conversation back to Nudger. "Are you still working on the nightlines case?"

"Yes, but not at the moment."

"What's it about?"

"Murdered women."

"Women who talked on the lines?"

Nudger nodded. Maybe he needed human contact too. He told her about the case. Not all about it, but almost all.

She was in an understandably somber mood when he'd finished, and he wondered if he'd regret sharing that part of himself with her.

"The wages of sin," she said, of the murdered women. She said it ironically, not in a serious religious context.

"Maybe not," Nudger told her. "There's nothing solid yet to link the deaths to the same killer."

"But you think there's a mass murderer using the lines."

"There's enough evidence for me to go on that assumption. But then I'm not a bureaucracy, like the police. They can't afford to follow hunches; I can't afford not to, because sometimes hunches and a client are all I have."

Claudia suggested that they return to her apartment. It was dark now, and the downtown area they were in was comprised mostly of empty office buildings and structures in various stages of renovation or construction. The city in the turmoil of rebirth. Not a safe place to walk. It occurred to Nudger that a mugger might appear unexpectedly and crack him on the head before finding out he was dealing with a tough shamus. Another tragedy born of misunderstanding. He didn't mind when Claudia picked up the pace.

Claudia's apartment building was in sight when Nudger said, "How long have you been a waitress?"

"Four years," she said. "Before that, I taught."

"Taught what?"

"Junior high school. Seventh grade. English and social studies."

"How come you quit?"

Nudger could sense her shrinking into herself again, as if to envelope a sensitive, vulnerable core that had endured all it could stand. And now he had come along and touched it and brought pain.

"I didn't exactly quit," she said. "I was forced out."

She didn't speak again until they were back in her apartment. She'd left the air conditioner on while they were gone, and the living room was comfortably cool. The wide window, without curtains or blinds and with a few half-dead viny plants in plastic pots suspended from the upper frame, looked out on soot-gray buildings across Spruce Street. The upper floors of the buildings were used mostly for storage, and their windows were blank. Some of the windows had faded remains of business names clinging in peeling letters to the glass. A few of them were boarded over with weathered plywood. The mercury streetlight down the block cast a sickly bluish light over it all, lending some of the grime and pigeon droppings a pale luminosity. Grim, Nudger thought. Grim. It would never make a scene in one of those crystal globes that you shook to make artificial snow fly. How would it be to live here? To look out at those buildings day after day?

Claudia walked to the kitchen door and turned to face him. "Do you want me to put on a pot of coffee?"

He shook his head. "Not for me. I've had enough coffee." He went to the sofa and sat down, listening again to the tired, complaining springs. "Are you glad I found you, Claudia?"

"I don't know." She absently fingered one of the scars on her wrists. "I'm sorry. I don't." Her fingernail lightly traced the scar down to the heel of her hand.

A cold wave of apprehension passed through Nudger, a mere tremor but powerful, like the shallow, rippling raw energy of a tidal wave in mid-ocean as it made for shore and shape and size and destruction. He stood up from the sofa and walked over to her. "Maybe I will have some coffee."

But she didn't move to make the coffee. "Will you stay here with me tonight, Nudger? Without sex, without any more questions, will you stay with me?"

"You're a beautiful woman who doesn't chew with her mouth open. How can I refuse?"

"I don't care if you wisecrack," she said. "It doesn't matter."

"I know, or I wouldn't do it."

She leaned into him and he put his arms around her, surprised by her thinness and the prominent contours of her ribs. There was about her a faint, clean scent of shampoo and perfume and onions.

"You did say no sex?" he said.

She burrowed her face into his chest and he felt the wet warmth of her tears through his shirt. "I don't want to be alone tonight," she told him, with a soft, vibrant desperation.

He hugged her to him and crooned comfortingly to her, as if she were a child awake from bad dreams, gently patting her shoulder. "You won't be alone tonight," he assured her again and again. "You won't be alone. And neither will I."

In the morning, as Nudger reached the second-floor landing on his way out of the building, Coreen Davis opened her apartment door and stared out at him with unmistakable reproach and warning. You couldn't help but like C. Davis.

EIGHTEEN

Nudger stopped by his apartment for a change of clothes, then drove to Danny's for a quick breakfast. Agnes Boyington must have been to his office and seen the sign hung on his door referring business messages to the doughnut shop downstairs.

"You had a visit from a cold-hearted woman with warm hands, Nudge," Danny said, placing a foam coffee cup and what looked like a hand-molded sugar doughnut on a napkin.

"She strikes everyone that way," Nudger said. Maybe he had risen a few notches in Agnes Boyington's estimation, if she was dressing up for him the way she did for her lawyer. More likely, his office was a brief stopover for her on the way to things really important.

"She asked me to tell you she'd been here looking for you," Danny said. "She wants you to phone her."

Nudger decided not to do that. Agnes Boyington could phone him. She could dial or punch out a number even with gloves on.

"Anything else?" Nudger asked.

"Naw. You want another doughnut?"

"I think not."

Nudger said good-bye to Danny and carried his coffee upstairs to the office. He checked his answering machine, expecting a call from Jeanette and possibly an innovative threat from Eileen. Instead he heard a Jehovah's Witness recording urging him to seek salvation. Then came C. Davis's thick, rich voice instructing him to call her. She repeated her phone number twice, slowly, like an announcer selling record albums or wonder cutlery on television. Maybe the supply was limited. Nudger immediately picked up the receiver, rang the number, and identified himself.

C. Davis wasn't one for preparatory small talk.

She said, "You know a giant honkie squeezes a ball?"

"What color ball?"

"Red," she said seriously.

"I know him, but we're not friends."

"Well, he was around here right after you left this morning. Stood

outside looking over the building, then came in and was eyeballing
the mailboxes."

"Then what?"

"I asked him what he was doing and he didn't have no good answer. So I told him he had no business here and to get his ass out and
away."

"What did he say to that?"

"He didn't say nothing. He left."

Nudger wasn't surprised. C. Davis would seem formidable to a
small country's army. "He's keeping track of my movements, Coreen, that's all. I'm sure he won't harm Claudia, but not so sure that
I'm not asking you to keep an eye on things if he shows up again."

"You don't have to ask, Nudger. Claudia's a beat-down fine lady,
and a friend. I ain't gonna let anything happen to her. Not 'cause of
you, neither. She told me before about how you talked to her on the
phone. I know about you and how she feels about you. And I'm
asking: You a one-nighter, or are you something more?"

"Something more," Nudger said.

"Then I think you better go talk to Laura Cather. You got a pencil?"

"With lead in it." Nudger jotted down the phone number she read
off to him. She repeated it with the same slowness and careful enun-
ciation he'd heard on the recorder. "Who's Laura Cather?" he asked.

"You the detective, Nudger. You puzzle it out." She hung up.

Nudger depressed the cradle button and pecked out the number C.
Davis had given him.

After three rings, a sleepy-sounding woman answered. She said
she was Laura Cather, and she didn't seem surprised when he told
her who he was and that he wanted to talk with her about Claudia
Bettencourt. C. Davis, mother-hen menace, must have paved the way
for him.

He made an appointment with Laura Cather for later that morning
at her apartment on Wyoming, on the city's south side. Then he sat
back in his squeaking swivel chair, played out a faint but shrill
rhythm by gently rocking back and forth, and thought about Hugo
Rumbo watching him and Claudia. Nudger didn't like it, not at all.
But he was sure that Rumbo's job was to watch him, and when or-

dered, apply direct pressure to intimidate. Rumbo really wasn't dangerous except in a shallow, ineffectual way. Partly because he was who he was, partly because he was an extension of Agnes Boyington, who was wont to maim souls and not mere bodies. It wouldn't be her style to have Rumbo harm Claudia to scare Nudger. Not only would that be too risky after what she'd told the police, but the weapons she'd chosen in the duel of life were more subtle and infinitely more dangerous. Still, Nudger didn't want Rumbo to frighten Claudia. Neither did C. Davis. It was good that she had called. It was reassuring that she was watching out for Claudia.

Wyoming Avenue was in the section of south Saint Louis that was a gridwork of streets named after states. As if that weren't confusing enough, the streets all looked alike, all straight and narrow, all lined with similar flat-roofed brick row houses or flats, with tiny square front yards bisected by short strips of concrete leading from steps to sidewalk. It was an old section of town that hadn't changed much in twenty years. Many of the houses had been in the same families' possession for twice that long, and it wasn't unusual to find people who had lived in the same shotgun flat for a quarter of a century without ever having signed a lease, paying monthly rent to the same landlord when he came around on the first to be sure the lawn was mowed or the walk cleared of snow. "Scrubby Dutch" the predominantly German Catholics of the area were sometimes called, and Nudger had often seen elderly women bent over scrubbing the curbs in front of their flats, or taping plastic flowers on the branches of dead shrubbery. There was plenty of front-yard religious statuary here, and more than a few plastic flamingos perched inelegantly on long spike legs. There were rough neighborhoods in the area, populated by rough folks, but for the most part it was one of the more stable sections of the city.

Laura Cather lived in a typical flat-roofed building on a drab, treeless stretch of Wyoming east of Grand. Nudger rang the bell to her second-floor flat and heard someone descending the stairs to her separate entrance. Taut white sheer curtains parted on the door's window, and a bespectacled blue eye peered fishlike out through the glass at Nudger before the door swung open.

Laura Cather was an emaciated-looking faded blond woman still in her twenties. She was narrow of bust and hip, and her blouse and slacks hung from her frame as if from a misshapen hanger. Her bare arms were a few ounces from bone. The only substantial things about her were an old-fashioned silver brooch whose weight was pulling the material of her blouse crooked, and her wide, round tortoise-shell glasses that threatened to slide down her narrow nose and shatter at Nudger's feet.

"I'm Nudger," Nudger said.

She smiled with terrible, yellowed teeth. Despite it all, she was somehow wanly pretty, like an ethereal consumptive. "I know," she said. "Coreen Davis described you. Won't you come up?"

Nudger followed her up the rubber-treaded stairs to her flat, which was larger than he'd imagined. Or maybe it seemed that way because of the bare wood floors and paucity of furniture. There was a worn modern sofa on one wall, on the opposite wall a director's chair with red canvas next to a squarish plastic table. On the far wall was a card table that managed to support a portable electric typewriter and some stacks of papers. There was a chipped white-enameled kitchen chair at the table, and a sheet of paper protruding rigidly from the typewriter's platen. Laura Cather had been busy when Nudger arrived.

"I'm typing resumes," she explained, noticing his curiosity. "Have a seat, please."

Nudger watched her settle her frail body on the couch as he sat down in the director's chair. He felt like yelling "Action!" to begin their conversation.

"Coreen thinks I should tell you about Claudia Bettencourt," she said. "If she thinks that, there must be a sound reason."

"There is," Nudger said. "Coreen Davis doesn't want Claudia to be hurt. Neither do I."

"Nor I, Mr. Nudger."

"What's the connection between you and Claudia?"

"I used to be a social worker for the Department of Corrections, a public employee doing pre-sentencing investigation. That was before the federal government decided policy was more important than people and cut our agency's funds." She waved a pale, thin hand in a casual gesture of helplessness. "I've been out of work for almost a year. I'm not bitching, because I'm not an isolated case."

Nudger was suddenly uneasy. His stomach let him know it was there. "You said pre-sentencing. Was Claudia convicted of some crime?"

"I'll tell you about Claudia Bettencourt," Laura said, in the tone that people use when they're about to begin at the beginning. "She was raised by a foster father who abused her as a child. Not sexually, but he beat her. That leaves its mark, Mr. Nudger. It stays in the mind and body like an infectious disease. Real child abuse isn't what most people imagine. It's not some frazzled parent losing control under stress and lashing out in a fit of temper. It's systematic and frequent. And unbelievably violent. It's not a bloody nose, it's blood on the walls. And the sickening truth is that neither the victim nor the perpetrator can help what's happening, or prevent it from happening again."

"Did Claudia abuse her own children?" Nudger asked, remembering his conversation with Ralph Ferris outside her door.

"She did," Laura Cather said, not simply looking at Nudger, but studying him. "She was one of the smart and brave ones; she tried to get help. But four years ago, while she was undergoing therapy, her three-year-old daughter, Vicki, contracted influenza. A simple case of the flu. Only the child was found in a coma one winter morning with her bedroom window open. She died two days later of pneumonia."

"Are you saying Claudia deliberately left the window open?"

"I'm not. But that's what her husband claimed when she was tried on a child-abuse charge, a second-degree murder charge."

"What was her defense?" Nudger asked. He felt hollow yet heavy, as if the thin canvas of the director's chair might at any second rip to dump him onto the floor. Maybe he could have Laura Cather play that last scene a different way. Take Two, with feeling.

"At first she denied opening the window. Vehemently denied it, as the lawyers say. Her lawyers advanced the theory that maybe the husband or one of the other kids opened the window and forgot it. Or maybe the sick child herself had climbed out of bed to open it. They do that sometimes if they have a fever, trying to cool off. But the prosecution kept pounding away at Claudia, and eventually she didn't know herself whether she'd opened that window. Child abuse is an emotional issue, Mr. Nudger, and Claudia had a history of it. The jury knew that history and voted to convict. I was assigned to conduct the pre-sentencing investigation, learn what I could about the defendant and make recommendations to help the judge decide how severe her sentence should be."

"What did you find out?" Nudger asked.

"That Claudia Bettencourt—or Ferris, as she called herself then— was an intelligent, disturbed woman who was not innately violent. Her past wouldn't let go of her. Her younger sister had also been abused, and was a diagnosed schizophrenic who killed herself in a period of depression. Claudia was haunted by her childhood and doomed to emulate it through her daughters. Unfortunately, it's not an unusual situation, Mr. Nudger. I recommended leniency and therapy. The judge agreed. Claudia stayed out of prison. She was placed on probation and saw a court-appointed psychiatrist for several years."

"Did the psychiatrist help her?"

"Dr. Oliver helped her only to an extent. She understands her past now, and she's no longer compulsively violent. Toward anyone. She loves her children, as she always did."

"But she doesn't love Claudia."

Laura Cather smiled her frail and gentle smile at Nudger and nodded, pleased that he understood. "Claudia can't shake the guilt," she said, "because Ralph Ferris won't let her. He's the one who needs mental therapy now, but the law doesn't demand it."

"And Claudia can't forget Ralph Ferris because he's got custody of their daughters. He's a part of her life whether she likes it or not."

"Exactly. And he sees to it that she doesn't like it. He's never forgiven her, or acts that way. If he's so sure she deliberately left that window open to punish their daughter for some minor childhood transgression, maybe you can't blame him."

"I can blame him," Nudger said. "He's perpetuating pain."

"I've told Claudia to limit her involvement with him, send someone to get the children when she has visitation rights. Her psychiatrist told her the same thing when she was seeing him. Ralph won't cooperate. He demands to deliver the children to her door himself. He occasionally comes to see her alone, or taunts her over the phone.

There's no way to stop him. No way, Mr. Nudger. No way even to know if he's still a grief-sick father or simply a mean and vengeful bastard. But I know which way I'd bet."

Nudger sighed. The world was a swamp, and understanding was quicksand. And sometimes the log you were standing on turned and gave you a crocodile smile.

"Two years ago Claudia tried to commit suicide by slashing her wrists," Laura Cather said. "Coreen Davis found her, slowed the bleeding, and got her medical aid in time to save her. It wasn't one of those Russian-roulette suicide attempts where the victim gambles on help arriving before death. Claudia's was a genuine attempt to die."

"And you're afraid she might try again."

"It's possible, maybe even likely. Coreen and I wanted you to find out about this the right way. We want you to know that Claudia is on a dark edge, Mr. Nudger. We want to make sure you understand that." She frowned, staring into interior distances, as she sought words to make him grasp her compassion and meaning. "She's fragile. So fragile. We want you to be careful with her."

Nudger sat looking at Laura Cather. He'd developed a sense about people like this, gentle people who couldn't dissemble or deceive. He knew them. They were easy to read; they wanted to be read, to live in a world without deception.

"There's more, isn't there?" he said.

She knew herself, too. She'd been expecting him to ask, maybe hoping for it. "I don't think Claudia left that window open, Mr. Nudger. I think Ralph went to the sick daughter's room that night. Maybe Vicki was feverish, complained of being too hot and wanted Ralph to open the window for just a few minutes. The child had vomited; maybe Ralph opened the window to let out the stench of sickness and forgot and left it open.

"Child abuse brings out the vigilante in juries, Mr. Nudger. Claudia didn't have a chance. But I read the court transcript with an objective eye, and I got to know everyone involved in the case. Ralph left that window open, Mr. Nudger. He knew it and denied it and let Claudia be convicted so he could get the children in the divorce. It eats on the bastard and he can't let Claudia alone. Maybe he hates her because she put him into that situation. Or maybe he's got himself talked into thinking she's actually guilty as charged. But Ralph left that window open, Mr. Nudger. I'm sure of it."

She sat fondling her silver brooch. There was nothing more to say. Maybe she'd said too much. Nudger stood up and moved to the door, turned.

"Thanks for telling me about this," he said.

She walked over and shook his hand, squeezing hard.

"I promise to be careful with Claudia," he told her.

She watched him down the stairs, into the street.

As he drove away he saw that she had come down onto the porch and was standing hunched forward with her thin arms crossed, wondering if she'd done the right thing by talking to him.

NINETEEN

Nudger bounced along Grand Avenue in the Volkswagen, wondering how he really felt about what Laura Cather had told him. How would he feel about it tomorrow? He was shaken and befuddled, devoid of answers and afraid of what they might be when they took form. He couldn't imagine Claudia harming anyone, becoming uncontrollably angry, yet he had been told that she'd been caught in a pattern of pain and violence. Trapped by her past, and now trapped again because of Ralph Ferris. Claudia had been painted as victim rather than perpetrator by two people who knew her well and long. They had wanted to tell him about her to judge his reaction, to protect her. Nudger wasn't sure himself of his reaction.

When he saw a phone booth on the corner of a service station lot, he pulled in and parked next to it. Holding one ear with a cupped hand to block the sounds of traffic, he stood in the booth and listened to Jeanette's phone ring.

No answer. Maybe she was working again today for the temporary-help firm that sent her out on part-time secretarial jobs, and so hadn't made any nightline appointments. Nudger thought that would be all right. They might not make any progress on the case, but then they weren't exactly leaping from clue to clue anyway. And Jeanette would stay out of trouble for a while and be able to afford his fee.

He hung up the phone, got back into the car, and drove on toward his office. There he would check his mail, then phone Natalie Mallowan on the pretense of inquiring about Ringo's well-being and apply gentle persuasion in an attempt to hurry payment of his nine hundred dollars. It was lunchtime, but he wasn't hungry and wouldn't stop anywhere. There was no point in eating anyway until he'd checked the mail for McDonald's coupons.

As he parked near his office he forgot all about lunch and looking at the mail and phoning Natalie Mallowan. A Third District patrol car was parked at the curb in front of Danny's Donuts. As Nudger crossed Manchester, Danny appeared at the doughnut-shop window and motioned with a nod of his long head toward the car, indicating that it was there because of Nudger.

Nudger walked past the car, waiting for the voice he knew would come.

"You Nudger?"

He turned. There were two blue uniforms in the car. The one on the curbside had the door open and was leaning out, waiting for Nudger's answer. He had a deadpan face with eyes as full of expression as shirt buttons.

It suddenly occurred to Nudger why the uniforms might be there. Claudia! In that instant he knew exactly how he felt about her. It was the way he had felt before his conversation with Laura Cather.

"I'm Nudger," he said, walking toward the car. "What's this about?"

"Lieutenant Hammersmith sent us to pick you up and drive you to where he is. Wants you to get there before they remove a body." He climbed out of the car, a big man with the back of his blue shirt dark with perspiration. He held open the car's rear door for Nudger.

"Where is he, goddammit?" Nudger demanded.

The uniform looked surprised, but only for a moment. "Over on Utah at a murder scene," he said. "Woman got herself killed. The lieutenant thought you'd be interested."

Nudger breathed out hard. Utah Avenue! Not Claudia, a woman on Utah! His world had lurched to a stop, then started again. He nodded to the uniform and got into the car.

*   *   *

Utah wasn't far from where Laura Cather lived on Wyoming. They drove back the way Nudger had just come, down Highway 44, then south on Grand. The scenery was still vivid in Nudger's mind, only running in reverse, lending what was happening the air of a recurring bad dream. For a murdered woman on Utah it had been more than a dream; it had been the end of dreams.

The scene of this murder was a brick two-family flat on a good block of Utah. Property here had become expensive despite its near proximity to poverty. The higher tone of the neighborhood hadn't helped; sex murderers were more likely to be influenced by a full moon than by property assessments. The flat's front porch was wide, with brick columns, and featured the ornate stonework that was prevalent in this part of town and that "craftsmen" would charge prohibitively for today, in this the age of the plastic heirloom.

One of the blue uniforms directed Nudger to the door on the right, to the ground-floor unit. Nudger immediately recognized the faint odor of putrefaction as he pushed open the door and stepped into a spacious beige living room decorated with too many potted plants. Something bitter moved at the back of his throat.

"Déjà vu, Nudge," Hammersmith said, waving to him from a doorway in the hall.

When Nudger approached, Hammersmith said, "I leave it up to you as to whether you want to look at this one."

Nudger felt his stomach drop a few notches. Beyond Hammersmith, a couple of police technicians inside the bathroom were wearing surgical masks as they went about their specialized tasks. The stench here was horrible, much worse than at the Valpone apartment. Nudger wondered how Hammersmith could stand it.

"The heat did it to her," Hammersmith said, reading Nudger's sickly expression. "She hasn't been dead much longer than Grace Valpone was when we found her, but the bathroom faces south and catches too much sun. I'm afraid it'll make determing the exact time of death a little tricky."

"Have you got an estimate?" Nudger asked.

"The ME's preliminary guess is that she's been dead about two days, two warm days."

A plainclothes cop came out of the bathroom with an alcohol-soaked handkerchief pressed to his nose and mouth. He was greener than the giant who sold peas, and not half as jolly. He seemed to stagger slightly as he walked down the hall, then he got in a big hurry.

Nudger looked at Hammersmith, who gazed back at him and shrugged. *Here we go!* Clutching his roiling stomach, Nudger slid around Hammersmith and stepped far enough into the bathroom to see the body.

After a glance he backed away and hurried into the kitchen, where he immediately vomited into the sink. He saw that he wasn't the first to use the facility, as he reached up feebly and ran the cold tap water.

Hammersmith had followed him and was standing waiting patiently for the retching to stop.

After several minutes, Nudger finally straightened, his hands still resting on the sink. He felt weak and figured he must be as pale and green as the cop with the handkerchief. He thought he might start trembling; he didn't want that. There was enough machismo lost in being green.

"Let's go out on the back porch," Hammersmith suggested, "get some fresh air." He threw a sliding bolt lock, shoved open the kitchen door to the rear porch, and let Nudger step out in front of him.

They were looking out over a gray, freshly painted wood rail at a small but neat backyard. There was a two-car brick garage there, with a flagstone walk leading back to it. Thick white corner posts at the gray railing supported an identical porch upstairs. In a far corner of the porch were a metal pan half full of water and a thick china bowl containing a lump of fly-covered spoiled dog food or cat food, the kind pet owners buy because it resembles hamburger and they'd like it if they were in the role of pet. Nudger looked away from that.

"This one is even worse than Valpone," Hammersmith observed.

And the five-minute-old image was there again in Nudger's mind: a smallish dark-haired woman in her bath, nude, one breast gone, her throat slashed with such brutal force that she was nearly decapitated. This time there was blood on the floor and walls, not much, but some. Maybe she'd fought harder than the others; maybe the life force had been stronger in her.

"Her name was Susan Merriweather," Hammersmith said. "Twenty-seven years old. Too damned young to die like that. She ved alone, worked as a loan manager at a bank, and had lots of cquaintances but few close friends. She partied now and then, but ostly led a quiet life."

"And met a quiet, nasty death."

"Yeah." Hammersmith caressed the cellophaned tip of a cigar pro-uding from his shirt pocket, then withdrew his hand. "He worked n her systematically before or after she was dead, or both. Same ind of mutilation as the Valpone woman had, only more so. Much ore so."

"I saw," Nudger said, his stomach cartwheeling at the thought of ried blood, gristle, and bone; the Death inside us all.

"You want to sit down?" Hammersmith asked, motioning toward e wooden steps.

Nudger sat down. Hammersmith sat beside him, a step higher. hey watched the neighbor's sad-looking beagle amble over to the ence and gaze through the chain link, wondering what all the human uss was about, then amble away toward some shade.

"Things have firmed up, Nudge," Hammersmith said. "There was six-six-six number on a slip of paper near Susan Merriweather's hone. And the fingerprint team picked up some smudged prints in a lood smear. I sent them down to Headquarters for a rush ID"

"Hear anything yet?"

"Only that they match exactly the abnormally large size and spread f the prints found in Jenine Boyington's apartment."

Nudger nodded, thinking. He hadn't really doubted the connection etween the killings, but this confirmed it. More than that, it placed im on different, more dangerous, ground. It was assumed now by eople other than Jeanette Boyington and Nudger that a mass murderer as operating in the city, insatiable and unpredictable, taking his ictims in seemingly random harvest. Nudger experienced a fear he ouldn't quite define, as if the laws of the universe were, after all, a rce, a grisly celestial joke, and there was nothing but black chaos here he had assumed there was some kind of order and meaning. heory had become terrifying fact; madness had been stamped official.

"The murders figure to be done by the same perp," Hammersmith as saying. "Jenine Boyington, Grace Valpone, and now Susan Mer-weather, all killed more or less the same way and within a relatively

short time of each other. We checked on all similar murders, Nudge
put the old computer to work. There were several resting in the bac
files, four possible tie-ins and three that I'd bet were committed b
the killer who did the work on Boyington, Valpone, and Mer
riweather. They were there all the time in Records, dating back thre
years."

"Why didn't you draw a connection until now?" Nudger asked.

Hammersmith shook his broad head sadly, his jowls swaying
"There are hundreds of homicides every year in the metropolita
area, Nudge. The ones done by this killer before his last three wer
simply unsolved and categorized under 'inactive,' lost in the stati!
tics."

Lost in the statistics. Nudger remembered Jeanette Boyington say
ing that, when she'd hired him to find her twin's murderer. He ha
listened to her mass murder theory mainly because he was betwee
cases while his rent rolled on. The needy ear of poverty. Nobody els
would have bought the idea. Maybe you didn't have to be dead to b
lost in the statistics.

"Whatever our past oversights," Hammersmith said, "we have t
take it from where we are. The news media is on to this now, and th
case is top priority with the department. More manpower's been a!
signed and the Major Case Squad is involved. Leo Springer is i!
volved. You better walk easy, Nudge, thinking all the time abou
where you're stepping."

"Because of Springer and departmental politics and PR?"

"All that and something else. The killer is murdering more fre
quently, more violently. Even the computer noticed. The time spa
between Jenine Boyington and Grace Valpone was two weeks, bt
between Grace Valpone and Susan Merriweather, only days. He'
getting more careless, more frenzied, more dangerous. This killin
won't keep him satisfied and inactive for long. You clue us in o
what you're doing, huh? You still using the Boyington girl to mak
dates over the nightlines?"

Nudger nodded.

"Anything come of it?"

Nudger shook his head no.

"Reticence can get you killed or unemployed," Hammersmith sai irritated. Irritated enough to disregard Nudger's delicate stomach and unwrap one of his greenish fat cigars. He struck a match, puffed like the little engine that could. "*Shwoo* . . . loyalty to a *shwoo* . . . client has its *shwoo* . . . limits, Nudge."

"Legal limits," Nudger corrected. His stomach was going on carnival rides; bile rose in his throat. "Can I go now, or am I under arrest?"

Hammersmith showed mercy, withdrawing the cigar from his mouth and holding it out over the railing. Smoke drifted away over the backyard as if there had been an explosion. "The kind of case it's become, Nudge, if we can't collar anyone else, maybe we'll settle for you."

"Maybe I did it."

"You only think you're joking. This case can get out of control in ways you wouldn't believe. And other than the killer, nobody is more in the middle of it than you."

"You have a point."

"Think of our Chief of Police and the special problems of his office; think of Captain Massey and his Major Case Squad; think of Leo Springer and his maladjusted libido. Reputations must be protected."

"But not mine."

"No, not yours. Not as far as the powers that be are concerned. It'll be a bounty of luck if you come out of this without wearing some kind of goat's bell around your neck. Maybe they won't break the electric chair out of storage just for you, but there's your investigator's license to consider, your ability to work in this Baghdad on the Mississippi. You could be a stopgap suspect and a big loser."

"You always understood these things, Jack." Nudger stood up and tucked in his shirt. "I appreciate the wise words. Really."

"Do take care, Nudge."

Nudger went down the porch steps and cut through the narrow, cool gangway so he wouldn't have to walk back through the murder scene. He wondered if Hammersmith had been completely serious about the department's possibly being pressured into manufacturing a suspect to tide them over until the real killer was found. It had happened before and would happen again, so why not to Nudger? There were those who would smilingly attest to his bad character.

He reached the sidewalk at the same time as the assistant ME, who had left through the front door. The man recognized Nudger from Grace Valpone's apartment and nodded to him. "Déjà vu," he said. French was in the air.

Suddenly remembering that he didn't have his car here, Nudger decided that he didn't want to be driven back to his office by the same two blue uniforms. He hitched a ride with the ME to a sandwich shop on Grand, where he phoned for a cab and sat brooding over a diet cola, waiting, thinking about a maniacal killer who was like a time bomb with multiple warheads, each exploding closer and with more force than the last. Déjà vu! Déjà vu! Déjà vu!

TWENTY

Still feeling shaky and nauseated, Nudger didn't bother going back up to his office when the cab eased to a stop in front of Danny's Donuts. He paid off the cabbie, watched the dented yellow taxi leave a haze of exhaust fumes down Manchester, then crossed the street to where the Volkswagen was squatted patiently at the curb.

He drove around for a while without a destination, until most of his queasiness had left him, winding through the park, past the Jefferson Memorial and the Art Museum, finally exiting from the park on Hampton, near the Zoo. Then he stopped at a phone booth and used the directory.

Dr. Oliver wasn't difficult to find. Edwin was his first name. Only an answering machine replied at his office, but at his home number a woman, possibly his wife, told Nudger that he was on staff at Malcolm Bliss Hospital and would be there until eight o'clock tonight. Nudger called Oliver at the hospital and explained what he wanted. Oliver agreed to give him fifteen minutes that he couldn't spare but would anyway. The implication was that Nudger should be extremely grateful. Nudger understood; the golf season didn't last forever.

*　　　*　　　*

But it took him only seconds to decide he'd been wrong about Oliver. Being on staff at Malcolm Bliss was no fiesta. Nudger had been there before, as a patrolman. This was where the police brought the violent criminally insane and dumped them in the laps of people like Oliver. People who really *didn't* have fifteen minutes to spare. Nudger had forgotten what it was like here.

"Please sit down, Mr. Nudger," Dr. Oliver said. He was a young-ish-looking man, though probably in his forties, large, yet with a kind of leprechaun air about him.

Nudger sat in a small vinyl-upholstered chair near the door. Oliver sat behind a plain gray metal desk. The doctor's office wasn't much bigger than a closet—it might even have once *been* a large linen closet—and was painted a restful pale green that was probably sup-posed to soothe the patients. It had a window, but no view worth looking at. There was metal mesh over the glass anyway.

"You said you wanted to talk about one of my former patients, Claudia Bettencourt," the doctor said, hurrying Nudger along. "What's your interest in her?"

To the point: "I love her."

Oliver studied Nudger. Then he shrugged and his leprechaun fea-tures lifted in a grin. "I can understand why. Claudia is a very fine person. You do know I can't divulge any details of our doctor-patient relationship."

"Of course," Nudger said. "I'll speak in generalities. Is she cured?"

"Of what?"

"The tendency to abuse her children."

"Some generality," Oliver said. He thought for a moment. Claudia's conviction was a matter of public record; no need for Hip-pocratic secrecy here. "Yes, I think she could be described as cured. Her problems now are her own and don't affect others, at least not physically. Child abuse is a curse that runs in a lot of families, Mr. Nudger. It's passed on down the generations, a chain of violence that needs something traumatic sometimes to break it. Claudia is an intel-ligent woman; she understands that aspect of herself now, and so has greatly reduced, if not eliminated, her impulse to deal with people through violence. Unfortunately, understanding came too late to avert a tragedy in her life."

"I know," Nudger said. "I've been told about her daughter's death, the trial, and conviction."

"Who told you?"

"Other people who care about her."

Dr. Oliver ran a thumb along the edge of the desk, as if testing for sharpness. "I told her to leave town," he said.

"What?"

"I could have fixed it up with the Probation Board. She should get out of St. Louis, away from her former husband."

"I've met Ralph," Nudger said. "He's worthy of getting away from, all right."

"He's still a part of her problem. He's the key link in the chain that can't be broken, because he won't let go of the past; he won't forgive Claudia. He's punishing her."

"Is that why she attempted suicide?"

Oliver leaned back and played some kind of touch game with the fingertips of one hand against the other. "That's a tricky question. I don't think I'd better answer it."

"Okay. Do you think she might try suicide again?"

"For all I know, you might try suicide, Mr. Nudger. We're getting into speculation. I'm a doctor, not an oddsmaker. And remember, it's been over a year since I've seen Claudia."

"Why didn't she?" Nudger asked.

"Didn't she what?"

"Leave town."

"Ironically enough, because she loves her children. She doesn't want to move someplace where she can see them only infrequently. It seems to me—" Oliver caught himself, nipped the words before they could escape his lips, lips he probably thought had been too loose already. He smiled. "There are subjects I really can't get into, Mr. Nudger."

"Sure. I guess what I really came to find out, and what you've told me, is what you think of Claudia personally."

"She's a kind, decent human being who didn't deserve what she got," Oliver said. "I could introduce you to dozens of such people, right here on this floor."

"And all over the streets outside," Nudger said. He stood up. "One other thing, Doctor, while I'm face to face with an expert. Can you give me any insight into the mind of your average mass murderer?"

Oliver laughed at the abrupt and bizarre change of subject. "Only very generally. He—and the mass murderer usually is a he—is non-social, a loner, with a gigantic repressed ego. If he kills women, he despises a formative woman in his early life, his mother, usually. He wants to kill secretly, to get by with something few would suspect him of, but he also needs for people to know about it. He needs recognition, needs glory—or his idea of glory—even if it means going out in a blaze of it."

"Then he'd have to kill more and more frequently, until finally he was caught and exposed. After a certain point, he'd have no choice."

"That's the classic pattern. The killer might even feel remorse: the well-known catch-me-before-I-kill-again syndrome. You said you were a private detective. Are you looking for a mass murderer?"

"I might be." Nudger moved to the door and opened it. The quiet of the office was broken by the bustle of staff and visitors in the hall. "Thanks for the time, Doctor. I know it's scarce around here."

Oliver looked at his watch and grinned. "Fifteen minutes. That would cost you twenty dollars with a psychiatrist out in Clayton or Ladue."

"But not here, Doctor. I've been here before, as a cop. The people you help here are the ones who need help most and can afford it least. If you were in it for the money, you'd be in the other end of the medical business."

"And if you were in it for the money," Oliver said, "you'd be in the other end of the crime business."

Nudger considered the doctor's remark all the way home.

When he got to his apartment his phone was ringing. He heard it in the hall as he was fitting his key to the lock, but he didn't hurry, hoping whoever was on the line would lose patience and hang up. Now that he felt better, he didn't want his stomach needlessly aroused by someone wanting money or selling storm windows or urging him to see another dead body.

The phone didn't give up as he closed the door behind him and walked slowly toward the persistent ringing. Few things are more irresistible than a ringing phone. Usually Nudger would have done just as well not picking up the receiver. He knew that. On the other hand, it was always possible that he'd bought a lottery ticket and forgotten. Monetary magic might strike at any time. Might. With misgivings, he lifted the receiver and held it to his ear.

"Mr. Nudger?" Jeanette Boyington said.

Nudger grunted in tired confirmation.

"You took long enough getting to the phone."

"I was outside rotating my tires."

She ignored him, following her own script. "I have another appointment, for eight o'clock tonight at the Twin Oaks Mall fountain. This one calls himself Kelly. He says he's about six feet tall—but most of them say that—and he'll be wearing gray slacks and a black sport shirt with white buttons."

"Kelly at eight," Nudger said. "Gray, black, and white." He knew he was speaking with a kind of sad weariness, like a man who had just that day met a butchered woman.

"Make sure you phone me tonight if this works out," Jeanette said.

"Are you getting impatient?"

"No, I'm getting more patient with each meeting that doesn't mean anything. They only eliminate suspects and improve the odds on encountering Jenine's murderer."

"That's true only if our premise is correct," Nudger told her, thinking she should have been a cop. "If her killer did meet Jenine on the nightlines."

"That's how he selects his victims," Jeanette said. "I'm sure of it. That's why he hasn't been caught, because there's no connection between him and his victims other than a late-night telephone connection."

Nudger agreed with her, remembering the 666 number found in Susan Merriweather's flat, but he kept silent. Hammersmith might not want that information told about town.

"That Valpone woman," Jeanette said, "the one who was found murdered in her bathtub on the south side. I think she was one of his victims."

"It's possible," Nudger said, "but so far there's nothing to link the two murders." Jeanette would soon hear the news of Susan Merriweather's death, if she hadn't already. "There's been another bathtub murder," he said. "I've just come from the scene. This one has caused the police to come around to your way of thinking, but it hasn't made my job any easier."

"Tell me about it."

Nudger did, giving her a fair share of the details.

Her voice was tight and cold, as if mechanically forced between her teeth. "I don't want the police to find Jenine's killer before we do. I want to be instrumental in his capture, and I want him to know it."

"It might work out that way," Nudger said. "But either way he'll be caught soon. He's gone completely insane, out of control, killing more often and maybe not even caring now if he gets caught. Maybe he hopes he'll get caught. The question is: How many more women will die before that happens?"

"Maybe not one more, if Kelly is our man."

"Your mother left a message for me to phone her," Nudger said. "Do you have any idea what she wants?"

"It doesn't matter what she wants," Jeanette said. "You work for me, and don't forget it."

"Apparently Agnes can't forget it. She keeps sending a leviathan named Hugo Rumbo around to try to dissuade me."

"Why would she do that?" There was a tremor, maybe of anger, in Jeanette's voice.

"I'm not sure. You should ask her."

"Rumbo is an idiot who has to reason out putting one foot in front of the other to walk somewhere. Someone in your profession should be able to handle him."

"Should," Nudger agreed.

"Don't forget to phone me about Kelly," Jeanette said, and hung up.

Nudger replaced the receiver and stood in the quietude of his apartment, where everything was exactly the way he'd left it this morning. No one to misplace things or greet him. The refrigerator hummed a belated hello to him, that was all. A bachelor's life sure was a solitary journey. He walked into the kitchen, smiled at the refrigerator, opened its door, and reached in for one of the generic beers he'd bought on sale.

He sat at the kitchen table, sipping beer and waiting for it to be time to leave for his appointment with Kelly. There was a lot of time between now and then. It would take a lot of beer to get through it. More beer than Nudger cared to drink. Carrying his plain yellow can into the living room, he got out the phone directory and looked up Ralph Ferris.

Ferris lived on Nightingale Drive in Ferguson. Not far from Nudger in driving time, just a swift jaunt north on the Inner Belt highway. Ferris, who had gotten the house and children in the divorce. Ferris, who knew more about Claudia than Nudger did.

Nudger looked at the clock by the phone. He could skip supper, or stop for fast food if he regained faith in his digestive system. He gulped down the rest of his beer. There. That would fend off hunger.

He checked his wallet to make sure he was carrying enough cash to see him through minor emergencies, called in to the refrigerator that he was leaving, and went out the door.

A few minutes later he was in the Volkswagen, his bumpy course set for Nightingale Drive, his ear tuned to Jumbo Al Hirt's trumpet on the radio. Golden notes; a golden, temporary sanctuary from trouble and fear. From loneliness. Nudger turned up the volume. Blow, Jumbo, blow.

TWENTY-ONE

Nightingale Drive was a flat subdivision street of frame houses that had been built by the same contractor at the same time, about ten years ago, and were all one of three models with little variation. Ferris's address belonged to the largest model, a long ranch house with a picture window, an oversized chimney, and an attached two-car garage. Nudger bet himself that it was called the Executive Model.

He wasn't really sure why he'd driven here. Maybe he simply

wanted to see the house where Claudia had lived with Ralph Ferris and their daughters, where one of those daughters had died. It was an ordinary house that might have been the setting for a TV family situation comedy, a house you wouldn't suspect could harbor such problems and potential hells. Here was where a young family should be worrying about paying the mortgage, or whether they could afford to send one of the kids to a private school and get dental braces for the others. Child abuse, death probably didn't occur very often on Nightingale Drive. Or did they? Walls were walls, regardless of their contemporary middle-America facade. And people were people, and inside those walls they would behave like people, despite the visions of themselves instilled by current movies, sitcoms, and television commercials.

Nudger sat in the parked Volkswagen a few houses down and across the street from the Ferris house and tried to imagine Claudia living there. He couldn't. She did not belong in this stifling suburban sameness. Maybe that had exacerbated her problem.

Several young boys were playing in a front yard half a block down, crouching behind cars or shrubbery, dashing from cover to cover in some sort of game where they were trying to sneak up and surprise each other. Nudger looked around at the other houses on Nightingale, wondering what games were being played behind their walls this evening, between the boys' parents and the people like them.

He found out part of the answer.

"Can I help you with something?" Ralph Ferris was standing on the curbside of the Volkswagen, leaning down and staring in at Nudger. "A neighbor phoned and told me there was someone watching my house."

Nudger got out of the car, his mind whirling, plucking at understanding. Ferris had gone out his back door, then around the block, to approach the car from behind. Sly Ralph. As sneaky as he looked. Nudger saw the subtle lift of the man's bony features as Ferris recognized him.

"Hey, you're Claudia's boyfriend!" he said.

Nudger gave him a smile and slight shake of the head. "No, Mr. Ferris. My name is Nudger. I hope you'll forgive me for describing myself as a friend of your former wife. Actually, I've never met her. I'm doing some checking into her background for American Hosts,

Incorporated. She's applied for a job at one of our hotel restaurants. We routinely check into the backgrounds of all our prospective employees. We feel we owe it to our clientele."

Ferris appeared dubious, but he was close to buying Nudger's explanation. He put his hands in the pockets of his casual khaki slacks, shifted his weight on his blue Nike jogging shoes. He was willing to listen to more, but not much more.

Nudger handed him a business card. Nothing convinced like the officialism of print. Detectives and dictators knew it.

"It says here you're a private investigator," Ferris said, staring at the card as if it might at any second leap from his hand to his throat.

Nudger smiled again. "I do all of the regional American Hosts pre-employment inquiries. It's a contractual arrangement."

"But why are you watching my house? Claudia doesn't live here now, hasn't for years."

"Occasionally an inquiry takes on aspects that require deeper investigation, Mr. Ferris." Nudger made himself appear uncomfortable. It wasn't difficult. "Frankly, one of my operatives has reported some unusual circumstances in Mrs. Ferris's—"

"Ms. Bettencourt's—" Ferris interrupted.

"—Ms. Bettencourt's background. Now, I don't say that these rumors, if true, necessarily disqualify her from the job. But her application doesn't mention any such . . . trouble. Certainly American Hosts has a right to make inquiries before hiring someone, wouldn't you say? These days, with the unions so strong . . ." Nudger shrugged, as if once Claudia was hired she could do most anything she wanted at American Hosts' restaurants, including roughing up young customers who spilled the salt.

Ferris leaned back to rest his angular buttocks on the Volkswagen's fender. He removed his hands from his pockets and crossed his scrawny arms, settling down to talk. He was had.

"I'll ask directly so as not to waste your time and mine," Nudger said. "Has Claudia Bettencourt had any sort of trouble with the law?"

Ferris smiled. Very slightly, but he smiled. "Not if you don't count murder," he said.

Nudger appeared properly jolted. Then he grinned. "For a second you had me wondering. Now—"

"Oh, I wasn't joking, Mr. Nudger."

"No?" Nudger put on his gravest expression. He reached into the glove compartment of the Volkswagen and got out his spiral notebook and a pen. This was something American Hosts would have to know about in detail. "Suppose you tell me about it, Mr. Ferris."

To say Ferris was glad to cooperate was to say bears liked honey. "There's no way to really know the person you marry, not until it might be too late. I knew Claudia had a temper, that she'd hit one of the kids too hard now and then. But it got worse every year, then every month. She'd beat up on our two daughters regularly when I wasn't around—sometimes when I was around. I couldn't stop her; she was like she was crazy. Hell, she really *was* crazy."

"Did she seek professional help?"

"Yeah, she saw a shrink. It cost plenty and it didn't help."

"You mentioned murder," Nudger said, pen poised. He glanced down the street and saw two young, sober faces peering from the Ferris picture window. Dark hair, dark eyes. Nora and Joan. What did they think of their mother?

"Yeah, murder," Ralph Ferris was saying. "I told you Claudia had beaten our two daughters, but we had a third kid, Vicki. She was only three years old, and Claudia hadn't really gotten to her yet. At least not that I knew of. Then one winter Vicki came down with a bad case of the flu. She was puking and crying a lot, causing a fuss, making trouble like any sick kid would. Claudia went into her bedroom one night, opened the window, and left it open. The temperature outside was nearly zero. The flu became pneumonia, and Vicki died. Claudia left the window open on purpose. She murdered Vicki. A court of law said so."

Nudger pretended to take notes, glancing up occasionally at Ferris. The man was speaking in a kind of furious monotone, as if by rote, and seemed more angry than sorrowful over the death of his daughter. The righteous wrath of the guilty?

"She got probation, can you believe it?" Ferris said in disgust. "She never spent a night in jail. Nobody even mentioned the death penalty, what with the pansy-ass courts we got these days."

Nudger was surprised. "Do you think she should have been executed?"

Ferris stood up straight, his anger suddenly aimed at Nudger. "Sure, I think that! Don't you? An eye for an eye, the Bible says. She took a human life, didn't she?"

"I guess so," Nudger said, drawing another five-pointed star in his notebook without lifting the pen. He started a Terrible Swift Sword.

Ferris was grinning gauntly, like a cadaver aglow with a life not its own. "You're not here representing some hotel chain," he said. "Am I right?"

Nudger said nothing. He realized that he'd never had Ferris completely fooled.

"Sure, I'm right. You really are that murderous bitch's boyfriend, trying to find out if what you heard about her is true. Well, it is true, brother. But don't take my word for it; it's a matter of public record."

"So is the burning of witches."

"Meaning?"

"The people who did the burning, they were the real murderers."

The flesh around Ferris's mouth twitched involuntarily, not at all like a smile. He went pale and stood rigid with rage, eyes gleaming with a hate that needed fear to fuel such intensity. "We're done talking," he said. There was a fleck of spittle on his taut lower lip.

Nudger snapped the notebook closed. "All right."

"You've got more than your quota of nerve, coming around here spying and pretending to be what you're not. It's a good thing you outweigh me by twenty or thirty pounds."

"Don't let that stop you," Nudger said.

Ferris looked remotely puzzled and backed away. The perplexed expression changed feature by feature into one of defiance. "You threatening me?"

"You're a sick bastard, Ralph."

Ferris laughed and licked the fleck of spittle from his lip with a darting tongue. "You're just saying that because I told you what you didn't want to hear. But it's the truth, and you know it and have to eat it."

Nudger was struck by a wave of revulsion for this skinny, venomous, self-righteous antagonist. Or was it possible that the revulsion really was for what Ferris had told him? Either way, the anger would follow. Nudger could feel it building to bursting inside him. He

wanted to get out of there before it escaped and took control of him.
He tossed the notebook in through the Volkswagen's window, onto
the passenger's seat, opened the door, and got back in behind the
steering wheel.

"Did you learn more than you bargained for?" Ferris asked
tauntingly, as Nudger started the engine.

"Everybody always does," Nudger said. He worked the shift lever
into gear. "Incidentally, Ferris, she gets the job."

"Fine," Ferris said. "They can give her a mallet and put her in
charge of tenderizing the meat. She'd like that."

Nudger fought hard not to yank the wheel to the right and run over
Ferris, as he pulled the Volkswagen away from the curb and acceler-
ated down the street.

"Think about what I told you next time you're with Claudia!" Ferris yelled behind him. Probably everybody on Nightingale Drive
heard. Probably they'd heard it before.

Nudger still had plenty of time before his appointment with Kelly.
He stopped at a motel on Lindbergh and went into the lounge. It was
a quiet, dim place with a faintly dampish odor, as if the carpet might
be moldy. He got a draft beer at the bar and carried it to a booth near
the entrance to the lobby, where the dampness hadn't reached. He'd
decided to skip supper entirely and give his digestive system a rest. It
had to need it, after his conversation with Ralph Ferris.

Unpleasant though the experience had been, Nudger was glad he'd
talked with Ferris. If nothing else, it had convinced him of one thing.
It wasn't because he was Claudia's former husband that Nudger disliked Ralph Ferris; it was because Ferris was damned unlikable.
Nudger was pleased. Possibly that was what he had needed confirmed.

Halfway through his beer, he'd managed to shove the conversation
with Ferris to the back of his cluttered mind. He thought instead of
Jeanette Boyington. There sure was a lot of hate in the world.

He sat wondering about Jeanette. The woman almost vibrated with
her unbending commitment to vengeance. Maybe Hammersmith was
right about how the surviving twin of a murder victim might feel.
Maybe Jeanette thought that when Jenine had died, a flesh-and-blood

part of herself had been slain. Nudger remembered how Danny had acted while talking about his twin brother who had been dead for decades. And weren't there studies that showed how identical twins separated at birth developed remarkable similarities in their behavior even though they had never met? Who really knew what complex universal equations ruled the lives of twins? Ruled the lives of us all?

Nudger decided that he shouldn't be thinking this way after only half a mug of beer. It was unnatural and uncharacteristic. It could lead to error. Save the metaphysics for good Scotch, Dr. Shamus.

He went to the phones in the motel lobby and dialed Natalie Mallowan's number, hoping he could catch her at home and remind her of his nine hundred dollars.

When he got no answer, he called Claudia to try to arrange to see her tonight or tomorrow. No answer there, either. No one seemed to be home tonight. No one other than Ralph Ferris.

Nudger hung up the phone, feeling an unaccustomed emptiness after not being able to talk with Claudia. He was beginning to understand why he'd had to go to the Ferris house on Nightingale Drive. It was part of Claudia's past, which made it part of Nudger's future. He felt a need to acknowledge and fully reckon with her life with Ralph Ferris, to know what he could about it, place it in its proper mental slot, and so reduce it to a negligible factor in his relationship with her.

He felt an overpowering desire to talk with Claudia's daughters, to explain some things about their mother so they might understand her better. He could imagine what Ralph Ferris told them about her.

His drive to the Nightingale house on what had seemed a whim had been significant and irreversible, Nudger belatedly realized. That people had time to contemplate forks in the road of life was a lie. Usually they went one way or the other without realizing it, and could only gaze back over their shoulder as those fateful three-way intersections faded into the past.

He stood supporting himself with one hand fisted against the wall. It had been a depressing day and a demanding evening. For a moment he considered driving home, taking in the Cardinals' game on television, and forgetting about the appointment with Kelly. Forgetting about everything except hits, runs, and errors, and how nice it

felt to be dozing off on the soft sofa instead of meeting another
might-be murderer.

But he knew he wouldn't return to his apartment. He couldn't. He
was destined to remain a while longer in the legions of those not
home, doing his job. It was a job he often loathed, but it was all he
had, a burden and a salvation.

He went out the lobby door to the parking lot and walked toward
his car, trying to decide which was the most direct route to Twin
Oaks Mall, forgetting all about going home.

TWENTY-TWO

Or maybe Nudger was home. The area around the Twin Oaks Mall
fountain was beginning to seem as much like home as his apartment.
He settled down on his customary concrete bench to wait for Kelly.

The mall was more crowded in the evenings than during the after-
noons. And there were more male shoppers, more family units of
husband, wife, and trailing, misbehaving offspring. The tempo of the
mall was quicker. Fewer shoppers were here for idle recreation. Now
the real business of buying was being conducted by many of the people hurrying past. Mr. and Mrs. Consumer, marching to the rhythms
of the latest catch phrases and advertising jingles. Nudger sat back
and observed the orderly lockstep madness. It was enough to make
him wish he had disposable income.

A gray-haired man, easily in his seventies, sat down gingerly on
the opposite end of Nudger's bench and sucked on a nasty-looking
black briar pipe, all the time watching the passing parade of women
with his weary but interested eyes. A couple of young boys ran up to
the fountain and tossed coins in, then threaded their way at high
speed back into the crowd. Two teenage girls in tight jeans walked
past chattering and giggling. The old guy on the bench, probably a
retiree well out of the melee, useless now to the mall except as a
consumer of dentifrice and laxative, looked on with approval before

fixing his wandering gaze on a buxom woman yanking a pre-schooler along behind her. Nudger had played this scene over and over during the past week. Home, all right.

With the old man, Nudger watched the woman with chest and child until she veered and entered the drugstore. When he looked away from her, there was Kelly.

Nudger glanced at his wristwatch. Kelly—and he was immediately sure it was Kelly—was on time to the minute. He was indeed close to six feet tall, but he was so broad through the chest and shoulders that he appeared shorter. He was wearing a black shirt with pearl buttons, and neatly creased gray slacks, all as Jeanette had described. But what claimed Nudger's wary attention was Kelly's full head of very curly coarse blond hair. Nudger let his gaze drop to Kelly's hands. They looked as if they could crush a week-old Danny's Dunker Delite.

Kelly's features were broad and flat, and because of their blandness barely missed being handsome. He wasn't at all fat, but he was wide through the waist, hips, and thighs. His arms were tanned and muscular, dusted with blond hair, with wrists as thick as many men's ankles. Not more than two hundred pounds, but a born strong-man, the kind that made natural college halfbacks or ends that could block.

As Kelly rested a foot on a concrete planter and looked around with wide-set blue eyes, Nudger pretended to study the shoppers streaming toward him, as if someone were keeping him waiting. He felt Kelly's gaze slide over him like a cool wave that stirred the hairs on the back of his neck. Wearing a carefully neutral expression, Nudger glanced at the blond man with seeming disinterest.

Kelly was looking away from him now with those ominously guileless blue eyes, eyes so emotionally void that they must conceal much, placidly surveying the throng of shoppers. Then he walked over to the circular concrete bench encompassing the fountain, sat down as if settling in for a wait, and began gnawing on a hangnail on his right ring finger.

He gnawed persistently for quite a while, although without real concentration, his wrist twisted at an awkward angle to allow him to use his incisors. He was lucky not to dislocate his arm.

Finally he gave up gnawing, then waiting, and began walking toward the main exit. Nudger stood up from the hard bench and followed.

Kelly strode slowly past the cafeteria, toward the glass doors that would let him out onto the lower-level parking lot. Despite his bulk he moved in a glide, with a jungle cat's grace. Nudger's Volkswagen was parked on the upper-level lot. There was no time for him to rush to his car and drive to the lower level with any expectation of spotting Kelly again in the acres of parked cars. All Nudger could do was stay behind the blond man and try to get his car's description and license-plate number.

Nudger felt an undeniable shameful relief. Kelly was one of those men who had about him an air of controlled menace, of barely restrained, unpredictable violence seething beneath a crude, calm exterior. A gut-deep tough man, close to the primal.

He surprised Nudger. Instead of going to a parked car when he got outside, Kelly turned and followed the walk bordering Sears' display windows. He stopped and stood in a relaxed wide stance, with his hands clasped behind him, a few feet from a bus stop sign.

Nudger's cowardly relief left him and his stomach came to bothered life again, spurring him on as he hurried back through the mall to the escalators and the upper-level parking lot.

He didn't know if he was disappointed or not when he drove the Volkswagen into the lower-level lot and saw Kelly still lolling at the bus stop. Nudger found a parking space from which he could observe Kelly, positioned the Volkswagen between the yellow lines just so, switched off the engine, and waited.

Not for long. Within ten minutes the Cross County Express belched and snorted its way through the lot and hissed to a stop, blocking Nudger's view of Kelly. Half a dozen shoppers got out through the rear door. The bus rumbled mightily and emitted heat-shimmering black diesel exhaust, then disembarked from the curb.

Kelly was gone from where he'd been standing.

Nudger backed the Volkswagen out of its parking slot and followed the bus.

They drove east, through a string of west-county bedroom suburbs, all the way into the city. Kelly got off the bus near Oakland and

Kingshighway and stood at another stop on the west side of Kingshighway, waiting to transfer to a southbound bus.

As Nudger parked on Oakland and kept Kelly in view, he pon-
dered the fact that the man had used public transportation to get to his
intended meeting with Jeanette. Certainly the women Kelly met had
cars, or he would assume so. Kelly's own car—if he owned one—
would be a hindrance and possible incriminating complication if he
left it in a parking lot while he did murder. It fit, this use of the buses
to meet intended victims.

Or maybe Kelly simply didn't have a car. Or maybe he had one
and it was in the shop. Maybe Kelly wasn't a murderer, just a lonely
guy making blind dates by phone.

Maybe Nudger should be careful about leaping to convenient con-
clusions.

The Kingshighway bus rumbled to a stop, and Kelly and two other
passengers boarded. Nudger waited until the bus would be far enough
ahead of him, then pulled out into the Oakland Avenue traffic and
made a right turn on Kingshighway.

The bus was stopped for a red light a block ahead. Nudger joined
the line of cars behind it. He didn't have to worry about mistaking
another bus for it; this one sported a large liquor advertisement below
its dusty rear window, on which someone had lettered HOT STUFF
with red spray paint across the seductive likeness of a slinky blonde
in a black silk evening gown.

Nudger couldn't have gotten close to the bus if he'd tried. Traffic
was heavy on Kingshighway, moving irregularly as cars slowed or
stopped to make left turns into side streets. Nudger didn't regard that
as a problem. From the angle he had, he could catch occasional
glimpses of Kelly's blond head through one of the bus's side windows.

But when traffic thinned out near Magnolia, Nudger was surprised
to see that Kelly was gone.

Like that. As if Houdini had had a hand in it.

Possibly he'd switched seats. Nudger hadn't seen him get off at
any of the stops the bus had made. A horn blared as Nudger veered
the Volkswagen into the outside lane.

When he caught up with the bus, which now contained only a few passengers, he still couldn't see Kelly inside. He dropped back half a block and continued following the bus, but with a self-deprecating kind of hopelessness. He could actually taste the bitter frustration of having gotten so close to the man who might be Jenine's killer, only to lose him again through bad luck. Or through incompetence.

Nudger followed the bus all the way to its turnaround point, where it would stand empty before looping in a wide U-turn to make its northward run. The end of the line.

No Kelly.

Somewhere between Tholozan Avenue, where Nudger was sure he'd seen him through the bus window, and Magnolia, where Nudger was sure Kelly was no longer on the bus, Kelly had stepped from the rear door onto the sidewalk with some other passengers and disappeared. It had to have happened when Nudger was well back from the bus, when his view of the bus stop had been partially blocked by stalled traffic.

Nudger sat in the parked Volkswagen and slapped too hard at a mosquito perched on his forearm. He missed the mosquito. He hurt his arm. Letting two antacid tablets dissolve in his mouth, he turned the car around and drove back the way he'd come, ignoring his mosquito antagonist as it explored the far corner of the windshield. A truce of sorts.

Within fifteen minutes he caught up with a northbound Kingshighway bus. It had the same sexy advertisement below its back window, the slender blonde in the black silk gown. He noticed that the ad wasn't what he'd thought. It wasn't a liquor advertisement at all. It was an ad for Tabasco sauce, and the words HOT STUFF weren't sprayed on by a vandal but were made to look that way, part of the copy. Some ad man's contribution to creativity. A real eye-catcher.

Nudger actually groaned as he realized his mistake. Somewhere along the way he might have begun tailing a different bus. He had stupidly followed an advertising poster instead of Kelly. A poster that was probably one of hundreds being carted around the city.

In a burst of frustration, he slapped the bucket seat next to him, stinging his palm. He wondered if drinking an entire bottle of Tabasco sauce in one sitting might prove fatal. He wished he had an ad man to try it on.

TWENTY-THREE

"Have you ever worn a black silk evening gown while cooking with Tabasco sauce?" Nudger asked Claudia.

"No. It sounds kinky."

Nudger sat at Claudia's kitchen table, nursing an icy Budweiser and enjoying watching Claudia prepare dinner. She had every burner glowing on the old white four-burner stove, busying herself from pot to skillet to pot. She was a good cook, a practiced cook, though not necessarily the kind that could blend gourmet dishes. She was more of a specialist in the basics, in the sort of food that was no less tasty because it was recognizable on the plate. Corn on the cob was boiling in one pot, green beans simmering in another, potatoes heating in a third. In an old, heavy skillet, she was pan-frying the steaks Nudger had brought. Country cooking.

He liked the here and now of his life, he decided. There was a pleasant domesticity to it. Though Claudia wasn't wearing an apron, she was dressed in wifely-enough fashion in a sleeveless print blouse, denim skirt, and practical square-toed shoes that tried but failed to detract from the graceful turn of her ankles. Her dark hair was worn pulled back and pinned in a loose bun, emphasizing the symmetrical leanness of her face and making her deep-brown eyes seem enormous. She was obviously enjoying what she was doing, in fact seemed so absorbed in it that at times Nudger wondered if she remembered he was there. The simmering food gave off tantalizing cooking scents that mingled in the tiny kitchen. The beer was cold, the woman was warm. All very snug and right. Life on the upswing.

Nudger had thought his day was completely ruined when he lost Kelly. Listening to Jeanette's cold anger after he'd reported to her on Kelly hadn't improved his mood, either. But when Nudger had returned to his office, there was a new client, a six-foot-four, two hundred and fifty pounder who described himself as a small businessman, and who wanted his lawyer investigated. Nudger had taken the job, received a reasonable retainer, and immediately phoned Eileen.

What a princess! She had agreed to give Nudger more time to pay all back alimony on the condition that he mail her the retainer he'd just received. He'd gotten a money order made out to her, pocketed the part of the retainer he hadn't told her about, and mailed her the few hundred dollars to hold her at bay. It was something like tossing a cheeseburger to a trailing wolf.

Now here he was in Claudia's apartment, feeling content, knowing he'd staved off disaster at least through the weekend. That was about all you could ask of this world. He sipped his beer. Claudia turned the steaks.

"Black silk evening gown?" she said.

Nudger told her about his meeting with Kelly and his abortive attempt to follow the blond suspect. She listened attentively, automatically tending to the steaks.

"Do you think you followed the wrong bus?" she asked pertinently, when he'd finished.

"I think it was the same bus, the right bus, most of the way. But I can't be positive."

"Do you need to be?"

"No." He watched her switch off the burners, cross to the cabinets, and stretch to reach high for two dinner plates. It was worth watching. "But it would help immensely to be positive."

She set the plates on the counter by the stove and began deftly transferring food to them. "What are you going to do now?"

Nudger observed the largest steak, done medium and with just the right percentage of marbled fat, hoisted on the prongs of a fork and plunked onto his plate. "I'm going to eat," he said.

"I mean, about Kelly."

"I'm going to haunt the neighborhood between where I last saw him on the bus and where I first noticed he was missing from it. If he'd transferred again, I'm sure I'd have seen him standing at the stop where he got off, so I'm assuming he lives in the neighborhood, or at least had some business there."

"If you followed the right bus."

"If . . ."

"Well, it sounds like a reasonable plan," Claudia said, carrying the two heaping plates to the table in the small dining area. "Get yourself another beer."

"What about the wine I brought?"

"I forgot about that. I'll get some wineglasses."

She produced two stemmed glasses, one with a chipped rim. Nudger got the Gallo Brothers burgundy, of a vintage not yet ripped from calendars, out of the refrigerator, uncapped it, and poured. He gave Claudia the good glass.

The meal was delicious. Claudia had fried the steaks to exactly the point where they were done but hadn't lost much of their juice, and she had somehow seasoned the corn in the pot so that it didn't require salt or butter. She was in the wrong job at Kimball's.

Nudger raised his glass in a salute. "You're a world-class cook," he told her, meaning it. World-class. State of the art.

She seemed embarrassed. She actually smiled shyly and ducked her head, not knowing how to reply. "I use all cast-iron cookware," she said seriously. "It makes a difference." And so it must.

They decided to postpone dessert, then Nudger helped her to clear the table. She told him they'd wash the dishes later, after they'd had cheesecake and coffee. He didn't argue. She might think he was sexist.

"What do you want to do now?" she asked. "Watch television?"

"Too many commercials," Nudger said. "Watching television these days is like an evening with an aluminum-siding salesman."

"What, then?"

"I want to do this," Nudger said, and held her to him and kissed her mouth. He felt her arms jerk to life, coil around him, and her warm body levered forward and upward against his. He couldn't help feeling slightly surprised. It was as easy as in the movies.

She didn't want to pull away, but when she finally did, she looked up at him with dark crescent eyes and said, "I was hungrier for that than for steak. I'm not disappointed."

They were both in the movies. It was grand! "It has nothing to do with iron cookware," Nudger told her. Cary Grant.

She stared at him for a while, then nodded and smiled slightly. He knew that she saw the part of him that was detached from her and everyone else and would accept it. He could see the sweet sadness just below her surface. And her desperation, quieted at last, but patiently waiting. She led him into her bedroom.

The window was open, curtains swaying. Nudger could see the bright haze from the lights of the stadium, beyond the silhouettes of the buildings down the street. He heard the mass murmur of the night-game crowd.

As Claudia was methodically undressing, she saw the question in Nudger and said, "I had a tubal ligation. I can have no more children. Safe. Forever."

She made love violently and searchingly. There was a delicate sadness even in her letting go.

What they were doing must have been right. Thousands cheered.

By the time they were finished and lay quietly beside each other, the warm room held the musky scent of their perspiring bodies. A night moth found its way through the window, brushed softly against Nudger's bare leg, and then fluttered away. For an instant Nudger was with Eileen. For an instant.

"You were cautious with me," Claudia said.

"Yes."

"You don't have to be."

He laced his fingers behind his head, resting back on his pillow and listening to the faint sounds of the old building's concessions to time, the muted swish of traffic below on Spruce Street, the occasional stirring of the ballpark crowd.

"I've been doing some more detective work of a personal nature," he said.

"Oh?"

"I talked with several people who know you, your friends. Including Dr. Oliver."

She lay silently for a long time. When she answered, her voice held a flat tone of disbelief. "And you're still here with me?"

"I believe in you."

"You don't have any reason to believe in me."

"The best things in life are unreasonable."

She was reasonable enough not to argue.

"I want you to have faith in your future," he told her. "Hope."

She laughed her resigned, throaty laugh. "I can't keep hoping, and you can't stop hoping. Yours is a bigger problem than mine."

"When are you going to see your daughters next?" he asked. He felt the slight shift of the mattress as her body tensed.

"Next weekend. Remember? They're out of town this weekend."

"Let me go get them for you, bring them here or wherever you want to meet them. We'll make a day of it—the Arch, the Zoo, whatever you and they like."

"Ralph might not give them to you."

"I already told him I was your boyfriend. Must have been a premonition. Ralph and I have talked, so it's not as if we're strangers. You can phone him and let him know I'm driving by for the girls. Or you can go with me and sit in the car where he can see you."

"But you don't want me to see Ralph."

"Why should you?"

She didn't have an answer for that. Or not one she liked. She lay quietly beside Nudger, breathing regularly and deeply, almost as if she were asleep. He knew she was awake.

"All right," she said at last. He felt the light touch of her fingertips on his arm, tracing a feathery path from elbow to wrist.

"What about dessert?" he said.

TWENTY-FOUR

Early the next morning, Nudger began driving around the neighborhood of Kingshighway between Tholozan and Magnolia, when people were clustered at the bus stops on Kingshighway on their way to work. He stayed on Kingshighway for over an hour, bouncing along in the overheated Volkswagen, watching the number of people at the stops decrease, not seeing the ominous blond Kelly.

At eight-thirty he turned onto Magnolia and began cruising side streets lined with similar brick homes and apartment buildings, gradually working his way north to Tholozan. He noticed that the tires had begun humming on the rough pavement. The day was heating up, softening rubber and resolve. Summer in St. Louis. Wouldn't it be nice if the Volkswagen were air-conditioned?

The feeling that he was squandering his time crept into Nudger and spread delibitating tentacles. He had cause for discouragement. Not only might he be wrong about where Kelly had gotten off the bus, but Kelly might not even be the man he sought. "Murderer" wasn't a label to be pasted on lightly; if it didn't stick, there was trouble all around. Nudger had considered telling Hammersmith about Kelly, but there really wasn't much to tell. A vague match-up of descriptions wouldn't excite the police, and Hammersmith was no longer in charge of the investigation anyway. Captain Massey of the Major Case Squad was now running the operation, a meticulous officer competent at police work but overly concerned with PR and politics. Nudger knew Massey wouldn't take the information about Kelly seriously. And if by chance he did, he'd inundate the Kingshighway area, where Nudger was searching, with enough blue uniforms and news-media people to force Kelly, all traffic offenders with unpaid tickets, and all owners of unlicensed pets to flee the neighborhood and go into deep cover. Some things were better left unsaid.

Nudger drove around the neighborhood until noon, then dug deep in his pocket, gassed up the Volkswagen, and drove to his office. He didn't want to go there. The place was beginning to wear on him. It was becoming a den of depression.

He parked the car, then checked with Danny before going upstairs. Nobody had been by to see him on business, or to try to corrupt, coerce, or concuss him. Odd. But then, these things ran in cycles.

"Any sign of the monolithic Hugo Rumbo?" Nudger asked.

"Nope," Danny said, absently flicking his towel at a fly. "You miss him?"

"Like a fever blister."

After persistently declining the offer of a brace of doughnuts for lunch, Nudger went up to his office and checked his mail and answering machine.

Nothing interesting in the mail except a special offer on a quick-draw holster. The manufacturer promised it would shave half a second off the time between slapping leather and squeezing the trigger.

If Nudger had owned a gun, he would have been intrigued. It might be fun slapping leather and yelling at people to freeze, then commanding them to thaw.

There was nothing on the answering machine other than some adolescent giggling and a loud raspberry. It cheered Nudger considerably.

He phoned Hammersmith and asked him to check Records for a rundown on Roger Davidson, the new client's suspect lawyer. Hammersmith told Nudger he shouldn't make a habit of using the tax-funded police computer for private business, especially since he probably didn't earn enough to pay taxes, then said he'd get back to him by phone when he had something on Davidson.

The instant Nudger replaced the receiver, the phone jangled to vibrant life beneath his hand, startling him. He raised the receiver to his ear and said hello. He wished he hadn't.

"This is Agnes Boyington, Mr. Nudger."

"This is a recording. Mr. Nudger isn't in the office. At the tone, please leave a message and he'll return your call."

"I know that's you—"

Nudger whistled a high *C* into the phone and hung up.

The phone began ringing again almost immediately. He let it ring twelve times before picking up the receiver again. He didn't want his phone line tied up. He didn't want to leave. He didn't want a headache.

"What is it, Agnes?" he asked.

"It's Mrs. Boyington. I've been trying to get through to you all day, Nudger," Her voice oozed annoyance.

"My answering machine was on. You could have left a message."

"I don't choose to talk to a machine, then be ignored by you."

"I don't choose to talk to you, then *not* be ignored by the police."

"Let's call that a misunderstanding."

"No."

"All right. However you view the matter makes no difference to me. I called to demand a report on what progress you've made in tracking down my daughter's murderer."

The lady had chutzpah in all its pronunciations. Nudger was awed, but it wore off fast. "I'm working for Jeanette," he reminded Agnes Boyington. "Any information I obtain will be reported to her."

"Any and *all* information, Nudger?"

"Of course, Boyington."

"I've given more consideration to your proposal that I pay you to withdraw from the case without informing Jeanette," Agnes Boyington said slowly and precisely, choosing her words with a care that suggested she thought the conversation might be bugged or recorded. "I think five thousand dollars would be a reasonable sum."

"It was *you* who offered to pay *me* to drop the case," Nudger pointed out, also thinking the conversation might be bugged or recorded. Suspicion breeds suspicion.

Not differing with him now that they were both on record, if there was a record, she said, "I know that five thousand dollars is a great deal of money to a man who lives your sort of life. Think about it, right now. It could mean a lot to you."

Sitting there in his sparsely furnished office, gazing at shirt cuffs that would soon fall into the frayed category, Nudger couldn't disagree with her. He said nothing. He was afraid that if he did it might be yes.

"Are you considering my offer," Agnes Boyington asked, "or are you one of those increasingly rare Quixotic fools who won't put a price on client loyalty? On a dreamer's code of conduct that is nothing more than a vestige of youth. Or misplaced romanticism."

"You forgot professional honor," Nudger told her.

"There is no such thing in a dishonorable profession."

"Be glad you're not a windmill," Nudger said, and hung up.

He sat for a long time thinking about what he might have bought for five thousand dollars, not the least of which was escape from his creditors, and from troubled sleep fragmented by dreams of debt and destruction. Agnes knew how to negotiate, how to tempt. She hadn't offered him an astronomical amount of money, but when a man was treading shark-infested water, you might as well throw him a raft as a boat. He'd climb on. Usually. If he wasn't a Quixotic fool.

Then he considered the vulnerable position he'd be in if he accepted Agnes Boyington's offer. She would have him sealed like a bug in a jar, and she would remove the lid only to stick pins in him. He was sure that eventually he'd lose his livelihood as well as his self-respect. He told himself that, and not an antiquated code of honor, was why he'd hung up on her. It was an explanation he could live with and suffer no embarrassment.

As he sat staring at the phone, it occurred to him that he'd doubt-less be seeing more of Hugo Rumbo. An unsettling notion. Almost as unsettling as being five thousand dollars poorer than he might have been.

Nudger looked around the office to make sure he wasn't leaving anything switched on and unnecessarily running up his electric bill, then locked the door behind him and descended the hollow-sounding steep wooden stairs to the street door.

He would accept Danny's offer of a two-doughnut lunch, then re-turn to the neighborhood where he'd lost track of Kelly. If he didn't have persistence, what did he have?

Three days later he was wondering if persistence paid. He'd cov-ered the side streets along Kingshighway again and again, jarring over potholed pavement in the cramped, clattering Volkswagen, probably doing irreparable harm to his and the car's insides.

Time was becoming a prime factor. Nudger had only so much of it to waste. He'd phoned his new client yesterday afternoon and re-ported that there were three Roger Davidsons practicing law in the state of Missouri. None of them had the office address of the client's Roger Davidson; none of them had ever heard of Nudger's client. The Bar Association pleaded *ignorantia*. The Roger Davidson in question wasn't even a lawyer. Case closed. A nice profit for Nudger for doing nothing but making phone calls, but not so much profit that it amounted to more than carrion for his creditors. If something didn't happen soon on the Jeanette Boyington case, or if Natalie Mallowan didn't pay him for finding Ringo, he'd have to contact some bona fide lawyers he knew who sometimes threw business his way at the end of ambulance chases.

Nudger bounced in his seat, almost bumping his head on the car roof, as the Volkswagen hit a high seam in the pavement. The little car's suspension was about ruined, and the engine was laboring as if overheated. He decided to give car and driver a rest by taking time out for a cheap lunch at the diner on the corner of Kingshighway and Kemper; the place was built of glass and white metal and looked clean.

There was a shady parking space not far from the corner. Nudger

maneuvered the Volkswagen into it and listened to the tiny engine
putt and clatter for several revolutions after he'd switched off the
ignition. He thought it might be a good idea to pop the trunk a few
inches on the rear-engine car so the tired old motor would cool faster.

He'd just gotten out of the car and was about to close the door
when he saw Kelly emerge from the diner, clutching a white carry-
out bag beneath his arm like a football, and jog across Kingshighway.

Nudger caught his breath, then in one hurried motion climbed back
into the Volkswagen, bumped his knee on the dashboard, and inserted and twisted the ignition key. The engine turned over but refused to start, grinding and popping as if protesting this fresh abuse at
the hands of Nudger. He twisted the key again. Again. Heat-warped
metal ticked and moaned. The overheated little car sputtered something guttural and nasty at Nudger and the battery went dead. If yet
another war with Germany were in the offing, Nudger would be
among the first to know.

Legwork time. Nudger could still see Kelly walking along Kingshighway with his carry-out order. He wouldn't be going far if he was
planning on a hot lunch. Slamming the car door hard behind him, as
if that might cause well-deserved pain in the carburetor, Nudger followed.

Kelly didn't appear worried about being watched. He never
glanced back as he crossed Kingshighway at the traffic light and began walking east on Arsenal. Nudger stayed well behind him, watching his easy, powerful stride. Kelly looked as if he were merely
sauntering, but Nudger had to walk fast to maintain the same distance
between them.

When Kelly turned right on Morganford and was out of sight,
Nudger broke into a casual jog to close distance, then paused at the
corner and saw Kelly crossing the street to walk east on Hartford.
Nudger walked swiftly to the corner and peered down Hartford. Kelly
was half a block away, climbing some steps with a black curlicued
wrought-iron railing. He took the steps two at a time, effortlessly.

Nudger waited a few minutes, then approached the spot where
Kelly had gone up the steps.

The steps led to a small brick house with green metal awnings, almost exactly like the houses on either side. Without pausing, Nudger memorized the address as he walked past.

When he reached the corner and was out of sight of the house, he jogged back to his car. He was getting tired, getting old.

The Volkswagen was still miffed at him. Its engine had cooled, but the battery hadn't built up enough of a charge to turn it over. Nudger talked two summer-school students from the high school across the street into pushing the car down Kingshighway. They thought it was great fun, as they held their half-eaten hamburgers from the diner in their mouths like dogs with bones, and leaned into the task with strong backs and young legs. At fifteen miles per hour, Nudger popped the clutch and the engine thunked and clattered to life.

With a grateful beep of the horn to the two scholarly stalwarts, he drove for his office. In the rearview mirror a hamburger hit the pavement.

The three-year-old reverse directory Nudger kept in his filing cabinet listed the occupant of the Hartford address as Luther Kell. He looked up "Kell" in the phone directory, ran his finger down the page, and found a Luther Kell at the same address. So far so good. Unless Luther Kell had moved recently and the blond man was someone else.

There was an easy way to confirm his identity. Maybe. Nudger dragged the phone over to himself and punched out Kell's listed number.

"Hello," said a monotonous deep male voice.

"Mr. Luther Kell?" Nudger asked, trying to sound like Monty Hall.

"Yeah."

"This is Mike at J, T, and L Insulation and Remodeling. We understand you own your home on Hartford. We're running our summer special on insulation—"

"The house is warm enough," Kell said. "It don't need anymore insulation." A slight drawl now, distorted by the phone.

"What about siding? We're having a sale on our never-paint white vinyl siding."

"It's a brick house. It don't need any siding. Anyway, I rent."

"If you could give me the name of the house's owner . . ."

"Hey, get screwed, Mike! You friggin' pest!"

"You'll like our summer rebate offer."

But Kell had hung up. No tolerance.

Nudger sat back in his swivel chair, satisfied. He'd found Kell and knew where he lived. Damned if he couldn't do some mighty smooth sleuthing on occasion. The squeal of the chair's unoiled mechanism was like a trill of congratulation.

He reached again for the phone, to call Jeanette Boyington.

She didn't answer. It wasn't yet five o'clock. She was probably working somewhere on one of her Personnel Pool journeywoman secretarial jobs. He replaced the receiver and leaned back once more in his chair. *Greeeat!* it shrilly proclaimed again. It was a fan, all right.

But Nudger's mood was more somber. There was danger here in getting carried away, "full of himself," as his old grandmother used to say. It was just as well that he hadn't contacted Jeanette. Sure, he'd found out where Kell lived, but where did that leave him? Kell had used the nightlines to make a date with Jeanette, and he fit the very general physical description of the killer, including the oversized hands, but it was a long leap in logic to assume his guilt on that evidence.

It was a leap the vengeful Jeanette might make with room to spare.

Nudger decided that it might be better if Jeanette didn't know Kell's address immediately. That way Nudger could observe the man for a while without having to worry about Jeanette ringing the doorbell on Hartford on a mission of sisterly revenge, and confronting and possibly harming or killing an unsuspecting man whose compulsions were only the usual and understandable urges of the flesh. After all, sex and food were the only things Nudger had seen Kell pursue. Who could cast stones at anyone for that?

Nudger picked up the phone again, but instead of calling Jeanette he called Hammersmith at the Third District.

Hammersmith wasn't on duty yet. Nudger punched out another number and reached the lieutenant at his home in Webster Groves.

"I need another rundown from Records," Nudger said. "On a Luther Kell. Spelled like 'bell' but with a *K* as in 'kite.'" He gave Hammersmith the Hartford address.

"This Kell another crooked lawyer?" Hammersmith asked.

"No, it has to do with the Jenine Boyington case." Nudger explained why he wanted the information on Kell. He could have predicted Hammersmith's reaction.

"Something might be there, Nudge, but it's vague. I'd never get Massey to act on it."

"I'm not asking you to," Nudger said. "But the ground rules are different for me. It's a hunch I have to follow up on for my client."

"Jeanette Boyington? Professional surviving twin?"

"The same."

"No need to caution you to tippy-toe."

"No need."

"Seen anything more of the mother shark?"

"Agnes? She phoned and wanted to up the ante," Nudger said, "or at least define the terms."

"Which are?"

"Five thousand dollars. For not working. I declined."

Hammersmith didn't ask Nudger why. Nudger appreciated that.

"Which means," Nudger said, "I'll probably be saying hello again to Hugo Rumbo."

"You want protection, Nudge?"

"Tough guy like me? Naw, I can handle cheap gunsels."

"Good. I don't have anyone we can spare to assign to you anyway. You'll just have to rely on your gat. Where can I reach you with the information on Kell?"

"At my office," Nudger said. "Or at this number." He gave Hammersmith the phone number of Claudia's apartment.

"Sometime this evening okay?" Hammersmith asked.

"Fine. Thanks, Jack."

"Forget it," Hammersmith said. "Everybody in Records thinks you're on the payroll." He hung up to phone Records, then return to whatever he'd been doing at home. Probably sorting through the collection of old baseball cards that Nudger knew he kept. Hammersmith figured a 1954 Stan Musial was better than a triple-A bond.

Nudger looked outside and saw that a wind was swirling and light rain was falling at crazy angles, whipping across the face of the building on the other side of the street in graceful, breeze-flung patterns. St. Louis, making good on its reputation for unpredictable, instantly changeable weather. This staid and schizophrenic city was a meteorologist's nightmare and a sociologist's sweet dream. So waveless and conservative. So fractioned and fermented. So few meaningful changes on the surface; so many changes below that seldom reached the surface, or reached it distorted years later. People in this city could kid themselves, sometimes about which century they were in. Nudger and the city were not unlike each other. They were usually short of funds. They had problems. Somehow they lurched ahead, maybe toward better times.

Nudger had a key to Claudia's apartment. He decided to go there and wait for her, put his feet up on the coffee table, drink a few cold Budweisers, and listen to FM music on the radio. When Claudia arrived, he might brag a bit.

TWENTY-FIVE

"It's for you," Claudia said again.

Nudger awoke slowly and opened his eyes to see her sitting up in bed, carefully extending the phone's white receiver toward him with both hands, as if it were alive and fragile. Her dark hair was mussed in a way he liked, but her eyes bothered him. They seemed to be puffy from more than simply too much sleep.

Accepting the receiver, he pushed himself up to brace his shoulders against the headboard. Beside him, the sheets rustled as Claudia settled back down. The room was quiet, the air heavy, hazed by the morning sunlight knifing dustily between the blinds. Nudger pressed the cool receiver to his ear, managed to separate his dry lips, croaked a hello. Could that have been *his* voice?

"Are you awake enough to hear about Luther Kell?" Hammersmith asked.

"Sure, it's already almost seven o'clock."

"Folks like us have to rise before dawn to get a jump on evil," Hammersmith said. "Early birds of the law, foraging for the worm of crime."

"Luther Kell," Nudger reminded him.

"Oh, him. Mr. Anonymous. Male Caucasian, thirty-three, unmarried, no police record, no military service."

"Prints on file?"

"No. But then they wouldn't be, without the police, military, or Civil Service in his past."

Nudger felt weighted by disappointment. He'd hoped that Kell would have a police record with convictions hinting at or leading up to murder. He'd hoped Kell's prints would somehow match the smudged ones found in Jenine Boyington's apartment. These were the kinds of hopes that were bound to be dashed, but which Nudger seemed unable to cease embracing.

Hammersmith said, around a morning cigar, "Kell sheems sholid and waw-abiding." He puffed and wheezed repeatedly until the coarse tobacco was burning fiercely enough to trust not to go out in his desk ashtray. "Sorry, Nudge, the guy is a white-hat type."

"Not necessarily."

"Nothing is."

"Has the Major Case Squad come up with anything?"

Hammersmith chuckled. "Massey's as busy trying to placate the mayor and news media as he is trying to conjure up a reasonable suspect. Besides issuing not untrue statements and doing routine legwork, very little can be accomplished at this point. The idea is to quiet the clamor while gaining time for the machinery of the law to grind slowly and exceedingly fine."

"Makes sense," Nudger said.

"More sense than you're gonna like. Before we grind, we have to separate the wheat from the chaff. You're chaff, Nudge."

"There's not a grain of truth in that."

"Truth enough," Hammersmith said, puffing on his cigar. He exhaled loudly, maybe in an exasperated sigh. "Springer and Massey had a long talk about you. Springer thinks you should bow out of the case. Massey agrees. I wasn't consulted. That's a bureaucracy for you, Nudge."

"That's Springer for you."

"Yeah, he's a brass-knuckle political infighter, cutting down on the number of people who might get credit in the game he's playing. But why should you care; you're only trying to make a living." Hammersmith's tone left no doubt about what he thought of Leo Springer as a cop. "The thing is you've got no choice, Nudge. Bow out."

"I will," Nudger said, "as soon as I'm officially instructed."

"Fair enough. Springer's sent a couple of blue uniforms to your apartment and office to bring you in for a chat with him. A judicious use of manpower."

"Isn't it, though," Nudger said in disgust. "And just when I didn't want to be reined in."

"Sorry about this, Nudge. Life's a Popsicle with a sharp stick."

"And melting fast. I'll stay scarce. Thanks, Jack."

"For what?"

Hammersmith hung up abruptly. As far as he was concerned, the conversation hadn't occurred. He had a sane cop's knack of blanking out pieces of time. That's how a sane cop stayed sane.

Nudger handed the receiver to Claudia, who untangled the cord from around her arm and reached to the nightstand. Plastic clattered on plastic as she hung up the phone.

"Business call?" she asked, turning onto her side to face Nudger.

"The police are going to tell me to back away."

"What about Kell?"

"He doesn't have an arrest record. A solid citizen without blemish."

"Does that eliminate him as a suspect?"

"Not in my mind," Nudger said. "I saw the expression on his face while he was waiting for Jeanette Boyington in the mall. It was something more than lascivious, something more subtle and harder to read, but spooky."

"Maybe he was thinking of a lesser crime, like rape."

"Or maybe he was hungry and thinking about onion soup."

"That isn't spooky."

"You can say that, not being an onion."

"What are you going to do now?"

"Take you out for breakfast. Want to shower together?"

"Yes to breakfast, no to mutual shower."

She rotated on the mattress and stood up, her body a golden glimpse as she crossed a bright swirl of sunlight and left the room. A faucet handle squeaked, a water pipe rattled, and the shower began to hiss. Nudger patiently waited his turn.

From where Claudia lived, it was only a short drive to the riverfront. Nudger detoured through the brick-paved streets of Laclede's Landing and bought a morning *Globe*, then drove down a steep grade to the riverfront McDonald's.

He and Claudia sat at a deck table on the converted barge and watched the Mississippi roll by as they worried their Egg McMuffins. Nudger studied the newspaper for a few minutes. Hammersmith was right about the media's applying pressure. The suddenly discovered series of murders dominated the front page. Wily Captain Massey was quoted at length, saying absolutely nothing concrete yet somehow giving the impression that strides were being taken along the road to ultimate justice. A police artist had even whipped up a composite drawing of a suspect based on Grace Valpone's neighbors' description of a man they thought might have visited her occasionally. The drawing vaguely resembled Leo Springer, Nudger thought, and didn't look at all like Luther Kell. Not that it mattered. This suspect, if he even existed outside of police wishful thinking, would probably turn out to be a deliveryman or insurance adjuster. Or possibly Grace Valpone had had a fiancé *and* a male friend who hadn't killed her. Some women did.

Setting the folded paper aside, Nudger looked up to see that Claudia hadn't eaten any of her breakfast and was gazing at the dark, half-submerged humanesque forms of driftwood carried on the muddy current. She seemed to be staring into her own depths as well as those of the river.

"Is it that hypnotic?" Nudger asked.

Her body jerked and she looked up at him, interrupted from whatever she'd been thinking, wherever she had been. "I suppose it is," she said, turning back to the wide, sliding river. "Always on its way somewhere, doomed never to get there, like me."

"It's a strained analogy," Nudger told her. "I've never seen any barge traffic on you."

She smiled, nothing more than a twitch of her facial muscles, without humor. "Sorry, I didn't mean to be maudlin."

Nudger sipped his coffee and looked upriver to where the *Huck Finn*, an elaborate stern-wheeler excursion boat, was docked near the silver leap of the Arch. Beyond it, traffic was moving, distant and reflective, across Ead's Bridge into Illinois. A faraway tugboat whistle blasted a lilting note, like a sad warning. Nudger was afraid. He didn't understand the capricious dark wind that might at any time catch Claudia and carry her away from him.

"Are you okay?" he asked, resting his hand on her arm.

"Sure." She smiled again, this time maybe meaning it.

Nudger sat back and watched her try to eat. She managed a few small bites, then pushed the food away and concentrated on her coffee.

"Do you ever think about going back to teaching?" he asked.

"No, I haven't for a long time. I don't see why I should think about it. Anyway, I've got a job."

"You've got a profession, too."

"You mean I used to have a profession."

"I know a woman who's headmistress of a private girls' high school in the county. She owes me, or feels that she does. I could talk to her, see if there is or will be an opening to teach, ask her to interview you."

"I'd have to tell her the truth. Would *you* hire a convicted child abuser? A murderess? Someone who let her own daughter . . ."

"You didn't leave that window open on purpose, Claudia."

"My baby . . ." she said, simply and sadly, with a grief so vast her words seemed to echo in it. Her expression didn't change and her eyes remained dry; she was in a place beyond tears.

"You didn't deliberately cause Vicki's death," Nudger said firmly. "You should believe that. You have to believe it!"

"Sure. Dr. Oliver agrees with you. He used hypnosis, had me relive that night in my mind. But that was only in my mind."

"So is your guilt."

"Maybe all guilty people convince themselves of that."

"And maybe some who are innocent," Nudger said. "I'd hire you."

"Not if you wanted to keep *your* job. What would happen if the parents found out about my past?"

"Who knows? It might be rough, but maybe you could stick it out, with the proper backing. Enough of the faculty and parents might understand your situation and support you."

"Probably not."

"Then you'd lose your job. You'd get another job."

She bit her lower lip and studied Nudger with her dark, dark eyes. She'd artfully applied a lot of makeup around them, but cruel daylight confirmed that she'd been crying during the night. "Do you really think it's possible?" she asked.

"I can find out. I might be able to get you the interview, but from that point on you'd be carrying the ball on your own." He understood how important it was for her to feel that she'd be the one landing the job. "Do you want to teach again?"

She looked into her cup, then out again at the river that he knew was drawing her as it had drawn others. "Sometimes not at all," she said, "sometimes more than anything else." She raised her cup and sipped.

"Think about it," Nudger said. "Be sure before you let me know if you're interested. And remember, no guarantees. But a chance."

She stood up, leaned forward and kissed his forehead. Her lips were still warm from the coffee. "Thank you," she said, and walked away from the table, away from the cold, beckoning slide of the river.

Carrying his Egg McMuffin, Nudger caught up with her at the shore end of the wooden gangplank.

When they got back to Claudia's apartment building, she asked Nudger if he was coming upstairs. She had several hours before she had to be at Kimball's to help prepare for the lunchtime crowd. Nudger reluctantly declined. He was a workaday guy with responsibilities, he told her. She didn't seem to believe him. He kissed her. The Volkswagen was idling roughly, vibrating hard enough to jingle the keys dangling from the ignition switch. No place for a romantic tryst.

"Where are you going now?" she asked.

"To my office. Then to see if I can find out more about Luther Kell."

He didn't tell her what that entailed. If Kell was home, Nudger would wait for him to leave, then follow. If Kell had already left for work or wherever he went during the day, Nudger would make sure the house was unoccupied, then try to get inside and search for evidence pointing to Kell as a murderer. Illegal entry into the home of a possible killer was the sort of thing that frightened Nudger for a number of reasons; it was a game with a lot of ways to lose. But he had no choice. He hadn't much time to learn about Kell. Springer had seen to that.

Claudia kissed Nudger again, a slow, soft brush of her lips across his cheek, then got out of the car and closed the door without slamming it. Before walking away, she turned and leaned low to peer in at him through the open window.

"For both of us, will you be careful?" she asked.

"If you'll be careful for the same two people."

She nodded and stood up straight. Nudger shifted to first and pulled away from the curb. At the corner, when he checked in the rearview mirror, Claudia was gone.

TWENTY-SIX

"Ten thousand dollars," Agnes Boyington said to Nudger, sitting across from him in his office. She'd been waiting downstairs for him when he arrived, standing rigidly outside the doughnut shop, as if she'd rather endure the heat than enter.

Nudger swiveled thoughtfully in his chair and stared across the desk at her, trying to grasp what she was saying. Ten thousand dollars. One hundred C-notes. *Mucho dinero.* All those dead Presidents . . .

"My final offer," she added, setting her mouth in a straight, firm line.

"Oh, everyone says that," Nudger told her.

"To earn the money," Agnes reminded him, "you have only to do nothing and keep your mouth shut. I'm sure that for you the former will be easier than the latter."

"You're trying awfully hard to corrupt me, Boyington. To lead me down the primrose path."

"You've seen the primroses in all seasons." She got one of her long brown cigarettes from her purse, manipulated the never-fail lighter, and touched flame to tobacco. Tilting back her head so that she could gaze down her nose at him, she blew a cloud of smoke that hung together in an oddly grotesque shape which drifted toward the ceiling like a medium's ectoplasm. "What is your answer?"

"I don't mind if you smoke," he told her.

She exhaled another cloud of smoke, this one not so dense. He was getting to her. "Just what is it about my offer that bothers you, Nudger?"

"The fact that you made it, and that you keep increasing it. And that if I accept it, you'll have me at a permanent disadvantage. I wouldn't like that."

"Those are logical reservations, though based on unfounded suspicion. Anything else? No more consideration for your professional honor?"

"That, too. And something more. It bothers me that I don't understand why you're making the offer."

"I told you, Jeanette is under great stress. She isn't thinking clearly, or she wouldn't have hired you. I don't want her hurt more than she is already."

Nudger shook his head slowly, not looking away from Agnes Boyington. "I'm sorry, Agnes, I can't accept your explanation of motherly concern. It fits you about as well as a size ten hat."

Something crossed her face, momentarily altered the ice-gleam in her eyes. A reflection of pain. It surprised Nudger. It was like glimpsing human emotion in a reptile.

"To be honest, Nudger, I don't care about your assessment of me as a mother, except insomuch as it affects this matter. I love Jeanette dearly, more dearly than you can know." The expression of deep pain again, as if she were finally leveling with him and paying the price.

"What about Jenine?" Nudger asked. "Did you love her?"

"No." She smiled faintly at Nudger, from an icy distance. "I told you I was being honest. I knew Jenine, the way she lived, the things she did. She generated grief; all her life she was a burden and a stigma."

"Maybe you made her that way."

"No one made her that way. It was her inability to control her animalistic instincts that made Jenine what she was, that eventually led to her death. She was a sinner in the eyes of God and man."

"Her libido might have been much like yours," Nudger said, "only channeled in a different direction, a direction that harmed no one but herself."

"I'm not here to talk sophomoric psychology. I'm here to talk mathematics, coin of the realm."

Nudger placed both hands lightly, palms down, on the desk. From God to U.S. currency in less than a minute. It was dizzying. "I'm sorry, Agnes, but there are too many unknowns in the equation. I won't accept your offer."

Agnes Boyington stayed sitting very still in the chair before Nudger's desk. Then, with a subdued, steely vibrancy, she began to tremble. She was even paler than usual as she stared at Nudger, for an instant with pleading in her eyes, then with hate.

"You don't understand Jeanette as well as her own mother can," she said.

"I'm sure you're right."

"There's a great deal about this matter that you don't know."

"I'm a willing student. No one seems willing to teach me."

She stood up, tucked her purse beneath her arm, and glared down at Nudger. She'd stopped the faint trembling and had regained what appeared to be total control of herself. Nudger had to admit he was impressed by her as she stood over him in pale wrath like a well-preserved ice-queen and dropped cold, clipped words on him.

"I tried, Nudger, but you refused to listen, to be realistic. You've made a tragic course of events irreversible. If you forget everything else, remember that. What occurs from this point on might have been avoided if you had shelved your shabby idealism and done what was right for everyone concerned. Whatever happens now is on your head."

"Come off it, Agnes. I didn't open a tomb, I turned down a bribe."

She backed away a few steps, toward the door, and observed him as if suddenly he were miles away. She wouldn't attempt to buy him off anymore; he was sure of that. True to her word, she had made her final offer. She'd now accept what she couldn't understand. Money had talked, shabby idealism hadn't listened. That puzzled her, but in this instance that had been the undeniable outcome of her attempt to buy what she wanted. Life unaccountably worked that way sometimes. Mysterious circles.

"You'll be responsible," she said softly, as if to someone in the office other than the two of them. "As heaven is my witness!"

"Agnes, why don't you talk to Jeanette? Be honest with her?"

She disdainfully dropped her half-smoked cigarette on the bare office floor and ground it out with the pointed toe of her shoe. Without looking at Nudger, she opened the door and went out, leaving it open behind her. If he wouldn't talk sense, her brand of sense, then she wouldn't talk to him at all. So there. He heard her measured footfalls as she descended the stairs. The draft from the street door opening and closing rolled low across the office, stirring the ashes on the floor. He didn't like the look of those ashes, but then ashes seldom inspired.

Nudger was more worried than he had been, but he wasn't sure why. Possibly it was Agnes Boyington's mention of an irreversible tragic course of events. It seemed that she had turned a corner in her mind, and he had no way of knowing what street she was on or where she was going.

He shook his head as if to free himself from the after-scent of her tobacco smoke and disinfectant-like perfume, then stood up from behind the desk. He knew what street he should be on: Hartford Avenue.

After tossing the morning mail into the wastebasket and locking the office, he went downstairs and crossed Manchester to where his car was parked. The morning had been one of disturbing ambiguity. He longed for a problem he could grapple with and solve.

Trying not to think about Agnes Boyington and her ten thousand dollars, he drove toward the conservative, orderly neighborhood, the narrow, straight street, the neat little brick house of Luther Kell.

TWENTY-SEVEN

Nudger parked by a phone booth a few blocks from Kell's house. He left the Volkswagen's motor running as he entered the booth, fed in his twenty cents and dialed Kell's number. If Kell answered, Nudger was ready to see how he was fixed for magazine subscriptions.

Kell's phone rang ten times while Nudger leaned against the phone inside the hot metal booth and watched the traffic on Kingshighway. After the tenth ring, he left the receiver dangling out of sight, yanked closed the booth's folding doors behind him as he stepped outside, and drove to Kell's house.

He parked three houses down, slipped into his sport jacket, and tried to look like a pollster or Jehova's Witness as he walked with a sureness not felt toward the curlicued wrought-iron railing marking Kell's front steps. The antacid tablet he was chewing was dissolved except for its chalky residue on his tongue. His stomach moved and demanded another, which he promptly popped into his mouth as he unhesitatingly gripped the black railing and climbed the steps to Kell's front porch.

Even before he rang the doorbell, he could hear the telephone still jangling unanswered inside the house. He felt better now. He was sure Kell wasn't home. All he had to worry about was being unexpectedly interrupted. Or one of the neighbors seeing him as a suspicious character and phoning the police.

Nudger's Visa card with its carefully honed edge was ready in his shirt pocket. He nonchalantly withdrew it and fitted it between door and frame. The plastic made contact with the lock bolt, but met firm resistance. It took him only a few seconds to realize that the door was equipped with a dead bolt that wouldn't budge.

He backed away as if puzzled that no one had answered his ring, then he stood for a moment with his hands on his hips, as if innocently trying to decide what to do next. In feigned sudden resolve, he left the porch and walked along the side of the house to the backyard. It was all done with such accomplished acting that he almost hoped a neighbor was watching. John Wilkes Sleuth.

There was a chain-link fence around the yard, with a bulky padlock on the gate. Nudger saw no sign of a dog. He vaulted the fence and crossed to the back door. There was a screen door, which was locked. It took only half a minute and a minimum of trouble to slip that lock, but the main back door was like the front, equipped with a dead bolt and without windows.

Nudger knew he wasn't going to get inside without noise and dangerous long minutes, and in this neighborhood, where many residents were crime-conscious if not outright paranoid, he could afford little of either. He leaned to the side on the back porch and peeked through a window, through the narrow space between the frame and the drawn shade. If he could see inside the house, he might at least gain some impression of the man who lived there.

All he saw was a small, neat kitchen with a glossy green linoleum floor. A few of the furnishings were visible: a bare Formica table with metal legs, a high wooden stool, a smooth corner of a white refrigerator. The opposite window had a drawn shade, no curtains. He could hear the unanswered phone ringing more clearly here, reassuring him that Kell hadn't entered through the front door. But maybe Kell habitually came and went the back way.

Nudger's stomach growled something that sounded like "Get out!" He sensed that it was time to comply. Maybe past time.

A sudden breeze passed like a hot breath through the yard, rustling the leaves of the shrubbery by the fence as if there were something moving among them. Nudger hurried down off the porch.

He walked back toward the street the way he'd approached the house, with seeming casualness, noting that all of Kell's shades were lowered and that there were iron bars over the basement windows.

Sitting pondering in the sauna that was the Volkswagen, Nudger realized that all he'd learned was that Kell was very security-minded and kept a sanitary kitchen. But that was true of many of Kell's scrubby, conservative South St. Louis neighbors, who believed a pound of prevention was worth an ounce of cure, in battling bacteria or crime.

He started the car and drove farther down the street, then parked in the shade, in a spot where he could see the front of Kell's house in the rearview mirror. He settled back in the bucket seat to wait, always the dullest part of his job but a great instiller of the virtue of patience. Since it was one of his few virtues, he took pride in it.

*   *   *

After a while he moved to another spot from which he could watch the house. He didn't want to stay parked within sight of the same houses for too long, prompting a resident to wonder, worry, and phone the police to report a lurker in a Volkswagen.

At eleven-thirty Nudger went to lunch, ordering a carry-out hamburger at the diner on Kemper and Kingshighway, where he'd seen Kell yesterday. He'd allowed himself the faint hope that Kell would be there again today, but the only other customers were the summer students from the high school. It was tough catching up on classes during summer vacation. The thrust of their adolescent conversation was that they'd rather be someplace else. Welcome to the world, Nudger thought, juggling his coffee and hamburger and pushing out through the door.

He noticed that it had suddenly become cooler outside, and a line of dark clouds was closing in on the city from the west. Maybe rain on the way, maybe just show. Lightning flickered erratically out that way, like a celestial neon sign on the blink.

The hamburger was a culinary surprise. Better than franchise food. Nudger ate it one-handed as he drove to the phone booth from which he'd called Kell earlier.

The receiver was back on the hook. Someone else had used the phone, or some good citizen had noticed the dangling receiver and replaced it. Nudger hastily finished the last few bites of his hamburger and dialed Kell's number again. Still no answer. Still nobody home.

He folded the hamburger's waxed wrapper into fourths, placed it on the car's passenger seat, and brushed his hands together to rid them of salt and grease. Then he drove again to where he could watch Kell's military-neat brick house, parked, and leisurely sipped his coffee.

At ten minutes to three, when the coffee was only an acidic memory, a yellow station wagon pulled up in front of Kell's house and sat angled slightly toward the curb with its motor running. Luther Kell got out, said something casually to the car's driver, and the station wagon drove away.

Kell walked up the steps to his porch, jangling what looked like a ring of keys that he'd pulled from his pocket. He was wearing faded jeans and a sleeveless red T-shirt that emphasized the thickness of his sinewy arms. Maybe he was coming home from work, dressed as he was in summertime factory fashion. He keyed the unbeatable lock and disappeared into the house. The shades stayed lowered in Fort Kell.

Nudger felt better. Though another long round of waiting probably lay ahead, he at least knew Kell's exact whereabouts.

But this time the wait was a short one. Half an hour after Kell arrived home, he left again. He'd changed to dark dress slacks and a white shirt with the sleeves neatly turned up a few folds on his wrists. His long blond hair was carefully combed. He was walking fast, away from Nudger. It was the kind of walk that suggested a firm destination.

Nudger let him get a block ahead, then edged the Volkswagen away from the curb and followed. He drove around the block, waited a few minutes, and caught sight of Kell again at the corner.

Kell walked west on Arsenal toward Kingshighway. There was now an increasing eagerness in his stride; he crooked an arm and shot a glance at his wristwatch. When he reached the intersection, he crossed Arsenal and stood by the bench at the bus stop on the east side of Kingshighway.

Nudger made a right turn, drove a block past the stop, and pulled to the curb where he could still see Kell in his rearview mirror. An occasional droplet of rain softly patted the car's metal roof, or settled in a cool fleck on the back of Nudger's hand resting near the window.

Kell knew his bus schedules. Within five minutes a bus veered to the curb at the stop. It disgorged a few passengers from the rear door as Kell boarded through the front. The bus rumbled past Nudger, and he slipped the Volkswagen into gear and followed two car lengths behind.

This bus featured a cigarette advertisement below its rear window, an air-brushed photograph of a broadly smiling outdoorsy blond beauty who looked as if she could throw off lung cancer like a cold. This time Nudger memorized the company service number stenciled in neat black numerals high on the exhaust-darkened back of the bus. He didn't look again at the blonde.

When Kell got off the bus near where Highway 40 crossed Kingshighway, then transferred to the Cross County Express, Nudger suspected where he might be going.

Squinting through the rain-specked windshield, he followed the lumbering bus west beneath the low gray sky bent over them, toward the suburban land of mortgaged dreams and domestic delusion. And Twin Oaks Mall.

TWENTY-EIGHT

When they were half a mile from the mall, Nudger drove ahead of the bus and found a parking space in the main lot. Then he walked to the doorway of a shop that sold nothing but athletic shoes and stood where he could see the bus stop. He wondered how a place could stay in business selling only striped sneakers expensive enough to last forever.

The Cross Country Express lumbered around the corner by Sears, intimidated a few smaller vehicles into turning into intersecting parking lanes, and belched and hissed its way tentatively to a stop. Business was thriving at the mall today; over a dozen people stepped down out of the bus. The last one off was Luther Kell.

Kell stood still for a moment and looked around, as the bus emitted a noxious black cloud near him and eased away from the stop. Then he turned and went in through the mall's tinted-glass main entrance. Nudger noticed that Kell was wearing soft, black, crinkly leather moccasins. They were probably part of the reason the muscular blond man moved with such litheness and oddly ominous calm. Like the stillness before the storm.

Nudger followed, taking his time, sure of where Kell was going. Apparently the mall fountain was a favorite meeting place for people on the nightlines. Kell had probably talked on the lines last night and made a date with another woman. Unless Nudger was making false assumptions. He'd be disappointed if Kell simply shopped around for a while and then returned home with some new socks and shirts. For that matter, what was Nudger supposed to do if Kell did meet a woman here? She might be his regular girlfriend. Surely the man didn't murder every woman he dated. Possibly he had murdered no one, ever.

Kell slowed his pace as he approached the fountain, moving toward the center of the wide promenade, into the calm area between the thick streams of shoppers making their way to one end of the mall or the other. He ambled over to the raised concrete ledge that circled the gently splashing fountain, propped one foot up on the ledge, and began slowly rotating a toothpick between his front teeth. Sandy the vinyl-clad cowboy had picked his teeth in the same manner while waiting here. Déjà vu, Nudger thought.

Kell rotated the toothpick, absently rolling it between thumb and forefinger, for quite a while, then began diligently probing molars with it. Mr. Tooth Decay was no friend of his.

This time Kell wasn't stood up. Within ten minutes a long-haired brunette wearing a navy-blue skirt and red blazer walked up to him and they chatted briefly. Then she snaked her arm around his and walked away with him.

Nudger watched them stroll toward the mass of shoppers moving toward the east end of the mall.

Now what? Should he follow? Were Kell and the woman leaving the mall, or were they going to have a sandwich at the Woolworth snack counter and take in the mall theater movie? Or browse through merchandise at one of the department stores? Might they be shopping for her wedding gown? Possible. Shouldn't a model citizen like Kell, with a neat little house, have a neat little wife to go in it? Was all of this any of Nudger's business?

Of course not.

Unless . . .

He began walking in the direction Kell and the woman had taken. He could still see Kell's blond head, catch an occasional glimpse of the woman's flowing auburn hair and her red blazer.

Just as he reached the fountain, Nudger realized that, though he'd only glimpsed her from the back, there was something faintly familiar about the woman. About the compact, controlled way she swung her arms when she walked, and the way she carried herself, so smoothly and erectly.

An after-image flashed in Nudger's mind.

Her shoes! The dark-haired woman had been wearing high-heeled silver shoes with black bows! Like the shoes Nudger's former wife Eileen had worn. Like . . .

Like Jeanette Boyington's shoes!

Nudger sucked in his breath and plunged forward, skirting the fountain at a run to gain ground on Kell and the woman.

His leather soles scraped wildly on the synthetic stone floor and he did a mad little dance, almost losing his balance, as a weighty hand fell on his shoulder and stopped him as if his knees had suddenly locked tight.

"I been watching you, Nudger," a deep, thick voice said. "Mrs. Boyington says it's time me 'n' you had a little talk 'n' settled some things 'n' . . .

Nudger barely heard the rest. Hugo Rumbo, wearing a hideous green plaid sport jacket that made him appear even more gigantic than he was, prattled on about Agnes Boyington. The timing and setting for this encounter were absurd as well as inconvenient. Nudger didn't even have it in him to be afraid.

Rumbo came around in front of Nudger, moving closer, a gaudy muscular expanse of cloth. He was still babbling threateningly. "So whyn't you 'n' me take a little walk 'n' you can . . ."

Nudger squirmed loose from the painful grip and shoved hard at Rumbo's chest, slipping and falling to his knees with the effort. It was like trying to move a wall. Rumbo said, "Huh?" in delayed surprise, got his feet tangled with each other, and the backs of his knees struck the concrete ledge around the fountain. There was a tremendous splash. Nudger felt cold water on his face as he struggled to his feet and started after Kell and Jeanette. He saw people stopping, turning, gawking at the spectacle in the fountain pool, and caught a glimpse of what looked like a floundering green plaid whale, as he began to run.

He shoved his way through the mass of shoppers, hearing a heavyset woman grunt as his elbow sank into her doughy midsection. He stepped on somebody's toes, stumbled, nearly fell. Someone cursed at him as he ran past the drugstore: "Goddamn maniac! Gonna kill somebody!"

He stopped running outside a men's shop, jumped up on a bench and stared out over the heads of hundreds, maybe thousands, of milling shoppers. Everyone with a dollar to spend seemed to be here. Almost everyone.

Kell and Jeanette were nowhere in sight.

He dropped from the bench and ran for the escalators that led up to the second shopping level or down to the parking garage, trying to catch a glimpse of a red blazer or silver high-heeled shoes. All he got were curious amused stares directed at him by the lines of escalator riders gliding past with the calm, smooth precision of ducks in a shooting gallery. Nudger ignored the stares and sprinted for the exit to the lot where he'd left his car.

He drove the Volkswagen to the largest parking area driveway and pulled to the side, hoping to see Jeanette's blue sedan from where he was illegally parked.

Dozens of cars were streaming in and out of the lot, none of them Jeanette's. Nudger popped an antacid tablet into his mouth and chewed frantically, still breathing hard. His pulse pounded at his temples.

Five slow minutes passed. Nothing in the world changed.

Screwed it up, he told himself. Screwed up everything. He had a client who was on her way to kill an innocent man. Or kill a guilty man. Or be murdered herself. Whichever way fate moved the pieces, it was going to be a bad day for a lot of people.

Nudger squirmed in the little bucket seat. His stomach was zooming and twisting like a crazy carnival ride; his blood felt carbonated. He had to act, had to do something!

He restarted the engine, drove from the driveway and around the block, barely avoiding three accidents, his eyes in constant motion in a face immobile and stiff with concern.

He circled the vast mall twice, but he saw nothing other than red at his own stupidity for not realizing Jeanette might wear a dark wig and alter her appearance enough so her sister's murderer wouldn't recognize her.

Until she wanted him to know her.

Nudger yanked the steering wheel to the right, jerking the Volkswagen sharply to the curb, and sat while the idling engine perked rapidly, calling him a *dupe*! *dupe*! *dupe*! He couldn't agree more.

It occurred to him then that Jenine Boyington had been murdered in her apartment. Like Grace Valpone and Susan Merriweather. Like the women before them. If that was the killer's MO, it followed that Kell and Jeanette's next stop, if Kell had committed the murders, would be Jeanette's apartment. Unless they stopped somewhere for something to eat or a few get-acquainted drinks. Or unless Jeanette was crazy enough to try something in the mall parking lot or in a moving car.

Nudger slammed the Volkswagen into gear, stamped on the accelerator and shot back out into the flow of traffic. Horns were still blasting behind him as he veered onto the highway entry ramp and drove toward Jeanette's apartment.

Her door was locked. Nudger stood in the quiet third-floor hall of Jeanette's apartment building with his hand on the knob. A radio or TV was playing, very faintly, from the floor above. He breathed in through his nose. There was a damp scent in the corridor, and in one of the nearby apartments someone was cooking what smelled like vegetable soup. He pressed his ear to the cool, varnished door. He could hear nothing from inside.

After glancing around to make sure he was alone, he swallowed the fuzzy, square lump of fear in his throat and worked for a few minutes with the honed edge of his Visa card. The lock was a typical cheap apartment special. It slipped easily.

In everyone's life there are doors that shouldn't be opened. Though he suspected this might be that kind of door, he slowly rotated the knob and pushed inward.

The door swung open smoothly, scraping lightly on the carpet. Nudger was confronted by a low black vinyl sofa, modern glass-topped end tables, large chrome-framed indecipherable prints on white walls. There was a coldness and peculiar lack of color in the decor, and an almost geometrical neatness about the place. Curios were precisely arranged on glass shelves, and the few books in a white bookcase looked as if they had been bought yesterday and never read. Nudger was surprised to see that one of the curios was a blown-glass, artfully fashioned man and woman locked in blissful sexual intercourse. It didn't seem to fit with the surrounding souvenir-shop bric-a-brac. He checked the titles on the books, finding they were all of the vague and innocuous sort found in display furniture in department stores. Outdated sociology, regional history, obscure biography. The books were there for color, not content.

Nudger was alone. He knew immediately by the perfect stillness and staleness of the air that the apartment was unoccupied. Jeanette and Kell had either stopped somewhere before coming here or were due to arrive momentarily. If they were coming here at all. Nudger began to have his doubts. Or maybe his fear was finally catching up with his desire to intercept and face Kell. Maybe he wanted to doubt.

Natural to be apprehensive, he told himself, and thumbed several antacid tablets from the roll he kept in his shirt pocket. He tossed the tablets into his mouth like peanuts.

Chewing demonically, he closed and locked the door. That chased away the vegetable-soup scent that had followed him in, and he felt better. He walked around the apartment quickly to make doubly sure it was unoccupied, cautiously opening doors and poking his head into each room like a turtle exploring outside its shell.

When he checked the white-tiled bathroom, something stopped him and made him step inside.

The bathroom appeared antiseptically clean and unused, as if the apartment were vacant and displayed for rental inspection. In an instant he knew why. The shower curtain had been removed, its plastic hooks lined neatly along one end of the chromed rod. There were no towels on the racks, no rug on the hard tile floor.

As Nudger turned, he saw in the vanity mirror the partly opened door of the linen closet. The closet was stocked with cosmetics and folded towels and washcloths, and on its floor lay something black and glossy. Wet-looking.

He opened the door all the way, caught a glimpse of bare metal against the black, and drifted backward in spiraling horror.

A thick plastic drop cloth was neatly folded on the closet floor. On it were stacked several equally thick black plastic trash bags. On top of the trash bags lay a shiny new hacksaw and a wood-handled meat cleaver. They weren't there as bath accessories.

Nudger swallowed with a gurgling, cracking sound and left the bathroom, heading for the telephone in the living room. His discovery was more than he could cope with alone. Much more.

He had lifted the receiver and punched out two digits of Hammersmith's Third District number when he heard a slight scuffling noise in the outside hall.

The door burst open and Jeanette was propelled inside.

TWENTY-NINE

She skidded to a stop six feet into the room and stood with her arms raised shoulder-high and extended sideways, as if to keep her balance while poised on a high, narrow ledge. Jeanette's dark wig was askew, drooping low over one eye, and the eye that was visible was icy and inhuman.

Kell followed her inside with his lithe, confident swagger. He was smiling his barbaric little smile and holding a small nickle-plated automatic. Obviously he was a two-weapon man; the gun to frighten and order his victims into their bathtubs, the knife to operate on them at his sadistic leisure. Nudger wondered through his shock if Kell suspected that this tub had been especially reserved for him.

Kell looked at Nudger in surprise, his body still and tense, a wild and dangerous animal confronting danger, calculating on intinct. Then his pale eyes quickly adjusted and his subtle, scary smile was back. "I thought you lived alone," he said to Jeanette. "Didn't you tell me that in the car, bitch?" It was more than Nudger had heard him say on the phone. His voice was soft but with a nasty flat twang that Nudger placed as southwest Missouri Ozark. A mountain man.

"He's a friend," Jeanette explained. "His name's Nudger." She removed the dark wig and flung it angrily away, as if it were an animal that had snapped at her. Her own blond hair was tucked up with bobby pins where it wasn't standing out in wild tufts. Her eyebrows were somehow different, darker and arched higher on her forehead. She looked almost as terrifying as Kell, whose smile took on an even crueler cast.

"I bet you got lotsa friends," he said. He emphasized the "friends," so there was no doubt he didn't mean backgammon partners.

Jeanette ignored him and glared at Nudger as if everything wrong with the world were his fault. "It should have worked," she said. "I didn't think he'd pull a gun in the hall. I thought he'd wait and use a knife." Her voice took on a whiny tone, as if she'd been cheated. "He always used a knife!"

"I ain't gonna disappoint you," Kell said. "You're my type to cut up with."

"I knew I would be," she answered, without a sign of fright.

Nudger knew what she meant. Kell had gone after her sister, so while the dark wig and altered makeup would prevent him from recognizing his previous victim's twin and being alerted to danger, he'd still find Jeanette to his liking. Wouldn't any man, if he didn't know her?

Kell swung his gaze, and the gun, toward Nudger, who was still standing in shock holding the phone. Nudger tasted old metal in his mouth. It wasn't his fillings, it was the coppery taste of fear.

Kell cat-footed closer, keeping the gun leveled at Nudger's quivering midsection. Nudger's nervous energy reached critical mass, *had* to explode! "Put the phone down, pardner."

Nudger did. On Kell's head.

Kell yelped and the gun dropped to the carpet. A huge hand clamped around Nudger's throat, held him until its powerful mate could join it. In a paroxysm of fright, he clubbed Kell's blond head with the plastic receiver. Smashed down again and again! It seemed to have no effect. He could smell Kell's sour, hot breath, hear his own rasping struggle for air. He tried to shove the larger and stronger man away, and they both fell. The hard gun dug into Nudger's hip, sending a needle shower of pain down his right leg. Kell's hands retained their iron, unyielding strength, squeezing, digging . . .

Nudger felt his eyes bulging as his vision clouded with a thousand tiny red explosions. The room was tilting, swaying to slow dance music he couldn't hear. So this is how it is, he thought, at the still, hollow core of his panic. So this is death.

Then, without realizing how it had happened, he had the telephone cord wrapped around Kell's neck and was pulling it tight. Tighter! With a strength that seemed to generate from a point outside his body. It was *not* his turn to die! He wouldn't let it be! This was *years* too soon!

Kell's robotlike grip loosened slightly. Loosened again. Nudger called again on the strength of raw desperation, twisting the cord so tight he thought it might break. He heard muted, flesh-muffled cracking sounds, like tiny foam-wrapped firecrackers going off in a string.

Kell gagged violently and released Nudger, rolling away, the receiver dangling from his thick neck.

Nudger drew a shrieking, reviving breath and fumbled around behind him for the gun.

It was gone.

He looked up to see Jeanette holding it, waving it from one man to the other. Her wide blue eyes were wild with a sub-zero merciless glint. How she wanted to squeeze the trigger!

Kell, on his knees, still wearing his telephone-cord leash and collar, stared up at her in terror. His flat, deadpan face seemed incapable of containing such emotional intensity; its flesh undulated tautly, as if restraining great internal pressure. "Please, don't let her shoot me!" he pleaded with Nudger, not for a millisecond looking away from Jeanette. His voice was a croaking parody of itself.

"You killed my sister, and now I'm going to kill you!" Jeanette hissed, her jaws locked by fury. Her back was arched tightly with the rigidity of her rage; she was electrified with hate. "I'm going to kill both of you! I'm going to kill all the men I can find, before they kill me again!"

"Hey, listen!" Kell implored frantically, actually quaking now with terror. "I'll pay you to let me go, pay you plenty!" Spittle flew with the force of his plea. He recognized the nearness and implacability of death. He'd had experience.

"Every man I can find," Jeanette was crooning. "You're all rotten, rotten, rotten . . ."

A dreamy look clouded her eyes. The movement of the gun barrel back and forth from one man to the other slowed. She was ready for blood.

The dark eye of the barrel steadied at Nudger. He was first.

Jeanette spread her feet and tensed to absorb the gun's recoil.

Just then Nudger saw a representative of his much-maligned gender slip quietly through the door behind Jeanette. Knowing his face was registering what he was seeing, Nudger tried to look away and dim the desperate hope in his eyes. He couldn't do it.

Not that it mattered. Jeanette was possessed by her own dark world, and there was nothing in that world but the gun and Kell and Nudger and Death.

And right now Death was in charge.

Hammersmith glided as smoothly and silently toward her as one of those fat helium-filled balloons in the Macy's Thanksgiving Day parade. And he seemed to move about as fast. Nudger was close to screaming.

Jeanette was smiling. She leaned slightly toward Nudger. He thought she was going to say something, but she only licked her lips.

She hadn't the faintest idea Hammersmith was there until his wide pink hand closed on her fist clenching the gun and shoved it toward the carpet. She gave a low whine as Hammersmith squeezed hard.

Then her body sagged, drained by abrupt realization. What she had planned hadn't worked, couldn't work. It was over. Hammersmith calmly removed the gun with his free hand and slipped it into his pocket.

The blue uniforms streamed in then. Kell was jerked to his feet and frisked, revealing a long-bladed pocketknife with a yellowed bone handle. Jeanette stood quietly, her eyes wide and vacant, staring into cold distances beyond the apartment walls. Pain was already becoming resignation.

A Homicide plainclothesman hauled out a dog-eared card and read Kell and Jeanette their rights. They both stood unmoving, deaf to the carefully worded legalese. Neither of them looked back as they were steered from the apartment.

Nudger caught a glimpse of silver high-heeled shoes with black bows, of smooth trim ankles, during the momentary shuffling at the door. Then he heard policemen and prisoners move away down the hall.

Everything had become very controlled and efficient when Hammersmith arrived. Order had been wrought from chaos, in a routine, choreographed manner. Nudger was as impressed as he was grateful and bewildered.

"I could have sworn I didn't complete my call for help to you," he said, struggling up from where he sat on the carpet. The words came out as if they'd been strained through ground glass. His throat and the side of his neck were on fire. He felt a stiffness around his Adam's apple, as if he needed to swallow but couldn't.

"It wasn't you we charged in here to rescue," Hammersmith said. He fired up one of his abominable cigars with a connoisseur's quiet relish. "After our earlier conversation, I assigned a man to watch Jeanette Boyington. He didn't recognize her when she slipped out wearing her dark wig; had her confused with another woman who'd worn a hat going in. But when he finally realized what had happened, he phoned in and we rushed over here for the same reason you no doubt did. There was only one man Jeanette Boyington would want to disguise herself to meet, and this apartment figured to be their eventual destination. Our man stayed in place and saw you, and later the man and the Boyington woman, enter the building. We got here shortly after that. I guess you noticed we were almost too late."

"It hadn't escaped me," Nudger said in his new, hoarse voice.

Hammersmith puffed on the cigar and exhaled a cloud of noxious fumes, smiling through the greenish haze. The apartment would never be the same: Hammersmith was like a dog that had to mark its territory with a foul scent.

"You were right about twins," Nudger said, "about Jeanette's craving for revenge. Look in the bathroom closet. She was going to convert Luther Kell to pre-packaged meat."

Hammersmith looked. When he came back he was gazing musingly at his cigar. "It's a nice change in this job, to prevent a murder instead of investigating one," he said. He puffed, exhaled. "Two murders, actually. And colorful ones at that."

Nudger's mind flashed a slide of the black plastic trash bags and shining hacksaw and cleaver. The thing that had been fluttering in his stomach suddenly sprang claws and dug them in. Automatically he reached for his roll of antacid tablets, nimbly peeling back the foil with his thumbnail.

"Alive though you are," Hammersmith said, "you'll have a tough time collecting your fee."

"That doesn't seem important at the moment," Nudger said.

"It will, though." Hammersmith squinted at him, then motioned with the cigar. "You better have that neck looked at. Guy try to choke you?"

"Tried hard."

"Never know about those things. Lots of tender cartilage in the neck, little bones. Promise me you'll have it looked at?"

"Sure."

Hammersmith smiled his jowly smile. "The tech teams are on the way here, Major Case Squad, news media, everybody. In their numbers will be Leo Springer. We need your statement, say tonight, after you've had a chance to pull yourself together, get your story straight. I'm going downstairs and make some calls. It wouldn't be a bad idea for you to leave. On your own, you understand."

Nudger nodded.

Hammersmith flicked ashes on the carpet and glided out. He left the apartment door open. Nudger could see a blue uniform sleeve outside in the hall.

He jumped as something at his feet buzzed at him like a rattlesnake.

It was the damaged phone, its shattered receiver still off the hook. He picked it up with the futile idea of answering it, knowing he probably should leave it untouched for the print man and photographer, and it gave another dying rattle and was silent and useless. He started to replace it on an end table.

Instead he stood holding it, staring at its base, before finally setting it back down on the floor.

He raked clawed fingers through his tousled hair and drew a deep breath that seared his bruised windpipe. Suddenly he wanted to get as far away as possible from Jeanette's apartment. He wanted to run, but he walked.

At the open door he paused, leaning with a palm pressed high against the doorjamb, and glanced back. His gaze again fell on the phone, and he thought about all the late-night talkers and dreamers, all the agony and loneliness transformed to electronic impulses and sent out over the nightlines, seeking connections, searching for solace of whatever fashion. He thought about blown-glass erotica and a cold, agonized twin who was driven to attempted murder.

He walked out into the hall, nodding at the blue uniform on guard, and made his way unsteadily toward the stairs, wishing the damned building would stay still. There was somewhere else he had to go this evening, and Hammersmith was right; he needed rest and time to think before talking with the police, before walking the high tightrope that Leo Springer was sure to place him on.

There would be no net below.

THIRTY

Night hadn't fallen, but it was teetering, when Nudger turned the Volkswagen into the driveway of Agnes Boyington's fashionable white brick home in the central west end. In the dusk the house appeared even larger. The wide lawn, still damp from the afternoon rain, had been mowed recently and was rich with the sweet, pungent scent of summer. Deepening shadows softened the symmetrically manicured slope of the grounds. Lindell Boulevard didn't seem to be there at all beyond the spreading, sheltering oaks and maples. The area surrounding the Boyington house had about it the atmosphere of a groomed golf course.

When Nudger parked the Volkswagen near the columned front porch and got out, locusts in the nearby trees trilled like crickets, only deeper, more hoarsely. Katydids, children called them, mimicking their urgent rattling buzzing. The locusts existed noisily and briefly after long hibernation, then died and left behind only their dry husks. Nudger knew people who had done that.

As he stepped up onto the porch, he saw that there was a lamp burning at one of the front windows. Disdaining the brass knocker this time, he rang the doorbell, hearing chimes toll faintly inside. He waited for what seemed like five full minutes before Agnes Boyington came to the door.

She was wearing tight black slacks and a ribbed white sweater adorned with heavy gold chains. Her hair was rigidly engineered, as if she'd just returned from a beauty parlor. Earrings that matched the chains gathered and gave light as she moved her head. Nudger wondered if she'd been notified of Jeanette's arrest.

"It's time for us to talk," he said.

She studied him in the faint light, gazing at him as if he were a trespassing dandelion on the unbroken plane of green behind him. Finally she said, as if it were an order, "Come in, Nudger."

He entered, closing the door behind him, and followed Agnes Boyington through the hall and into an impeccably decorated, high-ceilinged room with pale, tiny-print wallpaper. There were soft blue chairs and a sofa with lots of light wood trim, and a dainty antique secretary desk with elegantly curved legs, just inside the door. The plush carpet was dead white and might have been laid yesterday.

"Sit down," Agnes Boyington said, pointing to a straight-backed chair with a modicum of upholstery. It seemed a device contrived by sadists.

Nudger sat. He was even more uncomfortable than he thought he'd be, but he made the most of it, scooting down and extending his legs, crossing his ankles. The chair creaked softly beneath his weight and then was quiet, as if afraid of being reprimanded for complaining. It was that kind of room.

Agnes paced to an advantageous position near the secretary and faced Nudger with the poise and presence of a stage actress. "I know about Jeanette," she said. "The police notified me this afternoon."

"How much did they tell you?"

"That she was being held for brandishing a deadly weapon."

"As soon as the prosecutor hears the facts," Nudger said, "the charge will be attempted murder."

"Oh? Murder of whom?"

"Didn't you talk to Jeanette?"

"No. I intend to do so in the morning, with my—her lawyer."

"She was going to kill someone named Luther Kell, the man who murdered your other daughter. I happened along. She was also going to kill me, as a bonus."

Agnes pursed her lips and tilted her head sideways, as if thinking over what Nudger had said, not liking it, but not disliking it all.

"I figured out some things," Nudger told her, watching her closely. He could hear the locusts screaming away their lives outside.

"That's your job, figuring out," Agnes Boyington said.

"Would you like to hear how well I've done my job?" Without

waiting for an answer, he continued. "When Jeanette was out of her head with rage, about to squeeze the trigger, she said something about killing all the men she could. '. . . Before they kill me again,' she said."

"Not surprising, if she was as hysterical as you describe."

"No, but it caused me to recall some things about her, like her familiarity with her dead sister's apartment the day she and I went there to search it. And the expensive but uncharacteristic piece of blown-glass erotica on the curio shelf in her apartment."

"Erotica?"

"Then, when I was about to leave her apartment last night, I happened to see a nightline number scratched on the base of her phone, the number Jenine had used, scratched on the bottom of her phone in exactly the same manner."

"Nightline number?" Agnes's voice was up an octave, oddly plaintive. Something in her was bending, and must break.

"Such a lot of questions," Nudger said. "You know what I'm talking about. Obviously, I was meant to find that number in Jenine's apartment when Jeanette took me there to search. The police hadn't found it because it had been scratched on the base of Jenine's phone *after* they searched the apartment."

The squareness of Agnes Boyington's deceptively youthful carriage melted. Her shoulders were slumped, narrow, and bunched. Her right hand flexed spasmodically and knotted into a fist around her thumb.

"How did you get the idea?" Nudger asked. "How did it happen?"

She sat down on the uncompromising sofa across from Nudger, a middle-aged widow by lamplight. To see her age that way, almost with the rapidity of movie magic, depressed Nudger.

Her voice was a defeated monotone now, lacking entirely the cold fire and authority of only five minutes ago. "Two months ago Jenine made an appointment on the nightlines with a man—Luther Kell, as I've learned today. Kell was alone with her in her apartment, but someone interrupted them. They made another date; Jenine gave Kell a key and he was to let himself in and wait for her to arrive home the next evening. But Jeanette dropped by unexpectedly to visit her sister. Kell arrived, assumed she was Jenine, and murdered her." Agnes drew a deep breath and thrust out her chin. "My slain daughter is Jeanette."

Nudger felt a melancholy satisfaction. He had figured things right, but it was as if he'd lost something in the process. Kernel of wisdom, kernel of sadness. He was familiar with the sensation.

"Jeanette was dead," Agnes continued. "Nothing could alter that. But why couldn't tragedy also be opportunity? Jeanette's death was a chance for Jenine to shake free of her sinful past. The twins had done everything together, gone to the same schools, acquired the same meager skills, so it was simple for Jenine to slip into Jeanette's itinerant part-time office work; and Jeanette hadn't lived long in her apartment, so it was easy for Jenine to begin living there as Jeanette without attracting suspicion." She dropped her gaze and frowned in annoyance. "If only she'd listened to her mother! I figured out everything for her, every minuscule detail! If only she'd listened!"

"Jenine wanted something more," Nudger said, "something you might not understand. She loved her twin sister, felt as one flesh with her. She identified with Jeanette to a greater extent than either of you had planned. The masquerade was complete; a part of her became her murdered twin, breathing and walking around. She wanted revenge."

"Yes," Agnes said, "revenge." She stared at the white carpet. "But that posed problems. The double of the victim is handicapped in searching for the killer. And any radical change in Jenine's appearance would have caused the neighbors—Jeanette's neighbors—to look closely at her, requiring explanations and making her impersonation of Jeanette more difficult. Jenine realized this. She realized she had to hire someone like you."

"Someone to be her bird dog," Nudger said, "to track down and point out her twin's killer without arousing his suspicion. When I told her about following and losing Kell the day she was to meet him, she decided it was time to act on her own. She talked to him again on the nightlines, without my knowledge, and made another appointment. She didn't anticipate me following Kell to where she was to meet him in her disguise, meet him wearing a dark wig and makeup to obscure her resemblance to her dead twin."

Agnes said nothing, still staring at the spotless white field of carpet.

The identity switch would have worked, Nudger realized, except for the power of Jenine's obsession to avenge Jeanette's death, for which she must have felt responsible. And it would have worked if Agnes Boyington had been able to buy or scare him off the case and prevent him from running Kell to ground.

And there was more. Something was bothering him, something darkly laughing and obscene.

"How much did you know," Nudger asked, "about what Jenine had planned for tonight?"

Agnes raised her head high and her eyes glinted in the lamplight with their old brittle disdain. If she was in league with the devil, the devil had better watch out. "Everything!" she snapped.

Nudger felt his breath leave him, his stomach contract. It was true, then. He hadn't really expected this, even from Agnes Boyington.

"You!" she said accusingly. "When you wouldn't be reasonable and drop the case, I had no choice but to change tactics. So you might well blame yourself for what's happened!"

For an instant Nudger felt a rush of guilt, almost buying her twisted perspective. Then, "No," he said. And unbelievingly, "How could you let your own daughter sink into this?"

"Jenine didn't take advantage of her opportunity after Jeanette's death, Nudger. The opportunity I gave her. She fell into her old sinful ways, began seeing men, virtual strangers. Doing . . . things with them! I know; I had Hugo Rumbo follow her, report to me. Everything."

"And you had Rumbo follow me. When he stopped me at the mall today, he was really trying to prevent me from following Jenine and Kell."

"Of course he was!" Agnes Boyington said, as if Nudger were a slow study and she was becoming impatient. "And on my orders. I knew where Jenine and Kell were going, and what she was going to do—or he was. It was the kind of life Jenine lived that killed Jeanette. I gave Jenine a chance to straighten out her life, to recapture purity—"

"To become Jeanette," Nudger interrupted. "For you."

"Yes! Of course! And when she turned her back on decency and respectability, what choice had I left? She visited death upon her own

sister with her sin and negligence. And when she failed her test with
God, I planned on letting her live only long enough to avenge
Jeanette's murder!"

"You really do believe in God," Nudger said incredulously. But he
knew he shouldn't be incredulous. The damnedest people quoted the
Bible. And, if it suited them, the Constitution and Rod McKuen.

"Of course I believe in Him. Don't you?"

"I don't think so," Nudger said. "I'm not sure I want to."

He understood now. Understood more than Agnes would approve.
Agnes had used Jenine as Jenine had used Nudger, to find Jeanette's
killer, the man who had dared to violate *Agnes* by invading her ordered world and murdering her pure daughter. She intended to let the
soiled-beyond-redemption Jenine perhaps meet the same fate as her
twin, before she herself would enter the apartment and exercise her
own righteous revenge on Kell. Or on Jenine. Whoever was the sur-
vivor. It was the puritanical Agnes who had prepared the bathroom
for butchery. She was the woman in the hat who'd confused Hammersmith's man watching for Jeanette. Probably she'd left the building when he was phoning Hammersmith. She had been waiting
outside the apartment, but she hadn't entered when she'd seen
Nudger, then the police, arrive.

There were depths to Agnes Boyington, and depths and depths. If
she was capable of planning the murder and dismemberment of her
own daughter . . .

Nudger didn't move. Suspicion drifted into his mind through doors
suddenly sprung open; awareness bloomed from memory: the momentary whiff of the mingled, distinctive scents of cigarette tobacco
and perfume that clung to a room long after Agnes had left it, the
way death clung. The killer who wore gloves; the murder that never
quite fit. *How likely is it that a woman engaged to be married?* . . .
He didn't want to believe it, but it wouldn't go away.

"You killed Grace Valpone," he said, finding the revelation left
him short of breath.

He'd surprised Agnes. She tilted her head back and to the side in
the Boyington manner. Her wary eyes registered confusion. Then a
new respect for Nudger flared in them like a fierce, cold light.

"What you did to her," Nudger said softly. "What you did with the knife. I mean, how could you? What sort of monster lives in your skin?"

"The sort that does what is necessary. The Valpone murder, done the way it was, proved necessary. It was what a man would do."

"You killed Grace Valpone because of her dissimilarities to your daughters," Nudger said, "because she was older, led a different kind of life. You murdered her because she wasn't a talker on the night-lines, and if she became a victim in the series of murders, her death would lead the police away from the lines as a factor in the bathtub slayings, away from Jenine's nightline conversations and meetings with men. Away from closer investigation and the discovery of Jeanette's true identity. From stigma reflected on you. But where did you know her from? What was she to you?"

"Why, nothing. A stranger."

An icy sea engulfed Nudger, stunning him. "You murdered a complete stranger?"

"I murdered the Valpone woman precisely because she *was* a stranger," Agnes said. "So there would be no personal connection between us and thus no apparent motive. I chose her name from the list of recent marriage licenses in the *Daily Record*. If she was going to be married, she'd hardly be talking on the nightlines as Jenine had. I eavesdropped on her life to make sure she suited my purpose, then I killed her in the manner of the nightline women's murders. She might have been anyone. I simply wanted to alter the pattern of the murders, but not so much that they still wouldn't be tied together in the minds of the police. That way the investigation would be diverted away from the nightlines. It didn't have to be Grace Valpone. It was nothing personal."

Nudger realized he was squeezing the arms of his chair. *Nothing personal.* He was in the almost palpable presence of genuine evil; evil found out, unmasked, *real.* He was awed.

"The police will piece this together," he said, "from what Jenine will tell them, from what I'll tell them."

"And from what I'll tell them," Agnes Boyington said. "Do you think anything really matters to me now? My daughters are shamed, one of them is dead, everything I've existed for is dirty, dirty, part now of your soiled and grimy world. Do you think what happens now actually makes a difference?"

"Not to you, I suppose it doesn't," Nudger said. But he knew better. He knew her. She would think about it. She was a fighter, and she'd pull on her white gloves and see her lawyer and make denials; she'd make whatever moves she had. Which in today's crazy-quilt legal system might be enough to let her walk away from the game free.

He looked at her.

She looked at him.

"I have always done what I must in this world," she said firmly.

Nudger went to the white phone on the secretary desk and dialed Hammersmith's number. He told him, briefly, the nature of the deception and the true identity of his female prisoner.

Then he hung up the phone and sat quietly with Agnes Boyington in her calm, ordered home, listening to the hoarse screaming of the locusts, and waiting for the police.

THIRTY-ONE

By the time they let Nudger leave Headquarters it was just past dawn. The wavering orange sun hadn't yet burned off the haze of pollutants that had drifted across the river from the heavy industry on the east side, obscuring the graceful curve of the Arch above the downtown skyline. He crossed to the City Hall lot, where his car was parked, and sat behind the steering wheel for a minute before starting the engine.

Springer had prodded and goaded, and cracked the whip of the law, sending him through smaller and smaller hoops with the skill of a practiced interrogator. But Nudger had passed through them all. Finally, with the usual instruction to stay available, they had released him. The police might still be an aggravation, but they were no longer a threat.

Exhausted though he was, talked out though he was, Nudger needed to tell someone about what had happened, to share it with someone who cared. Some things not shared ate like acid.

He started the car and drove to see Claudia.

When he entered the old apartment building on Spruce and reached the second-floor landing, Coreen stuck her head out of her doorway and called his name. Nudger picked up something disturbing in her voice, a kind of vibrant apprehension. He stood for a moment with his hand on the banister, then turned and took a few steps toward her.

"You going to see Claudia," Coreen said, looking concerned, "I'll go with you. I been trying to call her on the phone, but she don't answer." She stepped all the way out into the hall and closed her door behind her.

"Maybe she's not home," Nudger said.

"She's home, all right. I seen her come in."

"Come in from where?"

Coreen shrugged. "Early morning walk, I guess." She led the way up the stairs, aggressiveness in the swing of her arms and the roll of her wide hips. "I wondered what she was doing out that time of morning. That's why I been trying to phone her, to find out."

"Maybe she couldn't sleep and felt like getting out," Nudger said.

Coreen snorted dubiously. "Anything else you feel like believing, Nudger? It ain't like Claudia to go roaming around in the early dawn. Not unless something's bothering her."

When they reached Claudia's door, Nudger rapped loudly on it with the edge of a half dollar. Slow minutes passed and Claudia didn't answer his knock. There was no sound from inside the apartment.

"Maybe she went back to bed," Nudger suggested hollowly, trying not to let Coreen's foreboding infect him.

Coreen wasn't having any of that explanation. She reached around him and rattled the knob. The door was locked. "You got a key?" she asked.

Nudger nodded. He dropped the half dollar back into his pocket, then reached deeper and drew out his key ring.

He opened the door to silence. He and Coreen stepped into

Claudia's apartment like two people entering a swamp of unpredictable sinkholes.

Maybe she wasn't home after all, Nudger thought. The place had the unbroken quietude of rooms unoccupied. A cup and saucer sat on the table by the sofa, the cup tilted crookedly half up on the saucer rim, the brown liquid inside it level and still. For some reason it occurred to Nudger that the coffee was exactly the muddy brown color of the sliding current of the Mississippi just a few blocks away.

Coreen had moved around him and was standing in the doorway to the bedroom. Nudger saw her body stiffen and jerk backward as if she'd been struck. Her voice was the softest, saddest he had ever heard. "Aw, Lord, no, no! . . ." She braced herself with both hands on the doorjambs.

Nudger leaped to her side, pulled her roughly out of the way and charged into the bedroom, knowing what was waiting for him.

He recognized the two ties that he'd left here, one brown-striped and one blue-striped, to go with either of his suits. Claudia had tied them end to end, knotted one around the inside doorknob of her closet, run the other tie up over the top of the door, and wrapped its end around her neck. She was nude, hanging limply against the door, like some kind of grotesque masquerade costume that had been casually placed there the night before, too real to be real. The blue-striped tie around her neck had dug deep into her flesh. Her eyes were bulging beneath closed lids, her tongue purple and distended. The kitchen stool she'd stood on and kicked aside lay upside down a few feet from her.

Nudger's soul was a thousand pounds of cold lead, for a moment weighting him motionless where he stood. Then he rushed to her, his agony welling from his throat in a stricken, pitying moan. He saw that her toes were barely touching the floor. Clasping his arms around her hips and buttocks, he raised her to relieve the tension on the taut ties, and hugged her to him as he pressed his head against the cool flesh between her breasts.

He couldn't be sure if the heartbeat he heard faintly was hers or an irregularity in his own racing heart.

"Call nine-eleven!" he shouted to Coreen. But she was already at the phone by the bed, punching out the emergency number.

Nudger reached up and flipped the blue tie out from over the door's top edge, allowing enough slack for him to lower Claudia gently to the floor. Hurriedly, but with a calm that remotely surprised him, he dug at the knot against the side of her neck. His fingernail doubled back, jolting him with pain, but the knot gave slightly. He couldn't undo it, but he managed to get enough of a grip on the material to pull the tie loose from around her neck. He felt a helpless fury when he saw the wide red gouge where it had sunk into her flesh.

After arranging Claudia carefully on the floor, with her hands at her sides, he pressed her tongue back into her mouth flat. Then he pinched her nose between his thumb and forefinger, bent over her, and began administering mouth-to-mouth resuscitation.

He worked frantically, rhythmically, pumping air from his lungs into hers. Breath for breath, life for life. Feeling her chest rise and fall mechanically with his effort. He was vaguely aware of Coreen standing over him, saying something he couldn't comprehend. Nothing mattered other than that he must not stop lending Claudia breath. When he stopped, her life would be gone, irretrievably. He learned the meaning of forever.

Claudia's shoulder twitched!

He saw it from the corner of his vision—not his imagination!

She vomited then. He tasted the bitterness of it in his mouth and jerked away, turning and spitting. Claudia was gagging, her head lolled to the side. The gagging stopped and she began gasping with a bellows rasp, kicking one leg feebly, slapping the floor with rigid hands. Breathing! She was breathing!

Nudger crawled over and held her hand, watching her chest heave as she sucked at the air. Sirens were screaming their frantic prolonged yodel outside, close by. Her eyes sprang open, rolled wildly.

He heard the sirens growling animal-like to silence, and seconds later the clatter of footsteps on the stairs and in the hall.

"We'll take it now," a voice said above him. There were pants legs and shoes all around him. A pair of scuffed brown slip-ons edged closer. He let himself roll out of the way, and someone gripped him firmly beneath the arms and helped him to his feet.

*   *   *

Nudger rode with her in the ambulance all the way to Incarnate Word Hospital, while a paramedic kept an oxygen mask pressed to her face. Claudia's eyes were open, unmoving. If she was still drawing breath, it was too shallow for Nudger to see the rise and fall of her breast. Her arms and hands, her fingers were still.

The paramedics and an RN wheeled her away and out of sight immediately, and Nudger was told to go to the Emergency admittance desk.

He signed Claudia in, scrawling his signature on a flurry of papers, assuming responsibility for payment. A stout redheaded nurse assured Nudger that the hospital would check with Kimball's Restaurant to see if Claudia had any employee group insurance there. None of that mattered right now to Nudger. He couldn't make them understand that, so he only listened to them, staring and nodding numbly.

For over an hour he sat in a molded plastic chair in a waiting area. Half a dozen other people waited there with him. Everyone's eyes followed the white uniforms who came and went through wide swinging doors. No one in the waiting area spoke except in soft and polite monosyllables. No one wanted to shatter the crystalline vessel of hope held out for whomever they knew behind the doors. Tattered *Newsweek* and *Time* magazines lay untouched.

Behind the admittance desk, the redheaded nurse sat joking with a bespectacled man wearing a white outfit with a name tag. Nudger thought he could make out the "Dr." before the name. Didn't the bastard have something more useful to do than chat with the admittance nurse? People in the building were suffering, dying. The man said something through a crooked smile and the nurse laughed like a giddy teenager. Nudger felt like walking over and punching them both through the wall.

Then the nurse busied herself separating carbon copies and placing them in the right file folders. The "doctor" straightened up from where he'd been sitting on the edge of her desk, came out from behind the low partition, slung a pushbroom and mop over his shoulder, and meandered away down the hall. Nudger told himself to take it easy.

His bout with Springer and Company at Headquarters had drained his body of resilience, but left him mentally hyped up and dazedly overreactive.

He slouched low in his plastic chair, closed his eyes, and half-dozed, his mind a writhing mass. He didn't like what he saw behind his eyelids, but maybe time would pass faster this way.

Snatches of the interrogation kept coming back to him: "You knew from the beginning that Jenine Boyington was out for revenge, didn't you, Nudger? . . ." "Co-conspirator . . ." "Withholding evidence . . ." "Hang your ass out to dry . . ." "Helped a potential murderer . . ."

Finally a louder voice said, "Mr. Nudger? I'm Dr. Antonelli."

Nudger opened his eyes and looked up to see an unkempt, frazzle-haired man in a dirty green smock. He looked as if he should be mopping floors.

"How is she?" Nudger asked, standing up with the slow tentativeness of an arthritic.

Dr. Antonelli narrowed his eyes and appraised Nudger. "Right now, she's not much worse off than you appear to be. The area around the cricoid and trachea wall is badly bruised, the hyoid and larynx to a lesser degree. And there's some muscle and tendon damage from the weight of her body. All that isn't as bad as it sounds. So far there seems to be no brain-cell damage from lack of oxygen. I think she'll be all right, Mr. Nudger, but we'll make her ours for a few days to be sure."

Nudger ran a hand down his face and grinned. He felt thirty pounds lighter.

"The ties she tried to hang herself with were cheap polyester," Dr. Antonelli said, "so the material stretched far enough to allow her toes to touch the floor and take some of the strain off her neck. That saved her life. If they'd been expensive silk ties, she'd be dead."

"Can I see her?"

"Sure. But not for long. She's under sedation. And she shouldn't try to talk for a while." Dr. Antonelli ducked slightly so he could see Nudger's neck more clearly. "Excuse me for asking, Mr. Nudger, but has someone been trying to strangle you?"

"What room is she in?"

Antonelli shrugged. He was busy enough with patients who wanted his help. "Four-o-five. Elevator's at the end of the hall and around the corner."

"Thanks," Nudger said. He patted the doctor's arm and hurried away.

Four-o-five was a semi-private room, but the other bed was empty. The walls were pale green, to go with the room's faint medicinal scent of mint. There were two small white metal cabinets, white bed-side tables, and matching blue chairs for visitors. A framed print of snow-draped pine trees silhouetted against a moonlit lake hung on the wall between the window and the door to the lavatory. A cool room, in decor and purpose.

Claudia lay on her back beneath a crisp white sheet. When Nudger entered the room, she didn't move her head, but her eyes picked him up when he got close to the bed. Her pupils were dilated and Nudger wasn't sure she could see him, but she smiled weakly, with obvious pain. She was barely conscious above the pull of the sedative, and her neck was swollen and turning a livid purple. She moved her lips, said nothing.

"We'll talk later," Nudger told her. He bent down and kissed her forehead. A nurse pushed into the room, made a note of something, then turned with a sole-squeaking swivel and dutifully scurried back out.

Nudger rested his fingertips on Claudia's cheek. "Don't try that again," he said. "Please. For me, don't try that again."

She nodded. The effort hurt her. Nudger shut up and just sat there with her. Neither of them moved. Claudia closed her eyes as the sedative gained ground on her.

Half an hour passed that way, and then the door swung open and Dr. Antonelli slouched into the room. When he saw Nudger he shook his head in a gesture of hopeless disapproval.

"She's going to be fine," he said. "Go home, Mr. Nudger. You're useless here. Come back this afternoon. She'll be awake. Bring flowers."

"What time this afternoon?"

"One or two o'clock. It's not visiting hours, but I'll see they let you up here. Right now, go home. Get some sleep yourself. I can see that you need it."

Nudger realized the doctor was right. It was pointless for him to be in the room now. Nothing more could happen to Claudia while she slept. He would come back later, when she was awake and aware.

"The nurses are watching her," Dr. Antonelli assured him. "She's getting good care. The best. Believe it."

Nudger stood up and almost fell. He'd been sitting in such a way that he'd impaired the circulation in his right leg. It had become numb, and was reacquiring feeling now with a tingling sensation. While he was waiting to be able to walk, he fished in his pocket for a scrap of paper and a pen. He scribbled his apartment and office phone numbers and handed the paper to Dr. Antonelli. "If there's any change, any trouble, have somebody call me, okay?"

"A solemn promise, Mr. Nudger. Go. Put ice on your neck. Sleep. Come back later. Good-bye."

Nudger nodded and limped from the room, gaining strength and feeling in his leg as he navigated along the hall. Through his weariness and his concern for Claudia, he began to feel a burgeoning optimism, only hazily suspecting that this cycle of harboring hope and then being disillusioned was his blessing and his curse.

He'd have to wait to put his mind entirely at ease about Claudia. Right now, he'd follow Dr. Antonelli's persistent advice and finally allow himself to rest. Claudia was alive. For the moment, at least, luck was on the rise. Life's direction was up.

He stepped into the elevator and descended.

THIRTY-TWO

He was plunging through cold blackness, gaining speed, trying to see what lay below, his scream and the wind's scream the same terrified howl.

He never landed.

Nudger was awakened by his phone and his alarm clock jangling simultaneously in an urgent mad symphony. He came awake confused, sat for a moment while consciousness flooded into him, then lifted the alarm clock and said hello.

That didn't work.

He shut off the alarm with one hand and answered the phone with the other. He noticed that the clock had only one hand, pointing straight up.

As he said hello into the receiver, he came fully awake and realized that the hour hand was hiding behind the minute hand. Noon

"Nudge," said the voice on the phone, "this is Hammersmith Were you sleeping?"

"It doesn't matter, Jack. I have to get up."

"I thought you ought to know," Hammersmith said, "Agnes Boyington's dead."

Nudger felt a stunned, light-headed disbelief. Impossible! The world's Agnes Boyingtons didn't die. Did they?

"She hanged herself in the hold-over cell," Hammersmith said.

"Hanged herself . . ." Nudger repeated. "Jesus! How did she do that?"

"Tore her dress into strips, tied them together, and made a noose then looped the other end around the overhead light fixture. It held her weight. She had to keep her feet off the floor until she lost consciousness, but she managed."

"She would," Nudger said. "And she'd allow for fabric stretch."

"Huh?"

"Nothing."

"You okay, Nudge? You sound strange."

"I'm tired, is all."

"Yeah." Hammersmith chuckled tonelessly. "I guess you got a right to be worn out."

"What about Jenine?"

"She already knows about her mother's death. She didn't seem sorry. But in her condition, maybe the news didn't register."

"Or maybe it did," Nudger said.

"Also, we picked up Hugo Rumbo as an accessory. He was down on Eighth Street, disguised as a wino, trying not to be noticed in an odd-looking shriveled plaid sport coat. He was about as inconspicuous as Frankenstein's monster at the dance. One of the street people tipped us."

"No matter how cunning they are, they always make one mistake don't they?"

"You got it, Nudge."

"Thanks for calling, Jack."

"Sure. Go back to sleep."

"You and Dr. Antonelli."

"What?"

"Never mind."

It was one o'clock when Nudger entered Incarnate Word Hospital carrying a dozen tissue-wrapped long-stemmed red roses. He had no trouble getting in to see Claudia; Dr. Antonelli had left word at the nurses' desk that he was to be let into her room.

She was awake, lying with her head propped up on the wadded pillow as if she'd been reading. But there was no book or magazine in sight. She was simply staring straight ahead. The other bed in the room was still unoccupied; she was alone.

When she saw Nudger she moved her head slightly in his direction and smiled. Her face looked better, fuller, as if she'd gained ten healthy pounds. Her neck looked worse. The livid purple bruise had spread to the underside of her jaw.

"Flowers," she said, in a voice so gravelly and low he could barely hear it. "Thank you, Nudger."

Nudger looked around for something to put the roses in. There was nothing, not even a bedpan. He laid them gently on the bedside table. Then he leaned over the bed and kissed Claudia on the cheek. She didn't move.

Her eyes slid sideways to take in the horizontal bouquet. "It's a solitary red rose that's an expression of unending love," she said.

"Then imagine what a dozen must mean," Nudger told her. "You're lucky that's a single bed."

She smiled wider, though it had to hurt. "They tell me I'll recover completely. I can go home and become an out-patient tomorrow."

He sat on the edge of the mattress and stared down at her. "Why did you do it?"

"I didn't do it. I tried and failed." She looked away from him, off to the side, and he knew she wasn't sure herself why she'd attempted suicide. The dark wind. "Everything seemed to be closing in on me again," she said, "and I was afraid."

"Afraid of what?"

"Partly, of loving you. The last time I loved a man it didn't work out very well for him or me."

Nudger sandwiched her cool hand between both of his. "Don't be afraid of that, ever. Things will work out. There's always reason to hope. Hope is nourishment for the soul."

"It's junk food."

Nudger shrugged. "That's the tastiest kind. Stay a kid and enjoy your cookies and candy. Have hope."

"I do. Right now. But I'm not so sure it will stay with me." She swallowed with obvious pain, her discolored throat working laboriously. "I guess they'll make me start seeing Dr. Oliver again."

"Do you mind?"

"No."

"Good. I think Oliver can help you."

She looked up at Nudger, her eyes so very dark against her pale flesh. Gypsy eyes. Angel eyes. The endless way out. "I think you can help me more," she said.

Nudger leaned forward and kissed her softly on the lips, careful not to hurt her. She'd said what he needed to hear. She would be all right; he would see to it. He wouldn't let her be devoured by her past. Or lose herself in the sad solace of the nightlines. He'd strengthen her with love and teach her the most valuable skill a person could possess in what the world had become; the Nudger specialty. He would teach her to survive.

The door swished open and Dr. Antonelli was in the room, flanked by two starched nurses. The attitude of the three of them was that of overworked, harried people making important rounds. Antonelli held a clipboard propped against his right hip, and the taller of the nurses was carrying a stethoscope, an instrument to measure blood pressure and a gleaming many-tubed contraption Nudger didn't recognize. They were here on doctor business.

When Dr. Antonelli saw Nudger he beamed amiably.

"Ah, Mr. Nudger," he said. "You're looking better. And you brought flowers! How nice! Hello. Good-bye. Get out. Go away."

Nudger went away, but not far.